Perfect Ice

Perfect Ice

Nicholas Mizet

JANUS PUBLISHING COMPANY LTD
Cambridge, England

First published in Great Britain 2016
by Janus Publishing Company Ltd
The Studio
High Green
Great Shelford
Cambridge CB22 5EG

www.januspublishing.co.uk

Copyright © Nicholas Mizet 2016
British Library Cataloguing-in-Publication Data
A catalogue record for this book is available from the British Library

ISBN 978-1-85756-849-3

Author's email: nicholas.mizet@gmail.com

Cover Design: Barbara Lee Art and Design
barbleeia50@gmail.com

Printed and bound in Great Britain

For Kristin

Abbreviations and Slang Terms

A and M (Texas A & M) Agricultural and Mechanical. Many states of the USA established institutions of higher learning for the purpose of studying those disciplines in the second half of the 19th century. They evolved into the modern universities of today, but the name of the original purpose remained. Texas A & M required all students to be in the Corps of Cadets for military training but was dropped in the 1960s. It continues to be known for producing professional army officers.

AFVN Armed Forces Viet Nam. The radio and television station established in Saigon by U.S. military forces.

AIT Advanced Infantry Training or Advanced Individual Training for other schooling, i.e. accounting, mechanics, etc.

AK-47 Named for Russian designer Kalashnikov, it was the weapon made in communist countries and supplied to their allies, such as North Vietnam. It was a magazine-fed 7.62 mm automatic or semi-automatic rifle. It was reputed to be more rugged than the American M-16.

ao dai (ow-zye, in northern VN, ow-yai, in southern VN) The traditional women's attire in Vietnam dating from the 14th century. With a Mandarin collar, long sleeves, form-fitting bodice, and floor-length skirt slit at the sides from the waist down, it is worn over pants of the same or contrasting colors.

ARVN Army of the Republic of Viet Nam. This was the volunteer and heavily conscripted army of South Vietnam allied with US forces.

AWOL Absent Without Leave. Term for vacating assignment by military personnel; not being accounted for; gone.

buku	A lot. Many. A corruption of "*beaucoup*" from French colonial days.
C rations (*Cs*)	Green cans of a balanced meal, such as spaghetti and meatballs or pork slices in juice, flat cans of peanut butter, jam or cheese, crackers, mixed fruit, pound cake, instant coffee, and a sheath of 6 cigarettes all contained in a quart-square cardboard box. A dozen of these individual meals came in a tough corrugated shipping container secured by a tightly bound wire which could sustain rough treatment, such as being dropped from a low-flying helicopter.
C-4	A pliable and very stable plastic explosive. With the consistency of modeling clay, it may be formed into any shape, such as a ring around a small tree to cut it down, yet it can only be set off by a blasting cap simply stuck into it and detonated by a an electrical charge. If heat such as a flame is applied C-4 will burn quickly and intensely.
Cadre	(kad-ree) Officers and enlisted men as permanent party at a military facility engaged in training.
CEO	Chief Executive Officer
CIB	Combat Infantry Badge. A silver musket on an infantry blue rectangle the length of an index finger, awarded only to infantry soldiers who have been in combat. It is always the uppermost badge or ribbon on a uniform for those eligible to wear it.
claymore	An anti-personnel mine encased in a hard plastic shell packed with C-4 behind a slightly convex-shaped board to which 100 steel balls have been adhered. The bottom has pointed metal legs to stick in the ground. The top has an opening to allow placement of a cylindrical blasting cap at the end of detonator cord through which a hand-held plunger sends an electrical charge. Invented by Norman MacLeod and named after a Scottish sword of medieval times.
CO	Commanding Officer
CP	Command Post. Where the CO has established his or her position to command.
DEROS	(**dee**-ros—rhymes with gross) Date Estimated Return from Overseas. Everyone knew this date, as they counted down the days when their year-long Vietnam tour was over.

deuce-and-a-half	The work-horse two-and-a-half-ton straight truck ubiquitous in the US Army. Four-wheel drive, green canvas canopy over a truck bed with flip-down benches capable of transporting troops.
didi-mau	(dee-dee mau) Leave, move out, or vacate the premises. Sometimes just di-di.
dink	Derogatory term for Asians, particularly GIs referring to North Vietnamese enemy soldiers.
dinky-dao	Slang term for crazy, in Vietnamese.
DMZ	Demilitarized Zone. In Vietnam, the border at the 17th parallel between North and South Vietnam. A misnomer as the area was fraught with probes and combat incidents.
EM	Enlisted Men. Army personnel below the rank of sergeant.
FNG	Fucking New Guy. In a typical year, the American armed forces constantly rotated personnel in and out during a year-long tour of duty. New arrivals were derided for their inexperience and requisite counseling of how to make it in the Nam.
GI	Government Issue. Practically everything in the U.S. military inventory during WWII was preceded with G.I. for Government Issue. It evolved into a term for a U.S. soldier and is still used today.
gook	See dink.
grunt	Term for 11B20s, or light weapons infantry, the lowly soldier who pounded the paddies, humped his ruck, and engaged an enemy in adverse conditions.
HE	Hotel Echo in phonetic alphabet. It stood for high explosive in a variety of ordnance, such as mortars, artillery, rockets, etc.
KIA	Killed in action.
klick	1000 meters (.62 miles) Derivation is unknown, but came into extensive usage in the Vietnam conflict. Probably was the shortened word for kilometer by GIs in Europe during WWII.
KP	Kitchen Police. Designated workers in mess halls and cooks' helpers.
M-16	Standard issue weapon of U.S. military. Automatic or semi-automatic rifle firing a 5.56 mm round from a 20-round magazine. Very rapid fire with high muzzle velocity. Can fire 20 rounds in just under 3 seconds.

M-79	Grenade launcher firing a 40 mm grenade loaded like a single-shot shotgun into a barrel with rifling that spins the grenade, thus arming it after 20 feet. The stock is tucked underneath the armpit with the barrel at an upward angle for a parabolic trajectory. A maximum range of about 400 yards.
MBA	An academic degree defined as Master of Business Administration.
MIA	Missing in Action. There are still about 1,600 soldiers, marines, air force and navy personnel considered MIA in and around Vietnam.
MOS	Military Occupation Specialty. Every job in the U.S. military is identified by a numeric and alpha nomenclature. For example, 11C40 is a sergeant in a mortar section. Personnel specialist: 75B. Clerk: 71B. Light weapons, infantry below rank of sergeant: 11B20.
MP	Military Police
MPC	Military Payment Certificates. During U.S. pursuits in Vietnam, all salaries, payrolls and means of exchange were in MPC. With denominations of 5s, 10s, 20s, and 50s, they were about the size of monopoly money but with colorful printing depicting various American figures and events.
NCO	Non-Commissioned Officer. Personnel with the rank of Sergeant E-5 to Sergeant Majors E-9.
NDP	Night Defensive Position. Typically, units in the field would assume these circular enclosed positions with various methods of alerts and defenses.
NVA	North Vietnamese Army. Originally referred to as the self-named PAVN (Peoples' Army of Viet Nam). The US military began calling it the NVA, a less patriotic and popular-sounding force.
OCS	Officer Candidate School. After basic training an enlistee or draftee has the option, if eligible based on test scores, to attend a twelve-week course after which he or she is offered a commission as a 2nd Lieutenant. Some non-commissioned officers (NCOs) from sergeant E-5 to sergeant major E-9 apply and thereby, if successful, become officers.
OD	Olive drab. Practically everything in the U.S. Army is of this flat green color.

PFC	After basic and AIT, lowest-rank privates were promoted to Private First Class.
POW	Prisoner of War.
PRC	Portable radio communication.
PSP	Perforated Steel Planking. Developed for rapid airfield construction during WWII, these interlocking panels were used extensively for runways at U.S. air bases in Vietnam.
PX	Post Exchange. A duty-free store with non-taxable merchandise. Many PXs in Vietnam during the American war were filled with Japanese electronics and china, clothes, watches, jewelry, consumables, cigarettes, and anything you could imagine in a big box store in the USA. Every major post in Vietnam had one to varying degrees.
REMF	Rear Echelon Mother Fucker. The dichotomous relationship between those who were in harm's way and those in safe, easy duty was expressed by this acronym to the latter by the former.
re-up	The army had many enticements to re-up, i.e. sign-up for another five years or more. Of course it was a cost-saving initiative by the Defense Department, not having to train another inductee for their job. If anyone decided to re-up they were paid at least a bonus of $5,000 and the non-com who signed them could expect a reward, too. Another incentive was to allow an uneasy infantry grunt to stay out of the field if they signed on to an extended hitch.
ROTC	Reserve Officers Training Corp. In conjunction with colleges and universities who offered this as part of their curriculum over four years, a graduate became a commissioned officer with a three-year commitment to active duty.
RTO	Radio Telephone Operator.
SFC	Sergeant First Class, E-7. Three stripes and two rockers. Assists platoon leader lieutenant.
slick	Slang term for the omnipresent Bell UH-1 Iroquois (Huey) helicopter. So called because of undercarriage runners instead of wheels.
slope	See dink.
Specialist-four	U.S. Army rank of E-4 (enlisted level four) just below sergeant and above PFC. Rank of corporal seems to have been phased out.

tracers	Magnesium-laced bullets that glowed when fired. The M-60 machine gun had a tracer on its belt every five rounds to indicate direction of fire. NVA machine guns used them as well as AK-47s, and their tracers were bright green. GIs had one per magazine to indicate when the last round in a 20-round magazine was fired, which glowed white.
USD	United States Dollar.
VC	Viet Cong. A southern guerilla fighter allied with North Vietnam's regular army fighting a common enemy—the US forces and South Vietnam. VC, "Victor Charlie" in the phonetic alphabet, were organized as the NLF, or National Liberation Front. This sounded too positive so the U.S. and South Vietnam called them Viet Cong, a pejorative alluding to communists.
ville	From the French word for "town." Americans used the term (pronounced vill, rhyming with pill) as a carry over from the French colonial influence.
VND	Vietnam Dong. When North and South Vietnam were unified under the victorious North, called the Reunification, the currency adopted was the dong, thus replacing the South's piaster. Currently, the value is 20,000 VND = 1 USD.
web gear	Shoulder straps and belt to which ammunition containers and hand grenades were attached. Standard equipment for combat soldiers.
WP	White phosphorous. Whiskey Papa in the phonetic alphabet. Artillery and mortars used white phosphorous as marker rounds or anti-personnel. It burned on anything it adhered to and was not extinguishable by water or smothering. On impact, a not very loud "pop" sent up a white plume of smoke which was easily visible to a spotter.
WO	Warrant Officer. Equivalent to Sergeant Major E-9, they were under the rank of 2nd lieutenant, O-1. Thus they were in the enlisted echelon, not in the officer corps. Most of the helicopter pilots were Warrant Officers.

Prologue

Natalie handed her father the Far East edition of *The New York Times*. Her mother, Thuy, brought a copy home every afternoon from her book store. "Does America want to go to war again, *Cha*?"

Erik Thorvald was interested in his native country even though he hadn't lived there for thirty years. Now, with CNN and English newspapers, it was not difficult. "Why, what are they up to?"

"There's something about smoking guns and mushroom clouds," Natalie said.

Erik read the front page above the fold. "That's unfortunate."

"What?"

"Trying to justify invading Iraq. Americans will see through that *dong rac*." Erik and Thuy taught their children to be bilingual, mixing Vietnamese and English into their conversations. "Where's your mother, by the way?"

"She went to market. We're having fish for dinner."

"Why didn't you go?"

"I was practicing."

Erik looked at his daughter. Her black hair cut just below the ears gleamed in the natural light off the bay. "Well, don't let me stop you."

He walked to the veranda and, as always, was swept away by the panoramic view of blue South China Sea meeting green uplands rising sharply to imposing heights. Some of his Vietnamese friends told him that ghosts inhabit these mountains overlooking Qui Nhon, a city of a quarter-million people occupying a flat peninsula. They said if the ghosts are kept happy they will not bother anyone.

Through everything that had happened, Erik never considered leaving his adopted country. All he wanted was a life with Thuy, who would not break a spiritual connection to the land of her ancestors. He supposed that was one way to keep the ghosts happy.

When the American War ended in 1975, the North Vietnamese Army commandeered vast stores of weapons. Anything they couldn't use they put in museums and memorials which dotted the countryside. What Erik found hard to believe was how quickly they demolished any symbol left from what they considered an invasion by the United States. A few years after the Americans pulled out, on one of his many business trips to Saigon, Erik decided to take a side trip and see the Long Binh Army Post. It was the largest American base in the world in 1969 when he had first arrived in-country. He thought it might be converted to public housing or something useful. How wrong he was. It was totally obliterated. Not a stick remained. Where he thought it should be was overgrown with brush. He did find a couple of forlorn metal bunkers that guarded what was once a perimeter on the vast site, about as big as Sturgis, a college town where he grew up.

Erik was dumbfounded. Sixty thousand Americans were stationed at Long Binh for a one-year tour. Administration buildings and countless wooden barracks housed headquarters and support personnel for units up and down South Vietnam. It was as if the United States plopped a little version of itself in the middle of a foreign country.

What about the natives? Well, they gave them jobs, didn't they? In the meantime, officers, non-coms, and enlisted men indulged in all kinds of luxuries in restaurants, swimming pools, outdoor movie theaters, and massage parlors. What went on in those Erik didn't know since he wasn't there long enough to find out.

Large PXs offered Japanese electronics and Noritake china to ship home. Drinking clubs under parachute canopies were scattered across the vast graveled terrain in a grid of concrete sidewalks and blacktop streets. Stateside amenities were plentiful, such as pizza and beer deliveries by enterprising locals, probably gathering intelligence in the process. Wasted food in numerous mess halls was taken home by the Vietnamese kitchen help. No lowly GI had to pull KP, clean barracks or polish boots. It was colonial indolence all over again. Life at Long Binh was soft and easy and they weren't telling.

After a discharge from the U.S. Army and an MBA, Erik returned to Vietnam and worked for the Coronel Coffee Company. The communists nationalized it and many other enterprises at war's end, while military police rounded up so-called enemies of the state. Erik was arrested and placed in a compound for "misguided opponents to the revolution in need of re-education." Somehow he was released in a few months, which he still didn't fully understand, and got his job back. He figured officials of the company, now Vinacafé, wanted to develop instant coffee for supplying the new hotels on Vietnam's fabulous beaches. It had helped that he knew about the coffee business from the ground up, pun intended, he chuckled to himself.

A piece by Mahler enhanced the reminiscing, made all the sweeter by his change in fortune. Hard polished floors in their house with no carpeting, typical in this hot and humid climate, projected Natalie's violin in concert with a slow metronome of waves breaking on the sandy shore below.

The first assignment in the re-education camp, Erik recalled, was dismantling anything of value in the American Embassy before it was blown up with ordnance left by its former owners. From this high-rise redoubt sheathed in a concrete lattice, fleeing helicopters seared into memory the humiliating exit from this country that bedeviled the United States for a decade. Erik figured the victors were delighted at the irony of Americans destroying a vestige of their own country's failed attempt at bending Vietnam to their will.

Thuy, working at the Fahasa book store in Qui Nhon, took leave and helped Erik win his release. Their marriage produced a girl and a boy. Natalie played in an orchestra, and Kai was using his engineering degree to build roads and bridges.

Lord knows Vietnam needed those, Erik allowed. The only interstate highway in the whole country is twenty miles between Hanoi and the international airport. Otherwise, it's two-lane blacktopped roads teeming with men and women on motorbikes vying for space and enduring warning honks from trucks, busses, and intermittent cars, which they ignore. When Erik drove to the mountains near Kontum on business it was about four hours to go ninety miles on Highway 1, the main north–south artery with steadfast kilometer markers left by the French. The only thing slower than the traffic, Erik thought, is the modernization of villages and towns in bucolic settings. Simple concrete open-air houses on narrow dirt streets have, at the most, two appliances—a fan and a TV. Running water and a bathroom is hit and miss. If it's miss, residents relieve themselves in the nearest grove of palm trees.

Tourism had grown a lot in the 1980s, and the economy improved after the establishment of diplomatic relations with the United States in 1995, but Erik was becoming increasingly aware that a wide chasm divided the wealthy few from a vast majority with an average income of about one hundred dollars a month. His company's coffee pickers only made one hundred thousand dong per day, about five dollars.

The cities, such as Da Nang, Hanoi, and Saigon, are a different story because of foreign investments in high-rise hotels and apartment buildings. Erik was aware that lately, the Vietnamese are growing weary of the Chinese and their aggressive practices of paying off officials, who get rich.

Back to the newspaper; he wondered if America learned anything from that fool's errand forty years ago. Erik answered his own question; the president and military leaders would use an all-volunteer army for any foreign incursions. They probably thought Vietnam was lost because young men about to be drafted couldn't see any reason to get involved with the internal affairs of this faraway place. The peace movement during the Vietnam conflict had left its mark.

Oh my God, he thought as he read on. They're laying the groundwork for an invasion. They're really going to do it. He had a sudden vision of a savage tableau of killed, maimed, and emotionally messed-up young men.

Here we go again, he moaned, thinking his war had been a lesson learned and safely tucked away. He closed his eyes. The sounds in the night came back. It is 1969. A drop of water splashes on a leaf to his right. Outside the perimeter a mongoose is foraging in *C* ration cans for any leftovers. He is struggling to stay awake, which is weird, seeing as how the jungle mist is fear itself closing in on him. At least by sleeping he could escape this war for freedom. "What freedom?" he whispers, knowing it's not for the Vietnamese. They're terrorized by Americans and free-fire zones. The military is playing the patriotism card for this adventure.

Try to concentrate, think about something, he tells himself. Take patriotism ... please. He laughs ever so quietly. No, seriously, pressing on, where does the word come from? Greek or Latin *pater*, father, he presumes. He makes a mental list of related words: patriarch, patrician, patron, paternal, patronize—all about a loyal supporter and benefactor, such as a father. Hmm, he muses, that last one can mean to belittle or demean someone.

In the ominous silence among the shadows of giant trees, he thinks about his *pater familias* with warm memories, but they become clouded with judgmental criticisms. Probably a reflection of his state of mind, he thinks, but he's still bothered by it. How did his family get so screwed up when it had such a good start? Had he or his father changed along the way? He recalls some philosopher's advice that if you don't have a good father, you must invent one. Erik promises to work on its meaning if he ever gets out of this alive.

Traveling with his family from Iowa to visit relatives in southeastern Minnesota, Erik believed he was in a different country. The air seemed brighter and clearer with a woody fragrance, like freshly cut railroad ties. Steep bluffs appeared to be mountains, and the lowlands must have been made by a giant playing with a very big stick. When his father told him about glaciers, he could see where they had pushed up ridges called moraines. As the earth warmed, the bulldozing rivers of ice melted and left magnificent valleys.

Even in 1950 most folks around the little town of Reinberg still spoke Norwegian. This convinced Erik that he had crossed a frontier. His relatives were second and third generations in America, but their lives weren't all that different from the Bergensfjord in Norway where their family came from. That's what Harold Thorvald told his wife and children when he showed them where he grew up.

Like the glaciers, the Norwegians moved inevitably but slowly into mainstream America. If they spoke in English it was accented and sing-song, as Erik's Uncle Haakon said, "I tink it's going to snow on Tursday, then, you know."

Uncle Helmar made it a conversation when he replied, "Ja, I s'pose."

Erik heard many stories about growing up on a prairie farm. That's where Harold learned that hard work was a way of life. Every morning he had chores with his two older brothers, mainly cleaning out what the horses and livestock had deposited in the barn overnight. Walking a mile to the country school after that was the easiest part of the day. When starting first grade in 1920, he and his four classmates could only speak Norwegian.

Harold said the lessons taught by a solitary teacher in the one-room schoolhouse came easily to him. He began to stand out because of his ability with numbers and reading. Before long he was way ahead of his classmates. The county superintendent suggested that Harold skip fourth grade, and his teacher agreed. In a couple of years he still needed to be challenged, so they passed him through seventh grade too.

When Harold graduated from eighth grade, the highest level at the country school, he said his parents wanted him to continue his education. They told him that anyone who took to his studies the way Harold did should become a Lutheran minister. He would have to stay in a boarding house and go to high school in Lake Falls, a town about fifteen miles away. That was too far to make daily trips with a team of horses, so Harold lived in Lake Falls during the week and went home on the weekends.

Reinberg was about three miles from the Thorvald farm and had a railway station. Harold said his father took him there on Sunday evenings to ride the train to Lake Falls. He returned home the same way on Friday afternoons.

Erik and his sister, Helen, admired their father for being on his own at 12 years old. They listened respectfully when Harold told them how shy he was, which made it difficult to fit in when he was two years younger than his classmates. He said his work habit carried over to his academic career.

When he got back to his room after school, he had no one to give him help or sympathy, so he studied and read.

One of the family reunions took place on Christmas at the home farm. After dinner, the boys went outside to listen to the wolves. The warmth of the red brick two-story house was replaced by bitter cold that crept into every fold of skin and clothing. Deep snow glistened in the moonlight. From the dark outline of woods beyond the barn they heard a mournful howling. This *is* a different country, Erik thought as he shivered in the icy air.

Back inside, the younger cousins went upstairs to play something, anything to get away from the adults. The high school ones ignored an invitation to come with them, not even bothering to look up from their game of Rook in the dining room.

The second story had vents about a foot square in the floor of each room. These allowed heat to rise from the oil-burning stove on the main floor.

Erik knelt by one and looked through a metal grid to pine boards in the parlor. He could hear his mother, Marie, visiting with the other grown-ups in English since she was from Iowa and didn't speak Norwegian. They were talking about Truman firing MacArthur, whoever that was. Aunt Carol broke into the conversation. "Could we try to be more modern in our discussions and not be such provincial Norwegians? We should stop saying 'Ja, I s'pose' every time somebody says something."

The talking stopped. Erik couldn't see anyone, but he pictured some of the folks inspecting their fingernails, or looking at very interesting patterns in the floor. Finally, somebody said, "Ja, I s'pose."

Erik stood up to see what his young cousins were doing in their grandfather's study, a cozy room of bookshelves, an easy chair, and a desk. Helen and Martha were leafing through a few books while Richard and Larry snooped in some desk drawers. Funny, Erik thought, how the kids' names were so common and their folks had names like Ole, Haakon, and Helmar.

Richard pulled out a heavy green canvas bag. "What the heck is this?" he said.

Larry found more bags and everybody grabbed at the drawstrings to have a look inside.

Helen exclaimed, "They're all dimes! Roosevelt dimes!"

Richard turned down the desk on a leg that swung out and put all four bags on it. They each lifted one. "Cripes, it's heavy," Martha said.

Larry wondered how much money they were holding.

Richard quietly emptied one of the bags onto the desk. Everyone began stacking dimes in piles of ten.

"There must be a thousand," Helen whispered.

Martha accidentally kicked the support leg and the desk collapsed. Most of the dimes made a direct hit on the vent in the floor. Erik guessed the folks downstairs were surprised when a gazillion coins clanged out of a register in the ceiling. A loud crash echoed from the hard floor below. They all stared at the grill that ate their dimes.

Heavy footsteps clomped on wooden stairs. Erik scrambled with the others to pick up the little profiles of Roosevelt that missed the vent.

Harold walked in. "What do you think you're doing?"

Helen said, "We were just—"

Harold scowled. "You shouldn't be getting into other people's things. Go down, all of you, and pick up those dimes. Erik, stay and get the rest of these."

"Who was Roosevelt, anyway?" Erik asked his father as he started filling a green bag.

"He was the president during the Depression. Your grandfather thought he would have lost the farm if it hadn't been for Franklin Delano Roosevelt and the Agriculture Adjustment Act. He started collecting those dimes when they came out in 1946."

"Did you like Franklin Del … er, Roosevelt?' Erik said.

"Not really. He was an affected, scheming Brahmin who probably had a hand in the attack on Pearl Harbor. He had so much to gain."

This didn't make much sense to Erik, seeing as how he didn't understand the words, and also, didn't the Japanese bomb Pearl Harbor? He thought he would ask about it when his father was in a better mood.

Erik loved visiting this land that missed a few turns of the hourglass. Harold told his children that he never would have become a college professor if his parents hadn't insisted that he go to high school. Erik imagined a father and his boy sitting side by side in a horse-drawn cutter. It schussed through new snow in a concert of silence except for a steady pace of muffled hoof beats. The narrow road descended from the highland prairie into groves of hardwoods. Unlike the summer, when it was a green curtain, the two riders looked into deep woods. Leafless trees stood in stark contrast to the white forest floor until they blended into darkness a ways from the road.

As if on a Christmas card, Reinberg, in a secluded valley, came into view. The fine lines of a church steeple were shrouded in a bridal veil of gently falling snow. Lanterns on the corners of a station house glowed warmly in the fading light. A train whistle sounded far away, but suddenly a black, black as soot, steam engine appeared in a swirling white cloud. It huffed and puffed, venting its disgust at having to interrupt its hard-won speed for a few passengers. The train of several freight cars and one passenger car came to a stop. One of the boarding travelers was a boy carrying books, who found a seat and settled in for the long journey.

Chapter One

"Man, this stuff works," Erik said as he slathered on mosquito repellent. "I wonder what the hell's in it."

"You don't want to know. We'll probably find out it causes cancer or some other bad shit. Which reminds me, you got a light?" David Levy pulled out a cigarette from the box of six that came in the *C* rations.

Erik tossed him his Zippo. David hunched over and cupped his hand around the flame and took a deep drag. It looked so relaxing that Erik lit up when David tossed back the lighter. "I'm really a non-smoker," Erik said, "but right now I gotta smoke."

"Yeah right, I'm under the same delusion," David said. "How come you're not smoking some weed?"

Erik surveyed the perimeter they were in. The sweet aroma of marijuana hung in the humid air. "Nah, I don't have any and I want to keep my shit together. How about you?"

"Same here. Right now, anyway, but I might sometime," David said. "Christ, I can't believe how fast night falls in the tropics." He broke into his thickest Minnesotan. "Ja, I s'pose you want to stay awake first, then? All that shuffling dirt has made me tired, then, you know. I'll sleep first, if that's okay with you, then?"

Erik laughed because David probably thought he was exaggerating, but the tone was right on. "Okay, that works. How about I wake you at midnight?"

David said, "Yeah, four hours is good. Wake me if something happens." He stretched out on a poncho liner and covered his face with the standard issue, one each, OD, hat, jungle.

Erik looked into the tangle of brush and trees. The dark sky offered a few glimpses of stars. Every time he heard a noise he flinched and his heart pounded. He thought about history to keep his mind from acknowledging a dogged anxiety deep within him. He imagined it to be like a cancerous growth ready to metastasize into a panic. He ruminated on war and how it had been going on for as long as humans were on the planet. He pictured himself as a picket in front of Grant's position at Shiloh. Johnny Reb is just beyond those trees doing the same thing. He looked for the barely visible piece of white tape on the claymore mine thirty feet in front of him. It was still there. Despite the surreal nature of his present situation, he accepted the reality of an enemy out there wanting to make him a statistic. His mind wandered to halcyon days when the only fighting involved ripe tomatoes and apples in a lazy summer evening.

In the town where Harold and Marie bought their first house, Erik was all eyes and ears and grew to like it very much. He knew his sister, Helen, felt the same way. Now that he was in first grade he was past believing in Santa Claus. In his younger years he didn't question that jolly old Saint Nick could cover Gainesboro in one night, his world of eight blocks long and four wide. He was reserved around adults but had a lot of energy, which he tapped when playing in the neighborhood. In school he paid attention and found it interesting. He learned to read very quickly, but Helen had already taught him the alphabet and how to sound out words.

Helen usually had a book in her hands when not outside playing. At night, tucked in her bed, she read all the classics—*Little Women, Robin Hood, My Friend Flicka, Treasure Island, National Velvet, Little Men, Ben Hur,* and *The Door in the Wall.* When it was time for lights out, Erik knew she was in her room reading under the covers with a flashlight, but he didn't tell on her.

Since Helen was in fourth grade where her father was superintendent, Erik could tell that she was beginning to feel … what was the word? *Anxious,* that was it. He saw how his father would not listen to any worries or concerns that Helen wanted to talk about, such as being nervous in front of a group when she had to give a report or perform in music.

Helen was very quiet at school. Whenever Erik saw her, she was a model student. For class pictures she sat with her hands folded in her lap, and her feet were neatly placed together, but she wasn't smiling.

Erik sensed that Helen was more outgoing when not in school to let off steam. Lots of ideas for different activities were always popping up in her head. She and her best friend, Babs, made up their own languages so they could be mysterious strangers like the characters they knew in books. All the kids in the neighborhood tried to figure out how she and Babs could talk to each other.

One secret code sounded Asian. Helen and Babs worked it during the games. The trick was spelling words and putting *ong* after each consonant. The vowels were just spoken. "Look" was *long oh oh kong*. A conversation sounded like this: "*Jong ee rong rong yong, i song, song oh, cong u tong ee.*"

"*Cong u tong ee?*"

"*Yong ee song.*"

Naturally, Jerry would be interested in what they were saying about him and try to catch on. When anybody understood it, they would speak the language and be part of the in-group.

Gainesboro had a north side and a south side. The dividing line was Main Street, running east and west. Youths from the two sides didn't play much together, except on the ice skating pond in neutral territory on the west edge of town. Neither side had a shortage of kids. Harold said that soldiers had come back from a war to raise a family. Erik wasn't sure how that worked, but concluded that it took a mom and a dad to have children and then raise them. From what Erik could see, it was a good arrangement. Parents provided food, shelter, comfort when needed, and rules, and the kids had the run of the town without their involvement.

Everyone played outside in cold weather or hot, unless they were sick with the usual mumps, measles, or chicken pox. Erik's mother said his turn would come. As to playing games, anyone old enough to go to school was included. The older ones had better things to do, like school sports, or rehearsals for a play, which provided entertainment for the town. Erik's mom often played a role, as did other townspeople, when the high school needed more actors.

Erik never heard anything about being rich or poor. Everybody wore jeans and T-shirts when not in school, and they lived in similar houses, mostly two stories and a front porch with a swing to stir up a breeze on hot summer evenings. The families didn't own a lot of big things, except for a car and maybe an upright piano.

If anyone bullied somebody smaller they were yelled at by a whole lot of kids. There was no hitting, but teasing was okay and could happen at any time. It was part of the deal when a mob of different ages got together. Besides, Erik and everybody else had a bank of come-backs if teased that had to do with sticks and stones, pants on fire, or I know you are, but what am I? Grown-ups were never concerned about that. Erik heard his and other parents say, "You work it out or don't play." So the kids worked it out.

Just about any topic could be discussed, although sex wasn't among them. It wasn't on the radio, in magazines, or in the movies so nobody knew much about it. The F word wasn't even known. Erik would later say that he came from a time and place where MF stood for Massey Ferguson, the tractor people. Once somebody's cousin from out of town said "Jesus Christ" a lot, and threw in a lot of "goddamns," but they weren't adopted into the usual banter.

Sometimes, seeing as how Gainesboro was surrounded by farms, the word "shit" was well-known and used for emphasis, as in "What's a hundred times a hundred?"

"A thousand?"

"No, it's ten thousand, you dumb shit."

Paying attention in school, Erik decided, could be helpful in making one's way in the neighborhood.

In the spring, every moment when not in school, at piano lessons, or eating dinner was spent playing work-up softball in the vacant lot next to Our Savior Lutheran Church. Since it was a soft softball everybody caught with bare hands, a good thing because nobody had a glove anyway. Boys and girls played all the positions in the field as they worked-up to be one of three batters. If a batter made an out, they had to go to right field and start over while everybody moved up one position. It was a great skill builder.

In the summer every kid had daily chores, like cutting the grass, cleaning the house, washing windows, going to the grocery store, and whatever else their parents wanted them to do. When finished, everybody got together to play something, mostly because nobody had a TV in 1950s Gainesboro.

They played a lot of different games, such as Annie-eye-over, kick the can, or roller skating on Center Avenue's new sidewalk. Sometimes it was croquet with no boundaries. Having your ball sent over a couple of back yards built character. You tried like hell to get back in the game.

Most of the two hundred people in Gainesboro went to church on Sundays. First Methodist was the only church besides Our Savior Lutheran. The Lutherans were more in number, but the Methodists were an option. One Sunday, during the sermon about the meaning of Communion, Erik saw Mr. Gustafson, the postmaster, stomp out of church. Erik asked his mother about it. She whispered, "He wants to make a show of having a direct line to God."

After church Erik heard Mrs. Heglan say to Reverend Nuse, "He'll be starting his own church, as we Lutherans like to do, or joining the Methodists with his blessed opinions."

At dinner Helen asked, "How come Mr. Gustafson walked out of church?"

Harold and Marie looked at each other as though deciding who wanted to field this one. Harold said, "Well, I guess he thought that

Reverend Nuse wasn't saying enough about the bread and wine turning into the body and blood of Christ."

Helen said, "It sounds like cannibalism."

"We think, as do most Lutherans in their hearts," Marie said, "that the bread and wine are symbols of Jesus as we absorb his very being and what he stands for."

It was all very baffling to Erik. If anybody talked about religion in the neighborhood get-togethers, it took on all the features of a ghost story. One time Sally Grady had everyone's attention during a break from pom-pom pull-away in the churchyard. "My mom said that in the middle of the night once, she woke up to see Grandma standing at the foot of her bed. The next day, Grandpa called and said that Grandma died in the night, and they live in California." After a pause, Sally declared, "That proves there's a God and I'm going to devote my life to Jesus."

Gordy Halvorson sang out, "What, are you a nun or something? Hey, everybody! Sally's a nuh-un."

Sally pushed Gordy over. "Oh, you jerk! Be serious."

That was difficult since they were both laughing and tickling each other. They went back to playing pom-pom.

Toward the end of summer, backyard gardens were full of juicy tomatoes. Apple trees drooped with heavy bounty. A few tomatoes or apples taken for eating, or ammunition, wouldn't be missed by their owners. Erik learned that an apple or tomato fight could break out anytime because everyone was fair game, except adults, of course.

Mostly it was teenagers who started them, as on one humid August evening when the McLaughlin twins, Pat and Mike, were collecting for their *Des Moines Register* paper route. They saw Junior Thompson driving up Center Avenue.

Erik and his best friend, Arthur, were admiring the Jonathon and Cortland apples on the trees between Mrs. Waldron's and the Peterson house. The two boys were innocent of teenage pursuits, but were willing to learn. They stood near the twins who were about to help themselves to an apple.

As Junior's car neared, Pat said to his brother, "He's probably heading to Lenora's house."

"Yeah," Mike said, grinning.

Erik watched as Mike threw an apple like he did a baseball at shortstop when denying a single. This time first base was an unknowing and mobile Junior Thompson in the open window of a '49 Ford.

Splat! The four boys saw the missile disintegrate on Junior's front window vent, which stuck out like a triangle. Sure that Junior was going to slam on his brakes they scrambled for cover only to see him continue toward Main Street.

The twins looked puzzled. Dripping sweat at the sudden activity, they picked up their book of receipt stubs and continued with their collecting. Erik and Arthur tagged along, but Erik noticed they kept looking nervously behind them.

"We can be your lookouts," Erik offered.

"Huh? Uh, yeah, sure, you can be our lookouts," Pat said. He turned to Mike, "I bet he had bits of apple all over him. You got him good, Mike."

"Yeah, I guess so. I wonder what he's doing."

It was getting dark. The cicadas and crickets were warming up their instruments for a concert. Kids were heading back home from playing through the steam-bath heat. Erik knew of air conditioning in Storm Lake's movie theater, but he'd never heard of anybody's house having it, leastways in Gainesboro.

Reverend Nuse and Mrs. Nuse were on their porch swing, giving a slight push with their feet in unison every couple of swings. *Ozzie and Harriet* played on a radio.

The four boys met Gordy Halvorson on the sidewalk.

"Hey, Gordy, have you seen Junior? Mike nailed him with an apple when he was driving by," Pat said.

"Oh, shit. I haven't seen him, but if I know Junior, he'll be planning something."

"We gotta get some ammunition," Mike said. "Hey, Erik and Arthur, go over to the Petersons and Johnsons and get some apples and tomatoes. You know, not at one spot, but just fill up the front of your T-shirts. Then meet us back here."

"Yes, sir," Arthur said as he saluted. He and Erik headed for the Petersons'.

When they returned about ten minutes later, Gordy, Pat, and Mike were staring across the street. Rosalind Frederickson had just turned on some lights in her screened porch and was tuning in a station on the radio. Erik looked at her curvy silhouette, too, with an emerging hint of what was so fascinating.

Mike said, "Oh, man, would I like to—"

"Have a screened porch?" Gordy finished. "Yeah, that'd be nice."

"I'm not talking about the screened porch."

Erik had noticed that all the boys acted a little goofy around Rosalind. Her dad owned Frederickson's Standard at Center Avenue and Main Street. The three boys didn't notice how Erik and Arthur hung on every word when they talked about how they liked to go to Freddy's Standard to see Rosalind come out and pump their gas. Better yet, when she washed their windshield, the strain on her tight blouse looked as though a couple of buttons could pop right in front of their eyes. They hoped it would happen just once, and maybe, just maybe, she wouldn't be wearing a bra. When she dashed into the station to get change, they saw a very nice ... glancing at Arthur and Erik, never mind, they said.

Mike sauntered toward her yard and leaned on a streetlight. Patti Paige was singing "The Tennessee Waltz" on the radio. He called out, "Hey, Rosalind."

Rosalind turned down the radio. "Who is it, Pat or Mike?"

"It's Mike." He took a couple of steps towards the porch. "I was just—"

Something struck Mike on his left knee. He bent down and picked up an apple. As he straightened and looked around, three ripe tomatoes flew out of the darkness and hit him on his white T-shirt.

Mike darted for a tree away from the streetlight.

Gordy and Pat howled with laughter.

Rosalind came out from the porch and said between laughs, "What are you doing? Your T-shirt looks like a tomato strainer."

"Very funny. Were you a decoy for Junior?" Mike asked.

"A decoy? What are you talking about?"

"I hit Junior with an apple when he drove by and I thought he might be after me. You were a distraction and made me, um, forget about everything else."

Erik could see Rosalind's smile from across the street as she fanned her face with her hand.

Gordy said to Erik and Arthur, "Come on, bring the stuff."

They ran across the street. "Hey, everybody, grab a tomato and apple," Pat urged. "Let's go down the alley and head them off."

Erik was excited to be running with the big kids. They broke onto Main Street between the post office and the theater. They turned right towards Center Avenue.

"Hey!" someone shouted behind them.

They turned to see Erik's father with Junior, and his two buddies, Alan Angstrom and Walter Pusey. They were south-siders, thus the enemy. The three boys looked attentively at Mr. Thorvald.

Like the others, Erik covertly dropped his ammunition.

Pat and Mike said at the same time, "Oh, hi, Mr. Thorvald."

Rosalind added quickly, "We were just out for a walk."

Erik said, "Oh, hi, Dad. How are things at the office? Mom said you'd be working late. We were out chasing fireflies. It's a nice night, kinda hot though, and—"

"Stop. What are you doing?"

"Mom said I could stay out late and catch fireflies with Arthur."

"Looks more like you've been catching apples and tomatoes. What happened to you, Mike? Is that what the boys are wearing these days? I must be downwind, because I can smell something that makes me want to get a hamburger."

Mike stammered, "Uh, well, we—"

"Look," Harold continued, "I can put two and two together. These boys came tearing around the corner and literally knocked me over. I know what you're up to. School starts in a few days, so you're having a little fling. I don't think the good people of Gainesboro would appreciate having their hard work wasted like this."

"We could pay for everything," Rosalind offered.

Harold didn't say anything as he thought about it. He smiled. "That won't be necessary, Rosalind," Harold said. "I suppose our town wouldn't mind some extra throwing practice with a little bit of their harvest if it helps you win a close one this fall."

His dad was talking about fall baseball, Erik knew, because Gainesboro High was too small for a football team.

"Let's get this stuff cleaned up," Harold said.

Everybody quickly complied.

"Erik, you and Arthur walk home with me. As to the rest of you, I'll see you in school."

Reaching the corner, Erik turned and saw that Mike had his arm around Rosalind as they strolled the other way. He thought growing up looked promising.

On the way home Erik was proud of how his father had handled all those teenagers. He was funny and had their respect. He looked up at him with admiration and love.

Chapter Two

It was Erik's first night in the field. It seemed longer than a single day since they started that morning. No breeze stirred as the sun peeked over the eastern horizon. He wondered how it could look so friendly in contrast to its ruthless midday assault on sultry air that felt like a Turkish bath. A year of this seemed like an eternity.

Erik replayed everything from the time Lieutenant Cushman gave final instructions for the patrol. "Maintain recon discipline. Be quiet, be stealthy, be spookier than the spooks. Take enough Cs for three days, just a couple dozen cans dispersed around your ruck. Two bandoliers of ammo for your M-16s. One claymore mine apiece for everybody. No sleeping bags—just your poncho liners. When we come across a major trail, we'll set up a night defensive position, or NDP, so don't forget your entrenching tool and some sandbags for filling. Take three canteens. Any questions?"

"Yeah, El-tee," Clemons said plaintively. "I'm too short for this."

Lieutenant Cushman said, "How much time you got?"

"Three days and a wake-up."

The lieutenant thought for a moment. "Tell you what, Clemons. Get a radio over at supply. You're going to eat and sleep with it at *A* battery and be ready to deliver some 105s. We'll have our own frequency, twenty-five slash one thirty-five, and you stand by that fucking PRC and a map. I'm one, and you're three. Got it? Hosmer, can you get along without Clemons on this one?"

"Yeah, sure, Lieutenant. Fucker's too short, anyway."

Specialist-four Clemons looked relieved. "Thanks, El-tee."

"Just be ready to bring some high-explosives, you know, some bad HE, on Charlie's ass."

* * *

The platoon hiked north out of base camp on a dirt road. David was behind Erik. "Hey, numb nuts. How heavy do you think your ruck is?"

"It's gotta be about fifty pounds," Erik said. "I don't mind that. I'm just glad it's not monsoon. We wouldn't be walking along this dirt road free as you please if it was."

"Yeah, I wish I had left my book back in the hootch."

"What are you reading?"

"Caesar's *The Gallist Campaign.*"

"Sounds heavy. Hey, what does your father do—I mean to afford Brown and all?"

"He owns a small dry-cleaning shop in Brooklyn, along with my mom. I had some very good scholarships or I couldn't have gone there."

"Did you play football?"

"Brown doesn't give athletic scholarships, but playing football helped get their attention."

They moved into the thick forest. It was very slow going. Second squad took the lead. They soon strapped their M-16s in order to move vines and branches. Erik remembered Bodine saying that an ambush was unlikely if they weren't walking along one of the obscure trails that crisscrossed the wilderness of Vietnam.

Erik guessed it was already ninety-eight degrees in mid-morning and everyone's fatigues were soaked through. Fear wanted to walk with him, but he fought it off. Think of something, you dumb shit, he said to himself.

"Whose woods these are I think I know," Erik said.

After a moment David answered, "His ass is in a tunnel, though."

Erik said, "He will not see me stepping here," and waited.

David came through with, "All decked out as GI Joe."

The platoon got quiet except for the muffled curses of about thirty grunts as they made their way through thick foliage under towering trees that afforded a few patches of blue sky.

When they were loading magazines from the green bandoliers of M-16 ammunition back in Tay Ninh West, Erik noticed a young Vietnamese guy in camouflaged jungle fatigues carrying an M-16. He asked Bodine about him.

"That's Nguyen. He's a Kit Carson scout, a supposed jumper from the Viet Cong to the ARVN. Yeah, the ARVN are our allies, but they're worthless cowards. The lieutenant watches this guy like a hawk," Bodine said.

"How come he takes him along?"

"Every so often the RTO picks up radio traffic from the North Vietnamese Army and Viet Cong," Bodine explained. "Most people don't realize how sophisticated they can be with radios and laying communication wire, and shit like that. Anyway, Nguyen can tell us what they're saying if we pick up anything."

Sometimes the patrol came to a stand of bamboo that was so thick they had to go around it. They progressed only about two klicks due west. Erik figured if they didn't have a compass in such jungle, they would have gone in circles. Lieutenant Cushman signaled to break out the *C*s for lunch.

Erik and David hunkered down and had some spaghetti and meatballs. They listened as the other guys bantered back and forth. Hosmer: "Yeah, Snake, you go ahead and charge the dinks in an ambush."

"Well, that's what they said to do in AIT," Snake said.

"Yeah, I remember that, too, and I says to myself there's no fuckin' way anybody's gonna do nothin' but hit the ground. You go ahead and charge and get yourself a CMH," Hosmer said.

"A Congressional Medal of Honor?"

"No, a casket with metal handles."

Erik chuckled. He had brought along a can of pound cake thinking it would be a good dessert. Now the very thought of it made him thirsty. "Hey, anybody want to trade some pound cake for some fruit?"

That got howls of laughter. Snake muttered what accounted for such stupidity—"FNG." Erik learned that nobody, but nobody, brought along pound cake on patrols.

Lieutenant Cushman did a radio check on the PRC-25, which everybody called a prick twenty-five. "Three, this is one, over." The lieutenant listened. Then, "Three, one. Radio check. How do you read? Over." He waited for an answer. He finished with, "Three, one. Roger that. Out."

Erik took a sparing swig from his canteen, glad he had three. He lighted up a Pall Mall. David wrote in his notebook. All too soon the lieutenant told Sergeant First Class Anderson to saddle 'em up.

They continued in single file, going in the direction of 270°, due west. After about fifteen hundred meters they stopped. The point man signaled for Lieutenant Cushman, who moved up. He came back in a couple of minutes and told Anderson to have the platoon form a perimeter. He motioned for Bodine to come with him as he went forward again.

They returned in about ten minutes. The lieutenant talked in a quiet voice to the circled platoon. "It looks like a lot of slopes have been here recently. The undergrowth has been trampled, the vines have been cleared away, and the trees have a lot of branches broken off like somebody's been hanging their shit on the stumps. Bodine?"

"Yeah, I agree. It looks like a lot of NVA had a regimental powwow. Could be the 3rd NVA Division. They're supposed to be in the area."

Lieutenant Cushman said, "I don't know why here and above ground. They usually have their meetings in their tunnel complexes."

Sergeant First Class Anderson said, "Maybe they're too many. Maybe they're on the move. This could be major. Could be a big build-up for something in Tay Ninh City for Tet. Who knows?"

"They could have heard us coming and *didi maued* on the other side of that clearing," the lieutenant said as he wiped his dripping face with an olive-drab towel, which most everybody carried. "Sergeant Anderson, get the platoon on line with second squad minding our rear."

Soon the platoon was at the eastern edge of the clearing.

The RTO came up to the lieutenant. "You wanted me, El-tee?"

The lieutenant looked at his map. "Yeah, we're going to sight in some guns with Clemons." Sawyer handed him the horn. He keyed it, producing a momentary static. "Three, this is one, over." After a response, Cushman said, "Three, one. Coordinates six niner seven eight two three. One whiskey papa, over."

Erik heard distant thunder. Here comes the white phosphorous round, he assumed, amazed at how artillery could give them an umbrella of protection, if needed, anywhere in South Vietnam. In a second, a whine rose and fell in a Doppler effect as the round passed overhead. It landed with a small explosion that discharged a column of white smoke about two hundred meters beyond the clearing and to the right.

Anderson said, "Hey. Not bad, Lieutenant. Were you pretty sure where we were?"

"I had a pretty good idea. Wondrous things happen in the enchanted forest." He called again. "Three this is one, over." Clemons acknowledged. The lieutenant continued, "Three, one. Drop one zero zero, left two zero zero. Four hotel echo. Fire for effect. Out."

Four remote blasts reported execution of the fire mission. The high-explosive rounds screamed their arrival and landed in the darkness of low trees and bushes just beyond the clearing. They sounded like empty boxcars slamming together. Dirt and foliage erupted in fountains of orange and brown. The smell of cordite drifted their way. Erik could hardly believe the destructive power of the 105mm howitzer rounds. David looked so fascinated that he wasn't writing in his notebook.

Something hit the ground right in front of Erik. He looked down to see a piece of gray metal that looked like the sole of a size-four shoe. He picked it up and immediately dropped it. "Damn!" Erik exclaimed loudly. It was hot. "Is that a piece of shrapnel from the 105s? That is freakish. I can't believe it came this far."

Most of the guys in the platoon saw this and snickered. Snake said, "*Xin loi.*"

In a low voice Erik asked David what was the meaning of what sounded like "sin loy."

"I have it in my notebook. *Xin loi* means 'sorry about that' or, in our lexicon, 'tough shit.'"

Lieutenant Cushman said to no one in particular, "This meeting must have taken place yesterday and whoever it was has moved on. Let's get going."

The platoon advanced cautiously through the jungle for another klick. Third squad was leading. The point man stopped and held up a fist. He looked like he was standing in the middle of a trail going north and south.

The lieutenant came up as third squad gathered around. "What the fuck?" the lieutenant said. "This is not your typical gook trail. This has seen some serious traffic, like bicycles loaded with mortar rounds and who knows what ordnance."

"Yeah, what it is," said Reginald Robinson, a black guy from south Los Angeles. Erik heard he always volunteered to walk point. At breakfast that morning he had told Erik that he used to dodge a lot of gangs in Bellflower because all he wanted to do was play football, although he didn't spend much time in the library, which he planned to correct by using the GI Bill when he was back in the world.

"This is the way it's going in 1969," Lieutenant Cushman said resignedly. "We're trying to keep casualties low and they keep pecking away at us. What were our fearless leaders thinking to get involved here, trying to hustle the East?"

Erik recognized the line from Kipling.

The platoon established a night defensive position with fourth squad setting up parallel to the trail. First squad secured opposite them with second and third squads on the two sides. They cut down some vines and saplings with machetes so they could see one another. Cushman and Anderson established a command post at the center. Doc, the medic, dug a small latrine pit within the perimeter, complete with a couple of sandbags for sitting.

Erik and David dug a foxhole and filled up some of the empty sandbags they carried.

"Don't fuckin' tie those off," Snake said. "Just fold the ends under so they're easy to empty tomorrow morning."

Out in the field, Erik realized, they were all in the shit together. "Thanks," he said.

David said, "This is just like the Romans in Gaul."

"They used sandbags?" Snake said. He had white skin like the underside of a catfish and his thin sideburns protruded below the bows of his black horn-rimmed glasses. Erik had seen him playing poker the night before and he looked reptilian when sizing up the other players.

"No, I mean the Roman legions always fortified their position with a trench and palisade of logs around it for their camps during military campaigns," David said. "They did that for hundreds of years, even before Caesar went into Gaul. Not only were they prepared to fend off attackers, they slept better. That's partly why the Romans were able to conquer Gaul and other places. Another thing was discipline in tight formations with their short swords in upward thrusts. Any man is going to jump back in a reflex before getting a *gladius* in the gonads."

Snake went back to digging his foxhole with Mason as if he couldn't see anything to gain by listening to more history.

Erik said, "Do you ever think this is all a dream? I have a feeling that I'm going to wake up any moment and you'll be a faded memory of a fairly real conversation."

"How about I hit you upside the head and see if you dream up a welt?" David suggested.

"At least I didn't volunteer for this shit, you lifer."

David shrugged. "I don't know. Maybe I'm trying to prove something."

"Like what?"

"I'll tell you sometime. Hey, let's do some history shit. Who was the chieftain of the Averni in Gaul that Caesar finally defeated?"

"Vercingetorix?"

"Right! How the hell did you know that one?"

"I had two years of French in high school and college. I should say, *J'ai étudié le francais pour deux ans dans l'universitée.* We had a whole chapter on that French folk hero. My turn. What two guys were consuls in the triumvirate with Caesar?"

David swung his entrenching tool over an imaginary home plate. "*Ker-ack*! It's a long fly ball into deep center field. Back, back, back, and it's outahere! That would be Pompey and Crassus."

Bodine approached. "Listen up, third squad. The lieutenant wants two volunteers for a listening post by the trail. They'll set up two claymores. We're not going to take on a force bigger than a platoon, but a squad or so, we'll blow their shit away."

"Yeah, Sarge, I'll go," David said.

Erik gulped. "Me too," he said. That's what I've got to do, he told himself, get the hell out of myself. Be brave. A vision of his father standing back in a crowd flashed in his memory.

Bodine looked at David appreciatively. "Nah, Levy, you're too green. You too, Thorvald. Forget about it." Nobody else volunteered. "Okay, El-tee will have to get them from some other squad. Put out your claymores where you can see the white tape on the back. We don't want some gook turning that sumbitch around during the night."

Erik went to the latrine and heard the lieutenant running through some frequencies on the radio. Suddenly, a voice broke in speaking Vietnamese. "Tom, get Nguyen," the lieutenant said to his RTO.

Nguyen was reading a paperback and doing very little preparation for a fighting position near the CP. When he got to the lieutenant he smiled at the sound of his native tongue.

"What're they saying, Nguyen?" the lieutenant said.

"They tell dai wi to string uh …you say, uh…commo wire along trail, but hap to be off trail."

More words came over the radio. "What'd he say?"

"He ask if see any Amelican killers. Othah mothlefuckle say no hap seen."

"That's good," the lieutenant said. "Okay, Nguyen, you can go back to your digs. Thanks."

Erik could barely see Flattum and Downs making their way to the listening post. He had heard they were gung-ho guys from Oklahoma just out of high school.

What a day and only 358 to go, he sighed. Staring into mottled shades of dark half way through his watch, Erik felt a little more secure knowing that he was within a perimeter of guys just like him protecting one another. David was still sleeping. He looked at the foxhole to his left. There's Mason who said he was from Birmingfuckingham, Alagotdambama when he first met him. What's he holding? That's a pocket radio. No doubt he's listening to armed forces radio, AFVN, with an earphone stuck in his ear. Learning about the radio station that played rock and roll all the time throughout Vietnam was just one of the many surprises Erik had when he arrived in-country.

He was getting used to the quietness of the night and keeping his mind active. Aiming his M-16, Erik fired a mock burst at a charging hard-core NVA soldier with leaves sticking out of his pith helmet.

He felt tired. A long time had passed. He checked his watch. It was thirty minutes to midnight. Let's see, what is that in military time? Oh, yeah, it's 2330 hours if you're a lifer. For us draftees it's 11:30 p.m. He thought a moment. For you marines, the big hand is on the six and the little hand is between the eleven and twelve. He laughed at his little joke.

Suddenly, Erik felt alarmed. Something's different. How come everybody's so quiet? He could usually hear guys talking in low voices or somebody going to the latrine. He squinted into the perimeter and could make out forms frozen in place, except for Mason who was apparently grooving on some rock and roll. He was about to say something when he heard what had everybody's attention. It was the faint sound of movement on the trail—low talking, a twig breaking, the slap of a sandal on the packed ground, a branch being brushed back. He shivered. Some unknown force is making good time through the trail and now right beside the perimeter. Christ, that's got to be a large body of NVA. His stomach clenched. He slowly reached for his M-16. He heard little clicks all around the perimeter as he flipped the safety toggle past semi to full automatic.

"Don't blow the claymores," Erik whispered, willing Downs and Flattum to be still. "They're too many." He thought about the hundred steel ball bearings adhered to the *C*-four explosive encased in a plastic case about the size of a box of Grape-Nuts and knew they were lethal, those claymores, but they could only do so much.

He listened as whatever it was passed by. He could barely hear Lieutenant Cushman talking on the radio. Erik figured he was calling in a fire mission with a guess as to where those NVA would be by the time he got the guns on line. In a few minutes came the far-off reports of 105s being launched. Erik knew that artillery rounds traveled faster than sound but traced a high arc, so the banshee cries of hot, spinning steel piercing the humid night air came right after the sound of them being fired. Erik automatically looked up as the ordnance passed overhead. According to some of the guys, short rounds were not unheard of. It was a crapshoot, they said. About half a klick away the rounds impacted with four fearsome *karumphs*. Erik thought how the movies never duplicated the crack-of-doom of real artillery.

Erik's breathing gradually returned to normal. He considered what would have happened if the listening post had blown their two claymores. That would have ended the war for about twenty hard-core NVA, leaving maybe eighty to do their thing with us. If our shit was flaky, they could have overrun us. If our shit was together, the first wave would have been neutralized by our claymores. For the second wave it would have been automatic fire and hand-to-hand.

The artillery awakened David. "What's going on?" he said groggily.

"Good, you're awake. It's time to switch anyway. You missed some weird shit," Erik said.

"Yeah, right," David said in a yawn.

"No, really. About a hundred NVA went ditty-boppin' down the trail about twenty meters from us," Erik assured him.

"Are you fuckin' serious?"

"I shit you not."

After Erik described the soft, yet unmistakable sounds of a lot of people moving fast, he said, "I guess the lieutenant figured they were too many and same with the listening post, so they didn't blow the claymores. Whoever they were, they went on their merry way. That's some audacious shit!"

"Huh," David said. "I thought the NVA were disciplined, sneaky bastards. Maybe they were ARVN. Nah, Bodine said they don't go out at night."

"Yeah, I'm sure they were NVA. ARVN don't wear Ho Chi Minh sandals. From what I've seen tonight the NVA use trails and we got here by hacking through the jungle. Is that the way it always is?"

"I don't know," David said.

Chapter Three

Erik lay on his nylon camouflaged poncho liner. The mosquito repellent was still working. He felt he could drift off at any moment. Leaves above made silhouettes against the stars. Leaves, leaves, leaves he repeated in a dream-like state.

Every autumn, by the middle of October, Gainesboro was awash in a sea of fallen leaves. Strolling through the purple, red, and yellow remnants of verdant summer shade produced a *koosh, koosh, koosh* with every step. It was the kids who dispensed with them, but they first had to let the parents have some fun, scratching the ground here and there. In a short time, they asked the adults if they could try it for a while. Before long, the grown-ups were nowhere to be seen, and the children got to rake and even burn the crunchy piles. Once again, Erik thought, he and the gang had outfoxed the adults. A few years later, when Erik read *Tom Sawyer*, something about the episode of the whitewashed fence seemed vaguely familiar.

Mountains of leaves provided soft landings when everybody took turns with running leaps and disappearing in a noisy cocoon. The piles were restored on the streets, and the burning phase began. Gordy threw a lighted match into a bunch of leaves. That was all it took to get a fire going. Everybody had a poke-stick to tease the flames into consuming more leaves. Eventually the yellow and red mounds were reduced to yellow and red embers.

These Indian summer evenings were shrouded in sweet smoke that held the last rays of sunshine in a hazy embrace. Whiffs of burning leaves brought memories of the year before. Erik thought the fragrance was like nothing else. It was fall, that's what it was. It was crisp Cortland apples, a harvest moon, hay rides, carving pumpkins, frost in the mornings, and flannel shirts.

With a few leaves left, everybody gathered sticks and dead branches for a bonfire to roast hotdogs. Some kids put them in buns. Erik ate a couple right off the stick. For dessert, they made angel-on-horseback, which was a bronzed marshmallow squished on a square of Hershey's chocolate between two Graham crackers. Erik wondered how his mom happened to have these supplies on hand.

He and Arthur discussed cowboys as they roasted another marshmallow. They had listened to *The Lone Ranger* on the radio that morning, and last Saturday night's movie was *Winchester 73,* so westerns were on their minds.

"Roy Rogers is king of the cowboys and Gene Autry is king of the horses," Arthur stated.

"I bet Champion could beat Trigger any day. Besides, Roy Rogers movies are stupid," Erik said. "Real cowboys didn't have jeeps and stuff."

Babs said, "Are you going to the movie tonight, Helen?"

"What's playing?" Helen said, her face aglow in the circle of friends around the fire.

Rosalind Fredrickson said, "I think it's *The Yearling.*" Rosalind's attention had been on Mike McLaughlin. He had driven into town to burn leaves with her, and then take her to a movie on what Erik heard his sister call a date.

"Yeah, and in color," Mike said.

"Of course I'm going," Helen said. "It's Saturday night, isn't it?"

The only time Gainesboro's Bijou showed movies was on Saturday night. Some farm kids and most of those who lived in town went no matter what was playing. Not much else was happening for entertainment, except for *Your Hit Parade* on the radio.

Erik saw no adults, as usual. Girls sat with girls and boys with boys, except for the couples on a date. Everybody talked during the previews. A bright Technicolor picture got Erik's attention as Gregory Peck in *The Yearling* blazed across the screen. This looks promising, he thought. Someone off to the right wondered if the main feature had started. "Is this the movie?" he said loudly. It was repeated up front, "Is this the movie?" Somebody hollered, "Shut up! It's the movie."

Everyone got quiet. All eyes were opened wide and focused on the big screen. Erik had heard of television. He saw one in a store window in Storm Lake. It was like a radio with a picture of somebody talking in a snowstorm. He was sure that television would never replace going to a movie. Tonight, *The Yearling* swept him into a place that was bigger and more colorful than Gainesboro.

The picture was so captivating that everyone laughed or cried together, but talking was against the rules. Erik thought it was a lot more fun to watch in a packed house than if only a few people were in the audience.

Walking home with Arthur, Erik could name the people who lived in every house. It was very dark, except for an occasional island of light under a street lamp. Erik knew he could find his way home blindfolded just by the feel of Gainesboro under his feet. He wondered if it was scary in a big city at night, because here he had no worries. He saw other kids on their way home and thought, this is a great place to grow up.

He recalled a few Saturdays ago when the new sidewalk on Center Avenue was a yellow brick road, the girls wore ruby slippers, and the boys were ready to do battle with flying monkeys and a wicked witch behind every tree.

Erik didn't want to live anywhere else and thought that Gainesboro would never change. He was disappointed when his father told him they had to move to a bigger town next year. His doctorate was almost completed and he wanted to teach at a college.

It was four o'clock in the morning when Erik awoke from a surprisingly deep sleep. The sky was still a black dome with pin-pricks of twinkling stars. He was curiously relaxed and ready when the reality clock started ticking again. "So anyway, do you think when our company does search and destroy missions they use trails?"

"Yeah, I think so," David replied.

"Then it's just a roll of the dice if there's an ambush on either side. The war in Nam is just a question of probability. Sometimes you're the windshield and sometimes you're the insect."

"I have to take a crap," David said as he stepped out of the foxhole.

Kablam! Kablam! Two explosions rocked the NDP.

Chapter Four

Erik ducked. "Now what the fuck?" he whispered. "Are they back to mess with us?"

David was hugging the ground. "Could be. Who knows?" he whispered back.

Lieutenant Cushman signaled the platoon with palms down, barely visible as dawn was breaking. "Be cool," he said in a low voice. He scuttled toward the listening post in a low crouch.

He came back in about fifteen minutes. The sky was starting to lighten as the lieutenant told them what happened. "Here's the deal. The LP blew away four VC. Two males and two females. You can see it all when we cross the trail. Let's get some grub and pack it up."

After breaking down the NDP, everyone opened Cs. Several pocket radios were on. The DJ from AFVN radio screamed "Goooooooooood mooooooorninnng, Vieeeeeeeet Naaaaaaaaaaaaaaaam!" Erik and David exchange puzzled looks.

Bodine grinned at them. "Welcome to the Nam, boys."

"That's our fuckin' barber!" Sergeant Hosmer exclaimed, pointing to a corpse lying on the trail. The front of his civilian shirt was a bloody mess, and his right leg was folded under him in an impossible position. Three mortar rounds had spilled out of his backpack. "That's the gook who cuts hair at Tay Ninh West."

Snake cursed the Vietnamese barber. "The fucking, spying, turncoat, lying sonofabitch. Make nicee talkee with us during the day and tries to kill us at night."

Downs said, "Fuckin' A."

Erik figured such a rant came from feeling double-crossed by the South Vietnamese because of being told they would be loved as freedom fighters.

A female lay at the edge of the trail clutching an AK-47. Snake pried it from her hand. From what Erik could see she was pretty, but it was hard to tell when her eyes and mouth were black with flies.

"Huh, I wonder what those are," the lieutenant said, looking at triangular patches sewn on the VCs' shirts. They were messed up, but some words could be made out. "Hey, Nguyen, what does *Nha nyer Son My* mean?"

"It say 'remember Son My.'"

"What the hell is Son My?"

"That place with small village, My Lai and same-same othah village. They in Quang Ngai."

"Quang Ngai is a coastal province, but I've never heard of Son My or My Lai. Have you, Andy?" Lieutenant Cushman said.

Anderson shook his head.

The other two Viet Cong, a male and a female, were dressed in black pajamas, their black-and-white checkered scarves stained with blood. They died clutching each other. Enough of the steel ball bearings had found their mark. Flattum and Downs snatched up their two AKs, one of them with a shattered stock.

Lieutenant Cushman said, "Thorvald, bury the mortar rounds. Levy, look for paperwork on them. We'll leave the bodies where they lay. Anybody got a patch?"

Sergeant Hosmer tossed down a Twelfth Infantry insignia on the embracing corpses. Its motto read: "Deeds, not words."

David went through their pockets, looking nauseated. He found a folded piece of paper in the man's black pajama top. It was bloody and torn, but he gave it to Lieutenant Cushman. "That's it, El-tee."

Erik started digging a hole off the trail. Something caught his eye. "Hey, Lieutenant, there's a wire here."

Everybody crowded around. "I'll be damned," said the lieutenant. He looked at Sergeant First Class Anderson. "That must be the commo wire the dink talked about on the radio." He turned to Erik. "Thorvald, finish up. We'll be up the trail a ways. Catch us up when you're done. We've got to get away from these fucking flies."

Erik watched the platoon fade into the shadows of the rainforest trail. This is what we look like, he thought—large, sweaty, skin-headed, swaggering Americans who traveled eight thousand miles to invade their land. The Vietnamese must think we're crazy, and maybe we are, he admitted.

To get away from the smell of death in the tropical heat, he buried the mortar rounds quickly. He looked at the carnage and thought things over. Why are we here? Freedom? He turned and walked down the trail.

Why is the great republic falling for that? It's a deception in order to wield power for power's sake. Americans never think of the brutality visited on humanity and what it does to their own warriors who are KIAs or damaged goods. Young men go along for adventure, brotherhood, testing their manhood, and the thrill of being alive while the feared other lay dead and unthreatening. Move on, Erik, he told himself. Could he survive? Does life make any sense so far?

Chapter Five

"I'll see you after school, but I'll have to leave right after dinner to go over to Ferndale for a basketball game," Harold said. He kissed Marie goodbye. "Let's go, kids."

"Zip up that jacket, Erik," Marie said. "It's getting a lot colder. I'll miss you." She often said that when Erik left for school, now in second grade and Helen in fifth. "You, too, Helen," she called out.

"Bye, Mom. I'll miss you, too." Erik said. He liked walking to and from school with his dad. That's how he learned to count numbers, the days of the week, and the months of the year. He said those lists as they walked in step on the sidewalk.

Today, Helen had his attention. "Daddy, I like my piano lessons, but I don't want to sing in the trio."

"Well, why not?" her father said quickly, almost cutting her off. "Come on, now. You, Eloise, and Babs do very well for the school programs, and you can sing in the church Christmas program too."

"I just get scared."

"Scared? Scared of what?"

Erik thought his father's tone was sharp and would cause Helen to shut down the way it usually did.

But Helen replied, "I tighten up when I'm in front of people and get queasy in the stomach. I think you will find mistakes, and I will look uncomfortable and nervous."

"Well, you must be brave." Harold turned to Erik. "Erik, you didn't know your months of the year yesterday."

"Um, how did you know?"

"I happened to be outside the room when Mrs. Peterson quizzed you. I could hear through the vent."

"I got June and July mixed up," Erik said, amazed at how his father got around in the school building.

Erik, Helen, and their father crossed Main Street as Gainesboro woke up. Men were making deliveries in semis and straight trucks. Some grain-elevator workers came out of the hotel restaurant with toothpicks in their mouths as they walked past Heglan's grocery and dry goods store to the west edge of town only two blocks away.

Babs and Arthur yelled, "Hey, wait up!" Erik and Helen stopped and looked back.

Harold said he had to get going and walked ahead. "I'll see you at school."

After crossing Main, Babs said, "Do you know your multiplication tables, Helen? Miss Bjornson's going to ask us today."

"Oh, yes. I've known them for a long time."

"What's a hundred times a hundred?" Arthur asked.

"That's not the multiplication tables, but it's ten thousand," Helen said, yawning.

"Dang."

It was Sunday. It had been very cold, even for November. The fields next to town showed black dirt between rows of cut-off corn stalks. Erik remembered last winter when the snow covered everything and made it bright and smooth.

Marie had prepared roast beef before walking to church for the Sunday service at Our Savior Lutheran. After dinner, Erik spread the comics out on the living room floor, and Helen went to her room to read *Gone With the Wind*. Erik noted that his mom was in her usual Sunday afternoon place, lying on the sofa with sections of the paper covering her. He wondered where his dad had gone.

The back door opened. In a moment Harold appeared. "Erik, get your sister. We're going ice skating."

Erik looked up and saw his father's eagerness, which got him excited, too. He ran to Helen's room. "Helen, we're going skating!"

The green 1951 Ford trailed a swirl of brown dust as Harold drove on gravel roads. The sun shone brightly, high in a cloudless sky. It was as cold as any winter's day, but without the snow.

Harold said, "Now, kids, we're going to what is called a gravel pit. They were formed by glaciers that came down from the north and sort of pushed a lot of good soil in front of them. They also tucked a lot of rocks underneath the ground. Sometimes these sedimentary layers were exposed on top of the ground."

Erik learned a lot when their dad talked about different stuff. Helen listened, too, and asked if there was going to be a quiz.

Harold laughed. "No, honey, but companies that build roads discovered that these outcroppings of rock were a great source of gravel. So they, well, mined the rock and dug a big hole in the ground. Sometimes they went too deep, and springs filled the open pits with water and had to be abandoned. That's where we're heading—to a gravel pit."

In a few minutes Harold parked next to a cluster of trees, gray and leafless in drab contrast to a cobalt sky. "Here we are. Grab your skates and mittens. We'll put them on down by the ice."

They walked on a little path and suddenly came upon a protected valley with frozen ponds like black jewels cut in different shapes and sizes. Some were long and narrow like a canal. Others were large ovals surrounded by small birch and maple saplings. A filigree of connections tied everything together.

Erik's mouth dropped. "Look! It's so smooth. It's perfect. It's perfect ice!"

The three of them couldn't get their skates on fast enough. Harold carefully laced up his brown hockey skates with their straight blades of steel that gleamed with the promise of impeccable skating.

Helen had her white figure skates on and was about to tighten the laces, but asked, "Daddy, can you lace up mine tight like yours?"

"Sure," Harold said. He went to his knees and got Helen's skates nice and snug, all the while talking about his favorite subject, the weather. "This cold snap we're having is because of an arctic high-pressure stationary front, which means that these ponds of water froze without a wind to corrupt the process. Precipitation didn't disturb it, either, so we've got smooth ice that's a couple of inches thick."

Erik enjoyed the explanation of what he was about to skate on as he tied the knots on his hockey skates. He stepped on the unspoiled ice and pushed off. His first glide on one blade seemed to go on forever with nothing to stop it. "What is it that makes it go so easily, Daddy?"

His father and sister caught up with him. "Actually, the runner is carried along on a thin film of water briefly melted by the pressure of steel on ice. The friction is very minimal as you glide along."

For the next two hours the crisp fall air was filled with laughter and shouts of delight as the three Thorvalds explored the linked-up ponds and raced on straightaways. They etched figure eights on the pristine surface. Sometimes they fell quiet as they stopped to lie on the ice and hood their eyes with their mittens to peer into the hushed world below. They saw a small, yellow seahorse-creature among green plants with tiny leaves. In shallow inlets the fallen leaves of red, yellow, and purple were preserved as if under glass.

"Go down to the end of this pond and face me," Harold told his children.

Helen and Erik screamed with excitement to see their father bearing down on them at top speed. At the last moment, he flipped his skates to the right, sending a blizzard of ice flakes on them and stopping just in time.

"Okay, now I'm going to teach you the cross-cut turn," Harold said. "First, you skate along and then, to turn to the left, like you're going around a curve, you cross your right leg over the left like this."

Helen and Erik caught on very quickly and were amazed at their father's enthusiasm and ability. They tried everything he suggested. When they played tag, Helen and Erik knew that their father let himself get cornered. Their faces reflected total joy, with rosy cheeks and unending smiles along with cries of glee.

The sun had dropped below the treetops. When they first arrived it seemed as if it was cheering them on to enjoy this day. As its brightness waned, Erik knew that this wonderful afternoon was coming to an end. Snow would probably cover this magical place soon. Other years may not have the right conditions, but today it was perfect ice. Although Erik couldn't put it into words, he felt that all the forces of the universe had come together to produce this brief moment in time for three ecstatic humans somewhere in the Milky Way.

Chapter Six

With the March thaw, Gainesboro and its surroundings changed from monotonous whiteness to various shades of green which heralded warmth and renewal. It was Saturday, and folks in Gainesboro were emerging from winter's hold by taking down storm windows, laying out vegetable gardens, and planting flowers.

Swinging around a light pole in front of Heglan's store, Erik watched Main Street grow busier with shoppers. He heard a deep rumbling of engines and turned to see five motorcycles roll into town like a dark cloud bringing a storm. His father went into the store to buy seeds for his garden. The riders wore black engineer boots, leather jackets, and motorcycle caps. Two girls rode in back, hugging their drivers around the waist. They pulled to the curb and parked right in front of Heglan's.

Erik had never seen the likes of them before. The girls' lips were a deep red like a Valentine's heart, and their eyebrows were thin black lines. When the guys swung off their bikes, Erik saw they each had an oversized billfold in their back pocket attached to their belt with a silver chain. One had a vest that said "Harley-Davidson" on the back. The biggest one had long, greasy hair the color of wheat, combed straight back. He didn't wear a cap.

The girls, wearing blue jeans turned up at the cuff, removed their polka-dot scarves and fluffed their hair. One unwrapped a stick of Juicy Fruit gum and popped it in her mouth.

The big guy said, "Hey, Doogle-ass. Get me and Betty a Coke."

Erik was surprised to see he was talking to Douglas Torgerson, a senior at Gainesboro High. His hair was longer now, and he had gotten himself a black leather vest studded with silver designs. His black engineer boots looked too big for him. He seemed like a tag-along with an older crowd.

Douglas looked at Betty.

"Move your ass, Doug," the big guy said as he combed back his thick hair.

"Well, Marion," Doug said, emphasizing *Marion* like a taunt, "Who was your slave last year? And besides, I'm not thirsty." He glanced at Betty again.

Betty gave Doug a smirk. "What are you lookin' at?" she said. And then, "Don't even think about it."

Erik felt sorry for Douglas. He had heard teachers say he was a goof-off with too much time and money. He needed guidance from his mother instead of the cash paid by an insurance company when his dad died of a heart attack. He lived on a good farm east of town, but his mom just rented it out. Erik looked at Doug's light-blue motorcycle with wide tires and a "Fat Boy" decal on its gas tank.

Marion slowly stuck his comb into his back pocket and said with a smile that wasn't a smile, "Hey, Doogle-ass, were you lookin' at my woman?"

Doug swallowed. "Yeah, she's pretty, don't you think?"

Marion backhanded Doug across the mouth. Betty's nostrils flared with excitement. The other bikers leaned back on their Harleys.

Doug looked surprised. He hesitated and then punched Marion in the stomach.

Marion landed a roundhouse with his large fist on the side of Doug's head. Doug swung wildly at Marion, but mostly held his fists in front of his face to fend off blows. Marion took his time as he landed more punches.

Erik couldn't stand to watch. He ran into Heglan's and saw his father. "Dad! Dad! Douglas Torgerson is getting beat up. You gotta stop it."

Harold was talking to two of his high school students who worked in the store. He turned to Erik. "No, uh, I can't go out there right now."

Erik was surprised. He thought his father would drop everything and race out to stop the fight. He looked at the two girls to see if they were shocked, too. They showed nothing. He ran back outside.

Marion landed a left on Doug, who had given up fighting back. His nose was streaming blood. He fell forward, crying, with his forehead on Marion's bended knee. Marion had his arm cocked, ready to hit him again.

"That's enough!"

Marion held his fist in midair. He turned to see who had yelled at him.

A man with silver workpants stood on the sidewalk and took a drag from his cigarette. Over his white T-shirt he wore an unbuttoned light-blue striped shirt that had "Bill" embroidered above his left pocket. The open shirt revealed the start of a paunch, but the arms coming out of his short sleeves were muscular. He was a little smaller than Marion.

The other bikers turned to look at the man. The people in Heglan's came outside. Erik noticed his father standing well back among the onlookers, wearing a serious expression. Erik realized he was trying to look tough.

With a cigarette dangling from his lips, the lone man on the sidewalk said, "You don't do that-a-way to anybody. You're a goddamned bully." He took a drag on his cigarette and flicked it away. "Bullies usually get what they deserve." His eyes looked like blue ice, but his face was calm, as if he wasn't surprised at what humans were capable of doing to each other, and what he could do to Marion in particular.

One of the bikers sneered at him. "So who are you?"

"I'm the guy what's stoppin' this fight." He looked at all of them, one by one. "Anybody else have any stupid questions?" He stared them all down. "I didn't think so. Now get your ass on those bikes and get the hell out of here."

Marion scoffed as he swaggered toward his Tele-Glide where Betty waited, snapping her Juicy Fruit. The others attended to something on their cycles, but didn't look back at the man.

Marion grabbed a handle bar and put his weight on his left foot as though to swing his right leg over his motorcycle, but spun and attempted a sidewinding kick at the man on the sidewalk behind him.

The man called Bill was ready for him and caught his leg in his right hand. He jerked it upward and put Marion on his back in one easy motion. Marion lay moaning on the pavement with the wind knocked out of him.

One of the other bikers made a move toward Bill, but looked unsure of himself. Bill pointed at him. "Don't do it," he said.

The guy backed off and helped Marion get up. Marion shoved him aside and took a few steps to his Harley muttering, "I'll get you."

"No you won't," Bill said matter-of-factly. "Now beat it and don't come back."

The gang, minus Doug, mounted up without another word. They kick-started their engines into a deep rumble and roared up Main Street out of town.

The man in silver workpants turned and headed back toward the hotel. The wide-eyed bystanders watched him in silence. Mr. Heglan seemed to know who he was and said two words that Erik barely heard: "Iwo Jima."

Nobody helped Doug, as if to say this is what you get if you roll with those people. Doug crawled to his cycle where he pulled out a rag from his saddle bag and put it to his bloody nose. When the blood and tears stopped, he straddled his new Fat Boy and brought his weight down on the crank and took off.

Erik stood in silence as everyone went back into Heglan's. He was alone in the street, playing back the last ten minutes. Such violence had never occurred in his idealized Gainesboro. He had an empty feeling that was worse than when he learned there was no Santa Claus. Troubling thoughts about his father wouldn't go away. If growing up meant more disappointments, he would just as soon stay at 8 years old.

Chapter Seven

Erik learned about finances and status, totally new concepts, when the Thorvalds moved to Sturgis. He discovered they were very poor. His parents had many conversations that revolved around money and what they could afford. He knew that his father had spent his savings on getting a Ph.D. and providing for his family in married-student housing at the University of Iowa. He heard them say things like "poor neighborhood" and "not our class of people" when looking for a place to live.

Compared to Gainesboro, Erik thought, Sturgis was very exciting. It was the home of Sturgis State College, where his father was hired as a professor in the Education Department. The town had a lot of people and Erik didn't know any of them, unlike Gainesboro, where he knew everybody.

Erik could see that his parents were worried. They snapped at him, and Helen, too, about little things, such as their posture, and what people would think of them. That was new—being concerned about how they appeared to others.

After several days of looking they still hadn't found an acceptable place to live. Aware that his parents were under a lot of pressure as the start of school neared, Erik tried to stay out of their way, which was hard to do in a small motel room.

Something lucky happened when Harold went to visit his department dean. He came back smiling and said that Sturgis State owned a big house that was willed to them by a professor. It was used for special occasions, but the college was thinking of renting it to a faculty member or maybe selling it. It was available for a year at a very reasonable rent. This made Marie very happy. She said it was Providence. Erik wanted to meet that guy and thank him for making his mother very happy.

*   *   *

The colonial-style brick house had two white pillars in the front supporting a portico. The whole family agreed it was bigger than anything they'd ever dreamed of living in. An ample lawn lay between the house and College Avenue, one of the busiest streets in Sturgis. Erik had no doubt it would be well maintained because his father was a hard worker, and he wanted to help keep it nice, too.

Sturgis State was three blocks away. Next to the campus was the Square, a little business district with a few stores and eating places, including a place that served pizza, which Erik and Helen had never heard of. They were also surprised to see three bars, since Gainesboro had only one, and nobody they knew ever went into that dark and forbidding place, except some railroad and grain-elevator workers and a few hard-scrabble farmers.

The first day after moving in, Helen and Erik sat on their front porch and played a game with all the cars that went by, which was a big change from sleepy Gainesboro. Helen had Fords and Erik took Chevys. They kept a count to see which would win. Helen won with forty-two Fords to Erik's thirty-seven Chevys by lunchtime.

In the afternoon some neighbors from across the street came over and introduced themselves. Erik could see that his folks were polite and nice enough but lacked enthusiasm. Erik guessed that they were a little tired from moving and all.

As they met other people, Erik saw a pattern. If his folks found that the people they met were with the college, they turned on the charm and easy laughter. It looked as if they were showing off or something. What are they doing? Erik wondered. They weren't like this in Gainesboro, where they were the same with everybody.

"So where did you live before?" a next-door neighbor asked after shaking hands with Harold and Marie. He wore sneakers, dirty khakis, and a T-shirt.

"Oh, a little town you've probably never heard of in northwest Iowa," Marie said, "called Gainesboro. Have you been working in your garden?"

"Oh, yes. I'm pulling some maintenance on my flowers. You'd think I would do something else since I'm always lecturing about stamens, zygotes, pistils, and things about plant life."

"Oh, of course, you're Dr. Mershon of the Biology Department. I've heard a lot about you," Harold said.

Dr. Mershon grinned and said, "I hope we can still be friends."

Erik's mom and dad laughed.

Harold said, "Oh, yes, it's all good. I'm new in the Education Department, just a seedling in the Sturgis State garden. How about some iced tea?"

They moved to the back yard and sat on folding chairs at a card table. Marie brought out a pitcher of tea that had brewed slowly in the sun and a tray of glasses filled with ice.

"So what's it like in the hinterland and living in a small town?" Dr. Mershon asked.

"Well, it's very nice," Harold said. "The property taxes are low, everybody is friendly, the kids loved it, but it can't last. People are going to the bigger cities to shop."

"I suppose everybody knows everybody and what you're doing," Dr. Mershon said, "but that could be a drawback." He chuckled.

"It was tranquil and easy going," Marie said. "We were all from similar backgrounds with nothing to prove. Our church had a lot of social activities, and we had ladies' and mixed bridge clubs."

Harold said, "We had one potential problem, but not bad, really, and that was no law enforcement except for the county sheriff in Storm Lake. Once we had a motorcycle gang come into town and try to cause trouble, but a group of us confronted them and they took off."

Erik looked up from inspecting the grass for four-leaf clovers. He saw no indication that his father felt uncomfortable telling that story. But he knew one thing; he would never stand back when somebody had to do something. He didn't know what, but he thought he could figure it out.

Chapter Eight

The big college house sat on a deep lot that extended beyond the mowed lawn and double garage. At the far end Erik found a little wood with different kinds of trees, one of which was a weeping willow. His favorite escape was to sit under that tree and smoke a pipe he took from the collection his father started when he became a college professor.

Erik followed Helen's example and discovered the world of books. Now in fourth grade he was reading books at a junior high level and above. *Huckleberry Finn* was his favorite. Whenever Huck wanted to pause and reflect on the life he was dealt, he would light up a bit of tabac in his corncob pipe and mull things over. That's what Erik liked to do, although he would get along with a regular pipe until he found a suitable corncob to make his own.

When leaning back against that willow tree wafting aromatic smoke into the canopy of light-green branches, he felt a pleasant sensation in his groin that was both exciting and relaxing at the same time. He didn't understand what it was, but it felt good. He dreamed of floating on a raft down the Cedar River to the mighty Mississippi like Huck and Jim, and leaving this new situation behind.

Erik tried to think of why his parents were so different from a couple of years ago. He didn't know his father anymore. They didn't talk the way they used to. His mother didn't pay attention to him except when she came down on him for something. Neither of them responded to any concerns Erik had about being a new kid in school, which had started the week before.

Harold seemed a lot busier than he was in Gainesboro. After dinner he corrected papers and read reports from his students. He left them on his desk for days at a time. Erik often read these assignments, but was careful to put them back exactly the way he found them. He didn't want his father to know he was reading observations at the laboratory school where he and Helen attended.

Erik read of incidents he saw at school or heard about. News traveled fast in that small school. One report was about a new kid from Puerto Rico named Marco. He looked a lot older than the other sixth graders. He "inappropriately" flirted with a very attractive student teacher on the playground. The paper said the kid asked her to have lunch with him in the cafeteria, and then suggested that they meet on the Square for pizza sometime. He said he would be happy to polish her apples and pound her eraser any time she wanted.

The school was new, and often tried the latest methods that educational science had to offer. Erik was surprised to see the desks in his classroom arranged in groupings. He supposed it was to find out if students could "work well with others," one of the items on the report card that his teacher showed the class on the first day of school. When college students came in to observe, Erik could see that some of his classmates behaved in such a way as to draw their attention, sometimes in good and sometimes bad behavior. He thought it was like being at a zoo, except they were being watched instead of being the watchers.

One day after school, when reading one of the reports on his father's desk, he realized it was about Helen. He remembered a conversation she had a few days before with his parents.

"I don't know why she's doing it, but she's always putting me down," Helen said.

"Who?" Marie asked.

"Darlene Klinger. I try to be friends with her, but I think she thinks I'm coming between her and the twins. I'm getting tired of it. I'm going to smash her face one of these days," Helen said.

Marie jumped on that. "Never get angry or smash anybody. Just ignore her. She'll stop. Seventh grade is particularly difficult. You're becoming a teenager, and I'm sure you will be popular."

"Ye gods! It's just an expression," Helen said.

Erik remembered how Helen looked so upset and frustrated. He wanted to say it's okay to get angry if you're right, like that guy in front of Heglan's that time that he didn't want to talk about. It doesn't mean you're going to haul off and hit somebody. He thought his mother should be more understanding and listen and not blow it up as though it were a big deal.

The report he was reading said that a seventh-grade girl had passed a note during class. The teacher confiscated it. The writer of the report found it humorous how junior high students think a teacher wouldn't see a note being passed. She wrote:

> The note passer's name was Darlene and she had been observed making unkind remarks to Helen, a classmate in language arts. "Did your mom make that dress or did you get it at a rummage sale?" Darlene looked at Carolyn and Marilyn, classmate twins, for approval, but received a definite disapproval. Helen smiled at Darlene and said, "We're very poor. We're just getting on our feet," and took her seat. Helen was very attentive in class, but quiet. Darlene did not pay attention and was warned for passing notes. The second time, the teacher, Dr. Zimmermann, gave Darlene a detention.

Erik felt himself flush with anger. He knew Darlene Klinger. She stopped by their house with the twins on their way to school. He thought about what Huck would do in this situation.

Sturgis Laboratory School had kindergarten to twelfth grade in one sprawling building, two stories high. The elementary section was next to the junior high wing, so it was easy to follow Darlene in the morning and see which locker was hers.

At lunch Erik sat next to Donny who laughed at his jokes. "What happens when cows see something funny?" Erik said.

"I don't know."

"Milk comes out their nose."

Donny howled above the noise of a table full of fourth graders. Erik was glad milk didn't come out of his nose.

Erik said, "Hey, Donny, want to be my lookout?"

"What for?"

"There's this girl picking on my sister, and I want to put a note in her locker. I think we can do it on the way to the playground."

"Okay. What's the note say?"

Erik showed him the note: "YOU ARE MY DREAM GIRL! I MUST MEET YOU! IT IS DIFFICULT! I'M IN ANOTHER GRADE. MARCO."

"What are you planning to do?" Donny asked.

"After I put this note in Darlene Klinger's locker, you know that Puerto Rican kid in sixth grade? We gotta go talk to him right away.

Unfortunately, Erik learned that Marco wasn't at school that day.

At dinner that night Helen talked about her day. "Darlene was all giddy about something and told the twins she was walking home alone today because she had a detention and that maybe someone would be waiting for her, or some such thing. Carolyn told me when we walked home that she thought Darlene was mean and that she was glad Darlene wasn't walking with us. Marilyn said so, too. We all decided that Darlene tries so hard to be popular, and she's too boy-crazy. I like the twins a lot. They really helped me the first day. They laughed when I said Darlene was obviously in training—in a training bra, that is."

Marie said, "I hope you're not talking about bras and underwear a lot."

"Oh, Mother, really," Helen said.

Harold stood up and announced, "Well, I've got work to do," and headed for his study.

Erik watched his dad settle in with a pipe and a stack of papers. Despite a moment of nervousness about a missing pipe and hopefully undisturbed papers, Erik went in and sat down in a chair in front of the desk. "Hey, Dad, I was wondering, what do you do at the college?"

Harold looked up, smiling. "I teach students."

"What about?"

"Oh, psychology, behavior, how to be a teacher, classroom management, and things like that."

Erik thought this over. "Do you teach Helen and I?"

"Helen and me."

"Yeah, do you teach us anything?"

"Well, of course. I teach by example."

"Oh."

Silence hung in the air. Harold went back to his papers.

"Well, I guess I'll go up to my room," Erik said.

"How do you like living in this house?"

"It's great, Dad. Too bad we can't live in it forever."

"If the college wants to unload it, because there is a lot of maintenance, maybe we can buy it next year. We'll see," Harold said.

Out on the playground the next day, Erik and Donny found the Puerto Rican kid standing alone with a very bored look on his face underneath a mop of black, curly hair.

Erik walked up to him. "Marco?"

"Yeh."

"I heard your name was Marco. You're from Puerto Rico, right?"

"Yeh."

"Do you know Darlene Klinger?"

"Yeh. I know her. She's in seventh grade." He pointed around the playground, palm up. "These sixth graders are babies."

"Well, she wants to meet you."

38

"Yeh?"

"Why don't you put a note in her locker … er, wait, better yet, I'll put one in for you. I know where her locker is," Erik said, trying not to sound nervous about pulling this off.

"What's in it for you?" Marco asked, his eyes narrowing.

"Uh …" Erik decided to go the honest route. "Here's the deal. Marilyn and Carolyn Taylor, the twins, have really struck up a good friendship with Helen, my sister. Darlene keeps putting Helen down because she thinks Helen is coming between Darlene and the twins. But really, the twins and my sister have a lot more in common, and they're getting tired of Darlene's boy-craziness. When you talk with Darlene, and I have a feeling she'll be looking for you, maybe you could ask to walk her home and stuff. Darlene may forget about my sister and the twins."

Marco grinned at Erik. "You got it all figured out, huh? Well okay, you're watching out for your sister. That's cool. What the hell, maybe I'll get a little something outa this too. Darlene's pretty cute, and she's starting to fill out a little in the front, if you know what I mean. Go ahead and put a note in Darlene's locker saying that I want to meet her. We'll see what happens."

Erik inhaled deeply and exhaled, flicking not so imaginary sweat off his brow.

Harold continued to leave a gold mine of very interesting papers on his desk, and Erik continued to read them. Not wanting to show up in these reports, Erik didn't act out in class if any observers walked in. He didn't read any more about Helen, except for one about a quiet girl who made a brilliant book report about a new novel called *The Catcher in the Rye*, although her voice was a little shaky at first.

Marilyn, Carolyn, and Helen were inseparable. They played in the orchestra, were elected to student council, and joined a literary club. They had many sleep-overs together where they talked to boys on the telephone, especially if they had met them at Joe's Pizza on the Square earlier in the evening, as Erik discovered while eavesdropping.

He often saw Marco and Darlene walking to school together. Sometimes he noticed them deep in conversation in the hallway. It seemed like other boys became interested in Darlene after she got so much attention from the high-profile Marco. Darlene tried out for cheerleading and made it. Erik began to see her with other boys. The word was that Darlene dropped Marco because he wanted to get too serious, but everybody noticed how Marco had eyes for a well-developed girl in his own grade. Erik figured Marco felt up Darlene and had a big disappointment. Ah, well, Erik thought to himself, things have a way of working out.

Chapter Nine

Erik needed something to read. He glanced around the bookshelves in the living room. Between his folks and Helen, a senior in high school, they had accumulated a lot of books. He pulled out Tolstoy's *Anna Karenina* and opened it to chapter one and read the first sentence. "Happy families are all alike; every unhappy family is unhappy in its own way." Oddly, he felt his forehead break out in a sweat and his ears throbbed. "What the hell?" he exclaimed in a whisper. It dawned on him that his family was in the latter category and the sudden revelation of what he had buried deep inside hit him like a truck.

The Thorvald family, Erik realized, was uniquely in disarray. He and his sister had learned never to bring up feelings or problems to their parents. If they did, they were rebuffed and made to feel guilty for harboring any negative thoughts.

Harold and Marie were profligate with criticisms, but parsimonious with praise. Erik mulled over why that was. He came up with the idea that maybe they thought if they praised too much, their children would become complacent. Or maybe they didn't know how to listen to problems. At any rate, they enjoyed their collegial social circle of dinner parties and faculty activities, such as bridge clubs and Harold's poker club with some other professors.

By all appearances, as far as Erik could tell, they were considered a happy family. Harold and Marie blissfully carried on with their parenting by example, while Helen lugged around a lot of anxious baggage, and Erik knew he didn't try very hard to get good grades.

It was not the first time Erik thought about his family's relationships. Last summer he came to the conclusion that he and Helen shouldn't count on any praise for doing well in anything because that was expected of them. That's how Harold and Marie explained it when they came down on him for sneaking out of the house one night.

Erik and a few of his friends wanted to find out if beer tasted as good as it looked in the beer commercials. He knew these ads by heart because he watched the *Game of the Week* every Saturday during the summer. He sang one from memory:

> Falstaff beer, bright brew anywhere.
> Falstaff beer, brewed with special care.
> Smooth and golden, bright and clear.
> America's premium quality beer.
> Sing out now, the time is here
> For cool refreshing Falstaff.

When Dizzy Dean joked with his sidekick, Buddy Blattner, and drank that frosty glass of Falstaff on a hot day, it looked like nectar of the gods. Later, Erik noticed they didn't let Dizzy drink a glass on the air anymore. He really missed that, and wanted to taste a Falstaff all the more.

Erik and three of his ninth-grade friends had it all planned. They sneaked out after midnight on a balmy night. Donny, who said to call him Don since he was in high school, brought eight cans of Schlitz from his dad's large supply.

"You couldn't get Falstaff?" Erik said.

"Don't complain. What did you bring?"

"I supplied the plan."

They sat in a quiet, hidden place on the Sturgis State campus and talked about girls and baseball until the beer chilled in the ice that Alan brought in a cooler. The fourth accomplice, Jim, brought the opener, so he got to put the two little triangles on the top of a can, and there it was—the golden potion.

"Huh," Erik said. "It tastes sharper than I imagined."

"Yeah, but good," Don said between coughs.

Alan said, "I wonder if we'll get drunk."

Jim said, "Nah, my dad drinks about six cans before he gets lovey-dovey and chases my mom around the house."

Erik tried to picture Harold chasing Marie around that big house, which they had been able buy because of the extra money his dad earned for publishing articles and doing surveys for schools around the state. Jesus, what a hard worker, thought Erik, and felt a twinge of guilt about this little escapade.

By the time they had finished two beers each, they were a little silly and the night sky was giving way to a lavender pastel at 4 a.m.

"Yikes! It's getting light out," Erik exclaimed, grinning.

Everybody laughed as if dawn was the funniest thing they'd ever seen.

When the laughter trailed off, so did the boys as they split up, each taking evidence of their night out.

When Erik arrived home he tried to shinny up the white pillar that held up the portico by his room. If he hadn't drunk two cans of beer he might have done it, but he made too much noise, and his mom came out.

"Erik! What on earth are you doing? Come down from there before you break your neck," his mom hissed. Erik figured she was worried about putting on a show for the neighbors now that it was almost daylight.

Sliding earthward, Erik said, "Oh, hi, Mom. Did I wake you? Shorry, I mean, sorry."

Smelling Erik up close, Marie said through clenched teeth, "I smell beer. That's disgusting. Now get inside." She glanced around. "Wait till your father hears about this."

Erik said, "Gladly," as he walked in the front door, wondering what was worse for his mom, him out drinking beer or creating a spectacle for the neighbors.

After Erik caught up on some sleep, his mother summoned him downstairs. "You are grounded for ten days," she said gravely, "and so are the other boys. I assured their parents that we have high expectations of you and that such behavior is not acceptable."

Erik thought his mother was over-concerned about what his friends' parents thought of the Thorvalds, so blew everything out of proportion.

"How come if I do something good I don't hear a word about it?" Erik said.

"Well, of course, that's what we expect from you," Harold said.

"I'm just a high-school freshman and even I know about reinforcement. Isn't that kind of your field?"

Harold looked disgusted. "You are pathetic! You don't know how to work. You have it easy and you just get by. When I was your age I was about to start college in one more year, and in the summer, why I—"

Erik groaned. "Yeah, I know. You baled hay, picked cotton, and slaved in the hot sun for de massa. I don't want to hear it again."

Harold looked as angry as Erik had ever seen him. He grabbed Erik's skinny arms, turned him around, and shoved him onto the stairs leading to the bedrooms. "Go to your room!"

Marie called up to him, "We just want you to be responsible. We know you do a lot of good things."

Erik called down, "Oh, sure." He had a disturbing thought that maybe deep down his father was afraid. Maybe insecure is a better word. What deep analyzing, he thought; that's what reading books can do to a person. Maybe Dad doesn't want to be outdone by me, he continued. Either that or he is blinded by his career and doesn't care about anyone else. Erik couldn't remember a time when he got a "well done" or "way to go" from him. He never got any support for some goal he talked about, either. He recalled a conversation they had last fall on campus when he helped his dad move to a new office. He was not encouraging.

Erik walked in a cathedral of golden leaves in the crisp fall air with splashes of sunlight dancing on the sidewalk. No wonder the people in academia felt blessed and a notch above any crass business people whose only motivation was a profit, as his father had said. At least he got to work there in the summers mowing the grass and saving up for college.

The song "Gaudeamus Igitur," "Let us rejoice, therefore," from *The Student Prince* echoed in his mind. He soaked up the ambience of peaceful seclusion and ivied halls on green swards. The students looked so carefree and attractive. They seemed sure of themselves, a quality Erik wished he had.

He saw his dad waiting in front of Old Main. "Hi, Dad. This is pretty neat."

"What?"

"A beautiful campus. I would like to be connected with a college someday."

"I don't think you have the desire for learning," Harold replied. "It takes a lot of studying."

Erik wasn't discouraged. "I read a lot. I don't think anyone in my class has read as many books as I have. I think I have a desire. I'm only in ninth grade for chrissake."

"Watch the language and what books have you read?"

"*Hawaii, The Catcher in the Rye, Exodus, Ben Hur, Gone with the Wind, Peyton Place*—"

"*Peyton Place*," scoffed Harold.

"It's a good story. Well written. Sure, there are some sexy parts," Erik allowed, remembering how he had masturbated after reading a steamy scene of Rodney and Betty in a car.

"Your grades are mediocre. When I was your age I was two years younger than my classmates but got 'A's in all my classes."

"Okay, so you're smarter than me. Is that what you're saying? What is this leading to; I can't work at a college?"

"No, no. You're smart enough. I just don't think you want to go that route."

"Can you think of any mistakes you've made?" Erik felt like pointing out some flaws he thought were in his father's make-up.

Harold was silent for a moment. "No, not really. Can you?"

"Should a father encourage his son's dreams?" Erik asked.

"Should a father be truthful to his son?" Harold replied.

Erik perceived a lack of introspection in his father's answer. He saw no point in pursuing this subject. He knew from past experience that his father would look offended and end the discussion.

Chapter Ten

Helen was a good student through high school and participated in a lot of activities. She was quiet but well liked by everyone who knew her. Out of school, like in Gainesboro, Helen still read a lot of books and was clever in conversations punctuated with irony and humor. Erik imagined she was fun on dates, but nobody broke through her shell except Steve, whom she dropped half way through her senior year for some reason. She played oboe in the orchestra, danced in one of the musical productions, and was vice-president of Quill and Scroll. Not a bad record for someone who fought personal insecurities and persevered anyway, Erik said admiringly to himself. He dreaded her going away to college because he would have to be alone with his mother and father.

Erik filed away Harold's opinions. He loved sports and all, starting in football and baseball, and running track, but he buckled down and became a good student, making the honor roll in the second half of his junior year.

His self-image improved so that he actually thought maybe the girls he lusted after would find him attractive. Linda made the first move, seeing as how she probably wanted to go to the post-game football parties. After all, Erik was the fast running back that carried the ball a lot, although in a mediocre season.

Linda was a make-up girl for *Annie Get Your Gun,* in which Erik had a small part, but nevertheless a brief solo. He sat on a table in the green room as Linda stood in front of him applying make-up to his face. Erik soon felt Linda's crotch inside her leotard rubbing against his knee. He envisioned a lovely thatch of dark pubic hair. She moved ever so slightly as she did her task. Her face became flushed, her breathing heavier.

Erik was in ecstasy as his penis searched for ways to expand. He managed to ask, "You know the homecoming dance is a ways off, but do you think maybe you could go with me?"

Linda smiled impishly and said, "Sure."

"Well, alright then," Erik replied. "I guess the show must go on," he said with reluctance.

After the homecoming dance Erik and his date were invited to a party at a summer cottage on the Cedar River with the so-called popular group of his class. Erik felt he was well liked but realized he wouldn't be there if he hadn't mustered the courage to ask Linda to the dance. He often wondered why he lacked confidence with the opposite sex, but here he was with a fabulous girl overlooking the Cedar River on a balmy September night redolent with possibilities. Leaning on the deck railing he was enthralled with the moment—a harvest moon and the heady scent of Linda standing close to him in her formal gown. Her corsage was still pinned to her strapless bodice bursting with saucy breasts.

The other partiers were inside doing the Limbo to calypso music on the hi-fi.

Erik drank from one of the beers that the guys had conspired to obtain for this special occasion, Falstaff, of course. "Do you like baseball?"

"It's okay, I guess," Linda said softly. She reached out and ran her fingers through Erik's hair. She found the inside of his ear with her little finger and began moving it in and out, in and out very softly. They kissed, her tongue seeking his.

Erik was delightfully aroused. He gazed at the rounded fullness of her chest in contrast to her tiny waist and lissome arms. His hand on her back held her close. He pulled her zipper down just a teeny bit. She smiled. He continued tentatively with the zipper. The front of her gown fell tantalizingly inch by inch revealing a strapless bra which barely contained her breasts. Her dark areolas slipped out easily. Linda moaned with pleasure when Erik wetted his thumbs and caressed her nipples into a pointed fullness.

Linda assuredly pulled out Erik's shirt and slowly unbuttoned it. She ran her hands over his lean chest. Her soft fingertips rubbed his nipples, surprising Erik at their response.

Erik found this very erotic and exciting as they explored each other. Linda's skin felt as if it was charged with sensuous desire. Her lips were on fire.

Erik whispered, "Let's go downstairs."

Linda nodded.

They found a chaise longue and silently undressed in the warm, but autumnal, night. They found new ways to arouse each other until they both reached climax.

They lay together, spent, their legs intertwined.

Linda said, "Why did you do that?"

"Do what?"

"Pull out."

"I don't want to grow up too fast, and neither should you."

"I wasn't in the prime for pregnancy. I probably would have been okay."

"Does that mean you didn't enjoy it?"

"No, don't get me wrong. I thoroughly enjoyed it, but it might have been more, I don't know, fulfilling, I guess."

"Ja, I s'pose, is how my Norwegian relatives might answer that, although I don't think they ever had conversations like this," Erik said. He was very pleased with himself. He'd found the holy grail of teenaged boys, and it turned out better than he'd imagined in night-time fantasies. He remembered thinking that his mother would probably wonder how she could have put starch in his sheets when she stripped his bed to do the laundry.

"I guess we better get up before the others find us like this, but they're probably busy, too," Linda said.

"Who knows?" Erik said. "Who cares? I take it you weren't a virgin."

"Why do you say that?"

"You showed me what you like so easily and you did things to me that were so, so—"

"Erogenous?"

"Yeah, that's a good word. Where did you learn about that?"

"You know I was a foreign exchange student in Denmark last summer. They have a healthy attitude about sex. It's natural and good without guilt."

As they dressed Erik said, "I think I love you."

"Don't be silly and zip me up."

In the ensuing months, Erik and Linda enjoyed love-making when they could be alone in a car or one of their houses. Erik developed an attitude that was more mature and confident at school. In fact, when Linda dumped him after football season and took up with a basketball player, he was philosophical about it. It had been fun and she taught him a lot about life, sex, and their proper balance as adolescent hormones kicked in. He had plans to go far away, he assured himself. He had been applying to colleges out west.

Erik tried to understand his parents and wanted to maintain a civil relationship. Of course they were involved with college activities. Why shouldn't they? Erik thought. He remembered how they were a little scared when they first arrived in Sturgis. Now they were socially adept with sophisticated professors and their stylish mates.

It was clear to Erik that, aside from the good foundation he had in Gainesboro, most of what he learned came from books, not his parents. His father was making a good living, and his mother meant well. They thought they loved their children, but it seemed as if they put what others thought above a genuine relationship with them.

Erik came to his conclusions as an observer. Did parents think children are not capable of seeing what's really going on? He remembered once when he was 12 years old he left a Sunday school Christmas program rehearsal before it was over. He thought he was finished when his part was done. It was just a practice, for chrissake.

The program director, who was on the Sturgis State faculty, dropped by to tell Harold and Marie that Erik had skipped out. They didn't pay much attention to Erik's explanation, but went overboard with apologies that the director should be inconvenienced. Erik could tell the poor bastard was embarrassed at their carrying on.

When Erik went on a Tolstoy kick he struggled through *War and Peace* and then read *Anna Karenina*. In that book he thought he understood Tolstoy's portrayal of true love as being all-consuming, primal, and irrational. One particular passage resonated with him besides the one about happy families. He had written it in his notebook:

> Hypocrisy in anything whatever may deceive the cleverest and most penetrating man, but the least wide-awake of children recognize it, and is revolted by it, however ingeniously it may be disguised.

"Stop it!" screamed Kenny Swanson, interrupting Erik's train of thought and bringing him back from his daydreaming. Dr. Hapgood, the physical education teacher, was conducting an all-boy class in the wrestling room. He liked to lecture them from time to time, after some physical activity, on growing up and becoming men. For these occasions he had the boys bring their spiral notebooks to write down his frequent adages. This session was about understanding girls' menstrual cycles and the communist threat to the United States.

All eyes turned to see Kenny standing up and looking as if he was about to cry.

"What is it, Kenny?" asked Dr. Hapgood.

"Stanley won't leave me alone. He keeps flicking my ears and saying 'pussy, pussy.'"

Some of the boys snickered. Erik knew that Stanley was a sadistic cretin who liked picking on anybody who showed any sign of weakness.

Kenny was physically frail, very shy, and never participated in activities or joined clubs. Erik often saw Mrs. Swanson in the school office, probably with concerns about Kenny.

Dr. Hapgood called Stanley up front. "How lazy are you, Stanley?"

"Pretty darn," Stanley said.

This got a laugh from the class.

"You never do anything constructive," Dr. Hapgood said. "You're a big boy, but you don't go out for football where your mean tendencies could have an outlet. You could push people around who could take it and maybe push back. But no, you'd rather take up space, disrupt class, and pick on others smaller than you. Just remember: What you're going to be, you are now becoming."

Stanley grinned but cast his eyes down.

Erik decided that Dr. Hapgood must have a pithy saying for every occasion. Another of his favorites was "When the going gets tough, the tough get going." His solution to life's problems was to go out for football.

Erik wished Kenny would stand up for himself. He had asked him why he puts up with that bullying. Use a rapier of words, like Cyrano, to embarrass Stanley in public situations, Erik told him, and maybe he would not want to mess with you. Get out of yourself, Erik urged.

Dr. Hapgood told Stanley to sit down and went on with class. "Next week we're going to walk over to my house on a little field trip to see our bomb shelter. It's stocked with enough food and water for three months. Our country has got to be ready for a nuclear war with the Soviet Union."

Erik was not surprised that Dr. Hapgood had a bomb shelter since he often spoke about how the country was getting so soft that the Russians could merely walk in. A few other people Erik knew had a bomb shelter, too, such as Linda's father, but it was only an underground concrete-block room on a cement slab with standing water in it. Something else was on Erik's mind.

"Stanley," Erik called out as everybody walked back to the locker room.

"What?"

"Oh, nothing, just checking assholes."

Stanley stopped and turned. "What's your problem?"

"You're a goddamned bully, and bullies usually get what they deserve," Erik said.

"Oh, yeah?"

"Brilliant, Stanley, brilliant answer."

Some of the guys chuckled as they walked by. "You gonna stop me?" Stanley said.

"Let's put it this way. If you don't stop picking on Kenny, you'll be sorry," Erik said, singing the last three words. He knew fat old Stanley didn't want to tangle with his quickness. Erik walked on.

"You cunt!" Stanley called after him.

"How would you know, you've never seen one," Erik yelled back.

Erik had an idea to make Stanley look ridiculous. Kenny was still being bullied so Don, Jim, Alan, and Erik, the guys who had bonded during the late-night beer caper, came up with a plan to give Stanley Fager what he deserved.

Jim was the best actor of the group, a veteran of several school plays. He was to call the science office next to the biology room during a lab when everyone was dissecting frogs.

Erik practiced with Jim several times. He would use a pay phone in the front lobby and say, "This is Mr. Fager," in as deep and commanding voice as he could muster.

Erik heard the phone ring in the science office and knew that Jim would be saying, "The office connected me to your location where I understand Stanley has biology class. I would like to speak to him. This is his father."

Erik saw Mr. Schnoeble answer the phone. It looked as if he asked if it was an emergency, to which Jim was to say very casually, "No, no, I just want to give him a message."

Mr. Schnoeble nodded, said something, and put down the receiver. He walked into the classroom.

Alan should be standing by, Erik hoped, with a petri dish containing black tempura paint to slather on the earphone and mouthpiece as soon as Mr. Schnoeble left the office.

Erik could see the whole thing from the back corner of the lab. He saw Stanley poke his frog with a scalpel and chuckle. Through the door he could see Alan leaning over the telephone for a few seconds and disappear. Mr. Schnoeble found Stanley and said something to him. Stanley put down his scalpel and walked to the office. He picked up the receiver and spoke into it. Then he switched hands and put it to his other ear. Oh, even better, Erik said to himself. Stanley pulled the receiver away, looked at it, and put it back in the cradle.

Erik breathed a sigh of relief that the black telephone didn't show the paint. He saw Don stroll into the office with a wet rag to wipe the receiver clean. Stanley walked back to his station in the lab.

Few people looked up to see that Stanley had some yucky black stuff smeared all over his ears beneath his well-kept flat top, and that his black lips were accented with inky parentheses on the sides of his mouth. Those who did see this clownish sight, Erik observed, didn't guffaw loudly, but snickered as they looked away from direct eye contact.

Erik moved closer. He heard Stanley say to his lab mates, "What's the matter with you?"

The two students who had to put up with him as a lab partner said, "Oh, nothing, nothing. Did you get a phone call?" It looked like they struggled to keep the corners of their mouths from turning upward.

"Yeah, I think somebody pranked me. There was no one there."

Class ended and Stanley went into the hall and headed for his next class, leaving his lab partners to clean up. Erik lost sight of him but could see some giggling reactions as he swaggered down the hall.

Linda filled Erik in later. She said Stanley got to an intersection of hallways and she heard him yell, "What're you lookin' at?" Then the laughter got real loud. Stanley ran into the boys' bathroom. Everybody heard a loud yell and then the sound of breaking glass. He came out with a paper towel wrapped around his hand and went to the nurse. Linda said she could see kids looking and laughing at him as he went down the hall.

Of course there was an investigation. Everybody in the science lab was questioned, but nobody knew anything. Erik guessed it died for lack of enthusiasm. The word was that Stanley wouldn't be suspended for breaking the mirror, but his parents had to pay for the replacement.

The four boys who pulled off the payback of Stanley Fager never said a word about it. Stanley was more subdued in his cruel inclinations and kept a lower profile in the remaining two months of school. Erik didn't know if Stanley connected the incident to him, because he must have figured there were many potential candidates who could have done it. Erik concluded that Stanley was going to concentrate on graduating, probably just barely, so he could "get outa this fuckin' place," as he often heard him say.

Chapter Eleven

Erik found a fairly good school to attend at the University of Wyoming. He was happy to leave his parents, but appreciated his college education, although he helped pay for it with six summers of maintaining the grounds at Sturgis State. He was thankful for his home and having good food to eat. Things could have been a lot worse, and he shouldn't be critical.

He didn't declare a major since he was still undecided about what he wanted to do. He joined a fraternity but as he rode the train home for Christmas, he questioned the value of that decision. The raucous carrying on by privileged white guys along fraternity row was getting old.

The Greeks had just completed a traditional Christmas tree contest as the holiday approached. The fraternity council gave a prize to the house with the most attractive tree. It was a ridiculous event because the one Tudor-style house with its vaulted ceiling always won with a huge tree. This year, the modern-style house next door cut a hole in their roof and installed a towering evergreen. Erik had to admit the decorated tree sticking out of the roof looked hilarious. They seemed destined to win the contest. Trouble was, the night before the judging, some of the vaulted-ceiling crowd opened up windows that overlooked the exposed tree and blasted it with twelve-gauge shotguns.

The university administration gave that boys-will-be-boys fraternity a slap on the wrist with some kind of lame probation. This being Wyoming, Erik figured, the use of firearms in a social range war did not warrant an investigation and expulsion for over-spirited undergrads.

Helen picked up Erik at the train station. "I am so glad you came back for Christmas, too," Erik said. "Wow! A senior at Grinnell. That's pretty cool."

"Yes, one more semester. I can hardly wait. By the way, I guess since we're adults and in college, Mom and Dad invited us for their dinner party tonight."

"Great. I always wondered what those gatherings were like," Erik said.

When Erik walked into the kitchen, Harold gave him a warm hug. "Hello, Erik. How are things going, college boy?"

"Great, Dad. Just great. I've survived at least one semester." He smiled at his father's typical thoroughness when he pulled out a file box containing index cards on which he had written cocktail recipes. "Who's coming tonight?"

"Winston Walcott, Trevor Hastings, and their wives," Harold said.

Erik knew they were from Harvard and Princeton. He had noticed that Ivy League professors enjoyed a higher status than the Midwestern ones, and their self-assurance seemed a tiny bit higher. He looked forward to listening to their conversations.

The guests arrived. Erik took their coats up to a guest bedroom and flung them on the bed. He hurried back, not wanting to miss anything.

"You mean we should just write off Laos?" Harold said.

Trevor Hastings said, "Write off from what, our influence? Why should we try to influence that little, faraway Asian nation?"

"Should we let China take over the world and spread communism, one country at a time?" Harold replied. "Vietnam will be next."

Winston Walcott of the History Department said, "You don't believe that transparent rhetoric about dominoes falling in front of a monolithic communist juggernaut, do you? If you do, the defense industry is doing a better job than I thought." Walcott laughed. "If anyone took the trouble to read about Vietnam's history, they would see that their whole existence has been a single-minded effort to remain independent from China." He took a drink from his double Glenlivet scotch on the rocks. "China did conquer Vietnam once a long time ago, and by the way, the Vietnamese are not of Chinese extraction. They migrated from Mongolia, and the word *Viet* was the name of a migrating bird from the north. Let's see, where was I?"

Hastings, in a corduroy sport coat over his buttoned-down shirt and crew-neck sweater, said, "Yes, yes, Winston, but aside from that, Laos is a land-locked country, and if we were to strategically make a stand, it wouldn't be there."

"There is no definitive, one-size-fits-all, communism. We don't have to make a stand. The Chinese have their brand, and the Vietnamese have theirs. Other than that, they distrust—no, that's not strong enough—they hate each other. The Laotians will do their own thing. They and the Vietnamese are about as racist as our good 'ol boys from the South. They look down on the Cambodians because of their darker skin. Anyway, I was about to say that China conquered the kingdom of the Viets, which had been around since 500 BC. They were an independent country whose people lived by the rice-growing cycle."

Erik listened intently. Vietnam was a hot topic in the dorm bull sessions.

"China had its eye toward conquering its southern neighbor because, one, it was licking its chops about the fertile rice bowl the Viets had, and, two, China liked to maintain hegemony over surrounding countries as a buffer for its own borders," Walcott said.

Harold stood up. "Hold that thought, Winston. It's time to refresh our drinks." He went into the kitchen, with Erik following to pour another glass of wine for Helen and himself. The wives were making hors d'oeuvres.

"How's everything in here, ladies?" Harold poured more scotch for Walcott and the rest of the martini for Hastings. He refreshed his tumbler with rum and sour.

Marie cheerily replied, "Oh, we're just cooking up a storm. Take some hors d'oeuvres with you."

Mary Walcott said, "These stuffed mushrooms will hold you till dinner. Winston loves these."

Gloria Hastings said, "So, Harold, you've certainly made some friends in the Philosophy Department. Trevor was so gratified with your generous budget for the summer session."

"Well, thank you. I think philosophy needs to be taught during the summer. It's in keeping with what higher education should be. I can picture some of the students discussing their philosophy class over pizza and beer on the Square."

"I think that is so uplifting," Gloria exclaimed. "If you ever get tired of administration, Trevor could use you in the Philosophy Department. What is your official title now?"

"It's actually Assistant Dean of Instruction and Director of the Summer Session." Harold looked proud and turned to leave.

Marie said, "We don't let him get too uppity around here. He still has to do the laundry."

Winston was talking when Harold and Erik returned. "Where is Hank Wright getting those new hires in his Education Department, Harold? My God, they don't know a damn thing about anything." He took a sip from his scotch. "I really don't know why we need an education curriculum, do you, Helen? You're going to be a teacher."

"Most of the education classes I've had weren't worth much. Having a good general background and knowing your content area is what counts," Helen said, "especially in English."

Harold said, "I think Dr. Wright has a tendency to hire people who are not threatening to him. Why do you think they don't know anything?"

From what Erik could gather, he doubted his father would be in this social circle if he still taught education classes.

Winston said, "I had lunch with one of the neophytes in the faculty dining room. I made a reference to the Orwellian newspeak when it comes to ethnic sensitivities and how we are to refer to disabled people, or I should say persons with a disability. He didn't have the slightest idea of what I was alluding to, er, to which I was alluding."

Harold said, "How could we get along without the Education Department?"

"Well, let's say the people who went into education created an industry about concepts that are axiomatic, and tangential bureaucracies that are superfluous," Winston averred. "Naturally, a teacher who really knows his subject will be able to impart more knowledge and answer questions. Knowing the subject matter is key, as Helen said. I wonder if we are graduating prospective teachers who don't know their subject areas because they're spending too much time taking meaningless education classes. Math methods should be in the Math Department. Measurement is about statistics, which is in the Math Department, too. Child development, the Psychology Department."

"What were you saying about Asian history, Dr. Walcott?" Erik said.

"Yes, back to Southeast Asia. The Pathet Lao are going to win and take over Laos, and it will not make a bit of difference to us or anybody else, the CIA's opinion notwithstanding."

"Okay, that's what I'm saying," Hastings said. "We've got to make our stand in Vietnam. The president will do the right thing, just as he did with the Cuban missile crisis. We should back him and the military, come what may."

Erik recalled Kennedy's speech two months before in October. He was impressed by the president's coolness in demanding that the Russians get their missiles out of Cuba. It was gutsy, but there were probably some under-the-table deals, Erik suspected. In keeping with the zeitgeist of the 1960s, he was less inclined to take what old white guys said at face value.

"Vietnam, my friends," continued Walcott, "is a potential quagmire in which we should never muck about. Look, a while back I said that China conquered Vietnam. That was in 111 BC. China's rule over them lasted a thousand years. Lots of changes were forced on the Vietnamese, and some were readily adopted, such as the Mandarin social service system, and the way of Confucius. However, the Vietnamese never forgot their independent heritage, and we're talking over a thousand years," he fairly shouted. "They were determined to free themselves and resist foreign dominance at all costs.

"The first uprising was in AD 39. That was when the Trung sisters went down in history as icons of resistance, something that every schoolchild in Vietnam can tell you about. When the emperor sent an army to crush the revolt, the Trung sisters drowned themselves in a river before they would surrender. One thing the Vietnamese learned, though, was that to be successful against China, their army had to have the support of the peasants." Winston looked at the drink in his hand. "I hope I'm not boring anybody. This scotch is an excellent elixir for elocution."

Erik chuckled at the professor's alliteration.

Harold said, "No, no, this has been very interesting, what with Kennedy sending advisors, and all the papers have been putting Vietnam on the front burner."

Trevor said, "You know, Winston, I read an article about Vietnam, and what you said about the peasants reminded me of a Vietnamese saying, which is 'An emperor's rule ends at the village gates.'"

"Yes, that's very good, Trevor," said Winston. "Suffice it to say, the Vietnamese tried another revolt five hundred years later, and it was put down. Finally, in 938, Vietnam united under Ngo Quyen and broke China's control at the battle of Bach Dang, which is like Lexington and Concord in their history. One more thing, Kublai Khan tried to conquer Vietnam in the thirteenth century and was defeated. Vietnam was the only country to successfully resist that Chinese emperor on the mainland."

The ladies brought food to the dining-room table. "Time to sit down, everyone," Marie said.

"But the point I'm trying to make," continued Winston as they moved to the dining room, "is that if anybody says that Ho Chi Minh is just a puppet of China, and that we've got to stop this communist aggression, you can laugh in their face. Ho only wants an independent, unified Vietnam. He embraced communism a long time ago, when one of its tenets was to end colonialism, which Ho had experienced in his youth before wandering the world as a ship's cabin boy.

"As you know, the French overwhelmed Vietnam with their industrial technology and established a colony in 1870, as all the European nations carved out their piece of the world, but the Vietnamese considered it only temporary. Oh, and here's another indication of how the Vietnamese hated the Chinese. Jesuit missionaries gave Vietnam its Western alphabet, which they happily adopted because it wasn't Chinese characters."

Erik said, "I'm not exactly sure where Vietnam is, but what could it have to do with us?"

Winston said, "Good question, Erik. When I was at Harvard, I knew many scions of the defense industry who would figure out a way to make it important to us.

"Back to Ho Chi Minh. He would never put up with Chinese domination. The Nationalist Chinese under Chiang Kai-shek occupied Vietnam after Japan surrendered at the end of World War II. This was a problem for Ho, but the French wanted to restore their colony. They had been humiliated by the Germans when they marched through France like a hot knife through butter. But to my point, Ho let the French in without a fight. His advisors asked him why he would allow the French to come back. Ho said, and I give you the direct translation, 'I would rather smell French shit for two years than Chinese shit for a thousand years.'"

Mary Walcott said, "Winston! We're at the dinner table."

Winston forged on. "Well, that's what he said. So, the Chinese moved out when the French returned. When negotiations failed to satisfy Ho's plan for independence in 1946, he and the Viet Minh—a collective national movement, part of which were communists—took to the hills and began attacking French forces. A punishing guerilla war ensued until the French were annihilated at Dien Bien Phu and Mang Yang Pass in 1954. The French left in disgrace, rightfully so, since they had been so exploitive of the Vietnamese for the seventy years they had that colony. Elections were supposed to be held in South Vietnam in 1956, but the United States wouldn't allow them to take place because Ho would have won in a landslide. So we began to support the corrupt Diem regime which doesn't represent the people."

Hastings said, "You mentioned the French. How many Frenchmen does it take to defend Paris?" He paused and then delivered, "Nobody knows. It's never been done."

Erik laughed along with everyone else, but still worried about the direction his country was going.

Chapter Twelve

Helen and Erik sat in the living room. Their folks had gone to bed after the guests left. Helen pulled a Prince Albert tobacco can from her purse.

Erik said, "Do you smoke?"

"Well, I guess you could say that, but this isn't tobacco." She pulled out some cigarette paper and began to roll a smoke. "This is marijuana—grass, weed, dope or whatever you want to call it."

"I'm surprised. So why are you smoking marijuana?"

"It relaxes me. Let's go outside."

As she and Erik stood under the portico, Helen said, "I'm a teacher, or soon will be, but I still get up-tight when I have to perform. I should do something else, but what?"

"Oh, come on. You can do it. A lot of people start that way."

"Well, maybe, but I just finished student teaching and I had to go home and unwind every night."

"Do a lot of students smoke that stuff at Grinnell?"

"Oh, yes. You'd be surprised. There are some really neat people from all over. And they're so different."

"So why do you think you're so anxiety-ridden?"

"Repressed anger? I don't know. I could never express myself around here. I could never get angry, and it stayed inside me in destructive ways."

"Listen, it's okay to get angry. Mom and Dad gave you an education, but you can go and be your own person."

"I should be very happy, I know, but I just feel a lot of stress. Maybe I should see somebody about it."

"That's a good idea. Do you want me to approach Dad about it? See if he'd pay for it?"

* * *

"I'd be interested in what he'd say. In fact, you ask him. He'll probably blow up about it. Go ahead, you'll see."

At breakfast the next morning, Erik sat down with Harold. After some talk about the dinner the night before, Erik asked, "What do you think about psychiatry?"

"Why, do you want to go to a psychiatrist?"

"No, but I think Helen would benefit from having some counseling."

"Why, so she can blame her parents for whatever it is that's bothering her?"

"Are you serious? You're a professor and you would be that callous, and … and … unprofessional?"

"Listen, I worked hard to get where I am. If I had to go to a psychiatrist every time I felt overwhelmed with challenges, I'd still be on a farm loading hay."

"What did you do, skip the sensitivity line to go back for more smarts?" Erik said. "That is so uncaring. Why not encourage her to go talk to someone?"

"Helen is doing okay. She's about to graduate from college. Her hard work has paid off, so, no, I wouldn't support that."

That night, over what Helen called a joint, she and Erik had another talk under the portico. Erik told her what their father had said.

"Ha! I knew it. No big deal. When I graduate I'm moving to Berkley with my true love."

"Who's that?"

"Bernard Golding. He's a philosophy major from Chicago and he's going to enroll in graduate school. He wants to change the rules of stuffy old men, and Berkley is a hub for a new order of peace and harmony. He wants to meet Mario Savio, a student leader who's really stirring things up with his free speech movement. I'll get some kind of job. Bernie loves me, and I love him. At least I think I love him. It's hard to say since I haven't learned anything about it around here."

"Well, that sounds like a good plan. Look, Mom and Dad have their faults. They were under a lot of pressure to make it and they've given us a good home."

"Oh, sure, a good home. It's a perfect home by all appearances, but cold," Helen said.

"Remember the perfect ice?" Erik said. "If you're like me, I've been looking for that father who took us skating ever since. I don't think it's going to happen. It's seeking the unobtainable. We never had ice like that again. That day was just a blip in the ebb and flow of life that will never be repeated."

"My, aren't we waxing philosophical."

Erik grinned sheepishly, surprised at his own ramblings. "I read somewhere that people tend to pursue their whole lives a time in their childhood that made them happy."

"Hmmm, that reminds me of *Citizen Kane*, the movie. Did you ever see it?"

"No."

"The central character, Kane, built an empire of spurious newspapers. He speaks one word at his dying moment—Rosebud. That was the name of his sled when he was a child."

"Omigosh! That's it. Hey, let me have a drag of that." Erik took a long pull on the joint and coughed. "I understand that. When you are on your sled you're in your own little world and your eyes are inches away from the name of the sled, in my case, 'Flexible Flyer.' That's what I was trying to say about the perfect ice. It was such a happy moment in our childhood."

Helen smiled.

Erik said, "I wish we didn't have to go back to school so soon. This is great, Helen, our discussions and all. This is why I hated to see you go off to college when I was starting high school."

"Yes, I know. Oh, one more thing about my feeling vulnerable, or whatever it is. I had a lot of conflicting emotions about Mom and Dad. When children are not given a foundation of personal worth, they tend to be more dependent on their parents. That's why I complied with Mom and Dad's wishes when I was dating Steve in high school. What a sweet guy he was. We had plans, but his father worked in a factory, and Mother said our relationship would go nowhere because of our different backgrounds. Mother and Father didn't let me go out with him. I should have told them to fuck off."

"That's the spirit, but I've never heard you say that before."

"You should hear some of my friends at Grinnell. It works wonders. I feel better already."

Helen left with her ride to Grinnell. Erik sat with his parents in the living room.

"I haven't declared a major, you know. I've been thinking. I'm going to pre-register this spring and sign up for pre-med next year," Erik said.

Harold dropped the newspaper he was reading. "You're what?"

"I'm signing up for pre-med next year."

"You can't do that. You don't have the math background," Harold said matter-of-factly.

"I've got to have a purpose, a challenge, something with meaning. Maybe I'll specialize in psychiatry."

"You've never shown an interest in medicine before," Marie said.

"Don't be ridiculous. You'll never make it. You'll flunk out. I'm not supporting that," Harold said.

Erik was profoundly disheartened. Shouldn't his father be supportive instead of putting him down? What does math have to do with it? Again, Erik wondered if his father didn't want him to achieve anything that approached his success. Is he a Cronus, the mythical king who felt threatened by his children? Nah, that couldn't be, he concluded.

Chapter Thirteen

Erik wasted a year of taking classes and trying different subjects. Then he worked at a ski resort for a year, much to his parents' disapproval. He felt adrift, but forced himself to enroll again and major in history. It was not terribly difficult given his voracious reading habits. It allowed him to spend the next three years in a fog of beer parties, skiing, attending classes, and staying healthy with his grade point. His grades were not bad, but not outstanding. He joked that he was going for summa-cum-lager.

Vietnam was in the forefront of everyone's plans since the draft was in full swing. The war to stop communism in Southeast Asia was escalating, and Lyndon Johnson needed troops to carry out his plans as a wartime president. Erik supposed he didn't want to be considered weak and unmanly, attributes not in keeping with his Texas heritage. Johnson kept the National Guard and the reserves at home, so it was up to the draftees and regular army to do the job.

On the eve of graduation Erik sat at dinner with his parents and half listened to the conversation while he thought about the U.S. history he had studied. At this moment he felt he was a passenger on a slow-moving but inexorable train heading for something disastrous. Some were trying to change its direction, but the American special wouldn't be sidetracked. The weapons industry wanted to try out new products. The military's officer corps wanted to get their tickets punched with combat experience. A spineless Congress didn't want to appear soft and "lose" Vietnam, which wasn't theirs to lose. The only votes against Johnson's phony Tonkin Gulf Resolution were cast by Senators Wayne Morse of Oregon and Ernest Gruening of Alaska.

The words of Winston Walcott reverberated in Erik's head. He was prophetic. Why isn't there shouting from the rooftops that a war in Vietnam will be a huge mistake. Erik saw it as another example of complacent and remote professors. The Beatles' track "Revolution" resounded in his ears. In the pulsating beat of rowdy music he envisioned a lot of people his age beginning to resent the arrogant detachment in the halls of ivy.

Ten days after he graduated Erik received a letter that read, "Greetings from your president," followed by information about when and where to report for a pre-induction physical.

Harold and Marie had attended his graduation. Erik was thankful it was far enough away that they didn't have a graduation party for him at home with a bunch of professors drinking cocktails and giving him words of wisdom about being in the army, seeing as how a lot of them had fought in World War II. They probably would have romanticized going off to war as a rite of passage.

Erik's mother said, "Don't you have a special person in your life?"

"No, I just haven't found the right one yet." Being engaged or married was not on his mind with such an uncertain future. Besides, he truly hadn't found anyone that he thought was perfect. Maybe that was his problem, he thought. Looking for perfection would only end with disappointment. He wondered if his father would give him any advice before leaving. He didn't, which was just as well, because it probably wouldn't carry much weight with him anyway.

Marie gave him a small Bible and said to read the ninety-first Psalm whenever he felt the need for inspiration if he should ever find himself in a battle.

Chapter Fourteen

Erik sat with a group of draftees waiting at the Dallas airport for a flight to Fort Polk, Louisiana. Some of the guys talked about going to Canada. Being against the war was cool, but it was difficult to be cool with a shaved head, their fate in just a few days.

Erik watched as two of the guys with long hair affected a devil-may-care attitude and said "Peace, man" while flashing the vee sign at some passing servicemen. The rest of the more circumspect recruits laughed as if this was the height of levity. Classic nervous laughter, Erik thought, and asked himself why he wasn't laughing. He was nervous, too. What the hell, he decided. He was on vacation because he didn't have to make any decisions. The army would make them for him.

Fort Polk lies in the heart of Louisiana, a very busy post during World War II, according to the encyclopedia Erik consulted before leaving Sturgis. It lay dormant after the war until it was reactivated in the 1950s. Now its hot climate, most of the time, was ideal for training GIs headed for Vietnam. Did our government know something in advance? Erik wondered.

In a WWII-vintage wooden assembly building, some clerks passed out postcards for everyone to write home that they'd arrived and were having a good time at Fort Polk. A career sergeant with a gut attesting to throwing back beers at the NCO club came in and addressed the wide-eyed inductees. "The U.S. Army does not allow reading materials of a prove-ient nature. You will come forward with any printed material, and I will give you my okay or not. If you have a fuck book, you will leave it on the table." He paused for effect, then, "Move it!"

All the inductees began parading up with books and magazines they expected to read during basic training. No one had made a peep since they came in.

The first guy, looking as though he regretted having to bother the good sergeant with his book said, "I've got *War and Peace.*"

"It's a fuck book. Put it on the table."

"But—" said the bewildered recruit.

"You got a problem, slick? I said put the fucking book on the fucking table."

The sergeant was a bastion against trashy literature as he read the titles. "*Animal Farm.* Fuck book. What's with all these fucking animal stories?" he said as he looked at *Babbit,* declaring it a fuck book. "Don Quicksote? What's that about, a quickie? Fuck book. *Principles of Accounting,* Third Edition. Fuck book. *Tropic of Cancer.* Fuck book."

Erik laughed to himself. Okay. He finally got one.

A week went by. With shaved heads everybody looked alike. Erik couldn't even identify the long-haired ones from the Dallas airport. Now he was listening to one of the training cadre rattle off something about the form that lay in front of him.

"In box one, print you last name first, first name second, middle name last." The young and wiry black sergeant in starched fatigues darted among the tables at which sat sixty nervous trainees.

"Hey, slick. Is you last name Jimmy? I said last name first!" He snatched away the violated form and slapped another in its place. "You will not fuck up!" he shouted. "These will be perfect. The U.S. Army is interested in where you been, what devious people you know, and if shitheads like you are capable of being a security threat to this here republic. I personally don' see it. You dumb fucks couldn't subvert a dogcatcher in a clusterfuck. Hey, dickhead! Yeah, you. Don't get ahead. The onliest time you use them fuckin' GI pens is when I say print it now." He let this sink in. "If you know you home address, as difficult as that may be, print it now in box two. I guaranfuckingtee if you mess up, you will do it over."

It dawned on Erik that the army was a think-tank for inventing ways to use "fucking" or forms thereof. Adjectives are easy, as in give me your fucking attention. How about a verb? Joady is fucking your girlfriend back home. Yeah, he heard that one several times. He racked his brain for other examples. He remembered one of the drill sergeants saying he was fucking delighted to teach you pussies how to be men. Hey, that's an adverb. Another one nailed a gerund when he hoped y'all had a good fucking because y'all won't be getting any in basic. But leave it to the crème de la crème to jam it between syllables to increase its frequency, as the sergeant just did. He figured it wouldn't be long before he heard bayofuckingnet, bivoufuckingac, guardfuckinghouse, AfuckingWOL, and six o' fucking clock in the morning instead of 0600.

"You motherfucking buddies will have to wait just for you in this assemblage of assholes," the sergeant continued. Erik felt beads of sweat forming rivulets on his face. He wiped them with his GI handkerchief. He didn't want to ruin his paper with drops of sweat. An air conditioner hummed away in a window, providing little relief from the humid, still air. "You could be outside smoking some butts, so pay attention."

The sergeant had a CIB, a combat infantry badge, pinned above the left pocket of his starched fatigue shirt, as did most of the training cadre. That silver musket on an infantry-blue rectangle granted the owner an aura of respect. It meant they were infantry who had been in combat. "On the slim chance you know the name you mama was born with, print her first and last name now in box twelve. If you don' know who popped you out, put *DK*, delta kilo, for don' know in box twelve." He paused while he moved up and down the aisles.

"In box thirteen, you write what you mama's name is now, not all the assholes she married before, just her current name. If she didn't get married, which is prob'ly the case for you bastards, you put the same fuckin' name in box thirteen as box twelve." He moved deftly around the room checking papers. "And now for box fourteen. If you know the sumbitch who planted the seed in you mama that produced you sorry ass, print it now in box fourteen. If you don' know, meanin' most of you jerk-offs, print *DK*, delta kilo, for don' know in box fourteen." A few barely perceptible grumbles in the room had no effect on the sergeant.

"Box fifteen. If you are Croatian or any part Croatian, print *yes* in box fifteen." A few trainees raised a hand. "If you don' know what a Croatian is, don' fuckin' worry about it. Just print *no*, you dumb fucks." The sergeant mumbled something about idiots under his breath. Then he yelled, "You mamas are so dumb they prob'ly think Johnny Cash is a pay toilet!" Nobody laughed. If the rest were like Erik, they were biting their lips in agony.

"And now the last box." The sergeant seemed disappointed that his eloquence about dubious heritage on the sorry lot in front of him would come to an end. "If any part of you is Serbian, do the same fuckin' thing and print *yes* in box sixteen. Otherwise, *no.*"

Looking as if he was inspecting the terrain for a land mine, the sergeant's eyes flicked from paper to paper as he danced around the tables. "Now, look at the statement above the line for you signature. It say—since you couldn't read an Exit sign in a whorehouse—it say, I swear that all the above is true, and I have never participated in, nor will participate in, any covert or overt action detrimental to the government of the United States of America and any authority inherent therein. Sign you name and date it. If you lied, the army's gonna be down on you like Joady on you girlfrien'. Leave the form right where it is. Remember the army way to write the date: the date, the first three letter of the month, and then the last two digit of the year. So, 22 Aug 68. All U.S. Army document have the date wrote like that. They is the right way to do ever thang, the wrong way, and the army way. When you get to Nam and get you ass blowed off, at least you learned how to write the fuckin' date the army way. On you feet!"

The two harangued platoons filed outside while the other two platoons of Delta Company waited to go in. The drill sergeant yelled to those who were milling around outside, "All right, take ten and light 'em up. If you don't have any, get 'em from your squad leader."

Erik was smoking every chance he got. It was a moment for reflecting, and he felt things weren't so bad. He was a college graduate, healthy, eating all he wanted, and exercising every day.

LeDuc from Cleveland walked up. Erik smiled, remembering how the drill sergeant called out his French name, putting it together as *Ledduck* with the accent on the *led*.

"So, college guy, have you read Hemingway, Camus, Steinbeck, Sinclair Lewis, any of the above?" LeDuc said.

"Yes, yes, yes, and yes. Let me ask you a question," Erik said after a contemplative drag on his cigarette. "Which one of those authors started a book with 'Today my mother died, or was it yesterday?'"

LeDuc grinned. "Hey, not bad. Uh, that would be Camus in *The Stranger*, or *l'Étranger*. Some say *The Outsider*."

Erik laughed. "*Ooh*. French, even. So, are you an existentialist, too?"

"Yeah, I guess so. Here I am in the swamps of Louisiana when a month ago I was minding my own business stamping out lawn mower parts and trying to earn enough money to go to college. Now I'll be sent to a little, two-bit country on the other side of the world to get my shit blown away, for what? Where's the meaning in that?"

The drill sergeant shouted, "All right, men. Pick up them butts and put 'em in the cans. Then police up the area. Hop to. I wanna see nothin' but assholes and elbows."

Erik and his two buddies, John and Terry, had succumbed to the army's irresistible force. All three had gotten their draft notices shortly after graduating from college. A sense of fatalism made their situation more acceptable and even laughable. They conspired to challenge rules as cavalier rogues but never to confront their superiors or disobey a direct order. They discovered that if they acted as if they knew what they were doing, they could get away with just about anything. Their rationale for even trying was "What can they do, send us to Nam?"

One very hot morning in the early weeks of basic training, the whole company had to go to the post dental clinic. "Every swingin' dick is gonna see a dentist," the drill sergeant informed them. It was one of those times when even the lowliest grunt-to-be felt as if he was being cared for by a benevolent army, even though that army made him wait in formation a lot. At least this time, since it was so hot, they let everybody sit under some trees in a shady square until their squad was told to line up.

Across the street sat the Accounting HQ in air-conditioned splendor. Terry said to Erik, "Come on. You look earnest and innocent. Go smuggle out three ice-cold Cokes."

Erik said, "You mean the ol' act-like-I-know-what-I'm-doing routine?"

"Exactly," Terry said.

"Uh, I don't know. I—"

"Come on," John said. "This is a perfect time for it. Anyway, what can they do?"

"Yeah, I know, send us to Nam. The irony is that someday we'll be saying, 'what can they do, send us to Nam?' and we'll be ass-deep in Vietnam." Erik thought about it a moment. "I've got an idea. You got any quarters?"

Erik strolled away from his group and then walked purposefully across the street like a private who was sent to the accounting office with a pay problem. As soon as he stepped inside the air-conditioned office he was caressed with a blessed coolness. He wondered what it would take to get assigned in here. Okay, I'll sign up for another year, he thought.

He was in a large room with about a dozen desks occupied by clerk-typists in khaki uniforms, either typing or working an adding machine. Looking around, he saw a Coca-Cola machine in the corner. Next to it stood a large trash can. He started walking toward it. The specialist at the desk nearest the door said, "Can I help you?"

"I'm supposed to get the trash," Erik said, pointing to the trash can. He kept walking. When he reached the corner with the Coke machine, he looked back and the spec-four was hard at work. He lifted the plastic liner on the inside of the trash can. Just as he thought, it had a folded plastic bag on the bottom. He grabbed it and put the liner back in. He walked around the room emptying wastebaskets into his plastic bag.

This was going pretty well, he thought. He went to the Coke machine and put in two quarters and got one bottle. The office machines were making so much noise nobody noticed. He got another bottle and then a third and put them in the bag. He twisted the top of the bag and started walking toward the door.

Just as he was reaching for the door knob the spec-four said, "Hey!"

Erik gulped. Good try, he thought.

"You forgot the CO's office." The spec-four pointed to the office to his right.

"Huh?" Erik said. "Oh, yeah. Right! Right you are," he said as he pointed to the CO's office. "Thanks a lot." At the door he breathed a sigh of relief when he saw that the CO was not in. Probably playing golf, he thought enviously. Erik emptied the wastebasket next to the desk.

In a moment he was out the door and across the street. He took the three Cokes out and dropped the bag in a trash barrel. Thanks to Terry having an opener strung with his dog tags, the three gulped down their Cokes, which Erik thought was the best and coldest soda he ever had.

The inevitability of going to Vietnam hung around Fort Polk like Spanish moss on the surrounding trees. Some trainees went to extremes to avoid it. One morning Erik saw a guy from Oklahoma, named Greg, limping around in the barracks.

"Greg! What happened?"

Greg winced, "When everybody was at breakfast, I asked that idiot Herndon to jump on the side of my knee as I stuck it out from my footlocker. That sadistic bastard did it. But that's what I wanted, so …" He gritted his teeth in pain.

How that guy could have jumped on Greg's leg was beyond Erik's understanding. What's more, Erik asked himself, how could Greg, an otherwise sane, boy-next-door type, stand to have that done to him? "This is crazy. Absolutely crazy!" Erik whispered in amazement.

In the early-morning darkness, Erik sat with his feet hanging over a drainage ditch which all the barracks at Fort Polk had between them. The rains had tapered off in September and the mornings were cool.

The mess hall was a beehive of activity as breakfast was being prepared. Erik was glad he didn't have to do KP since his drill sergeant picked him to be one of the four squad leaders of second platoon. He wondered, why him? He didn't set out to be a leader.

Maybe that was it, Erik thought. Take life as it comes without thinking of personal gain. Whatever you undertake, give it your best, but don't calculate self-centered advancement. Is that what Jesus meant when he said "he who saves his life will lose it, but he who loses his life for my sake will save it?" Could be, he thought, but he suspected that the writers of the Gospel had added that part about dying for Jesus. The simple paradox without it sounded more like what Jesus would say. That is, if you are too tentative and act only in selfish motivations, that's not a life.

Bodine, another squad leader, was sitting nearby. "Hey, Bodine. Are you religious?" Erik said.

"You kiddin'? There ain't no atheists in foxholes, man. Yeah, I read the Bible every fuckin' day."

Erik laughed. "Did you hear about Herringdine?"

"No, what?"

"I guess he got a little homesick and didn't like the army all that much, anyway, so he got into his civvies and walked into Leesville last night. The MPs caught him at the bus station. He kind of stood out with the shaved head."

"Yeah, that's standard procedure for the MPs. They just go to the bus station and wait for the AfuckingWOLs."

"Where did you get all your military know-how, like marching and shit?" Erik said.

"I was at Texas A and M for two years. Everybody gets military training."

"So what happened?"

"I got drafted. I dropped one class that I was flunking, and it put me below a full-time student. My home county drafted my ass, and here I am."

"Too bad."

"Ah, it's not so bad. I wanted to go to Nam. I just won't be going as a commissioned officer, unless I go to OCS, you know, officer candidate school, which I'm thinking about."

"You actually want to go to Nam?"

"Yeah, I want to put some of my training to good use. I think I could save some lives."

"How about not going and saving a lot more lives? Do you think we should be there?"

"That's not for me to say. Our president wants us. That decision is above my pay grade."

"Christ! I can't believe how we're cut off from any news. I wonder what's going on in the world. Protests were plastered all over the newspapers and on TV before I came in."

"Yeah, people are getting sick of hearing about all the dead and wounded with no end in sight."

"I wish I could have gotten into a National Guard unit or the reserves," Erik said. "They don't have to worry about going to Nam. They must have pulled strings, or known somebody."

"Yeah, life ain't fair. You should fill out a T.S. card."

"What's that?"

"Tough shit."

Erik laughed. "The Democratic convention is coming up in Chicago. I heard all hell's going to break loose with war protesters."

"Yeah, it could be interesting. Hey, the mess hall's opening."

* * *

After eight weeks of close-order drill, a feeling of unity increased daily until *I* became *we*. Erik didn't totally understand it, but a group of young men marching in kinesthetic oneness brought about a release of self. It was uncanny, but relaxing, and he assumed everybody felt the same. They marched to all the training sites, most often the firing range. The days flew by and suddenly basic training was over. Erik had never felt so healthy and stress-free, which was funny, since he knew where he was going. He decided to think about that some other time.

After a parade in their dress khakis in front of the brigade colonel, all the new privates got their written orders. It was like a graduation day. The company area was tidied up for visitors.

The October sun shone brightly, and the temperature was a perfect seventy-two degrees. By late afternoon, the once-bustling company area was reduced to about a dozen trainees. These were the guys destined for AIT, Advanced Infantry Training. The rest of the company of three-year enlistees or draftees pleading a medical excuse were off to training in accounting, personnel, mechanics, radio, or some other non-combat school across the country.

Erik sat on a folding chair on the mowed grass with John and Terry. They were the lowest of the low—the 11B20s—which was "light weapons, infantry." He looked at the small but well-maintained headquarters office with its bulletin board and pathways defined with whitewashed rocks. The company's four maize-colored barracks lay in a line to the right and seemed to retain an aura left over from World War II.

"I'm going to miss this place," Erik said not too loudly. There's nothing like an army post to have an unlimited supply of fatigue details to maintain it, he thought. That's why he liked it, he supposed. It was orderly and well kept. He also enjoyed the daily exercises and eating well.

Despite the nostalgic feelings about basic training, Erik grew less enthused about getting on a truck and being hauled to the other side of this large training post. He would be starting over with mock-up villages, jungle trails, and M-16 training in Tigerland, a facility designed for training infantry bound for Vietnam.

"So, are you guys thinking what I'm thinking?" Erik said.

"What's that?" Terry said.

"We get to do this all over again."

"This is about as low as I've ever been," John said. "At least we'll be able to get some leave-time off this fuckin' place."

"First leave I get I'm getting Bonnie to come down," Terry said. "I'm horny as hell, and besides, I miss her."

"Yeah, Diane can come with her," John said. "Come on. We can survive this. Advanced Infantry Training, ooh, I'm scared. Hey, we'll get in terrific shape." Terry and Erik looked skeptical. "We gotta be resourceful if we're gonna make it. Remember our motto: Stay with it, get away with it. Or, put another way, if you have the balls, you make the calls."

Terry laughed. "Since when did we have a motto?"

"Since I just made it up," John replied.

"I thought our motto was 'what can they do, send us to Nam?'" Erik said.

"No, that's the Nam protocol. See, that's what's invoked if the motto doesn't work out," John said. He ducked when Terry threw grass at him.

"At least it's not hot and humid like when we got here," Erik said. "This Louisiana autumn is beautiful."

Two deuce-and-a-half trucks pulled up. They were the 2.5-ton multi-purpose workhorse of the U.S. Army. One of the drivers got out and yelled, "Hey, you guys goin' to Tigerland, hop in."

That's when the top sergeant chose to come out of his HQ office and taunt the remaining GIs. "Have fun in the Nam, boys." He laughed as though he had told a hilarious joke. "Good luck on surviving." He went back inside, still laughing.

Chapter Fifteen

The kid in the seat next to Erik on the Boeing 707 said over the noise of the four jet engines, "Who woulda thought we'd be goin' to war in a Pan Am jet?"

"Yeah, with stewardesses," Erik replied, thinking how beautiful they looked in their light-blue uniforms. "I had no idea this was how they flew GIs to Vietnam, already in their jungle fatigues. I don't think that's been written about in the newspapers. Here's a whole new industry that's benefiting from the Vietnam conflict."

The kid looked at him blankly. He must have been only 18 years old. "What do you mean, benefiting?"

"Well, here's a Boeing 707, chock full of guys going to war. Pan Am isn't doing this for free. Just imagine three or four flights a week, maybe more. They don't have to advertise to get people to take trips to beautiful Southeast Asia, either. That's got to be very profitable. It's probably true of other airlines, too."

"I see what you mean."

They both looked at a sea of green behind them. Stewardesses slowly wheeled a cart up the aisle. As it drew closer, Erik heard GIs ask for a beer or a mixed drink, knowing full well what the answer was. Still, the sympathetic stewardesses said, "Sorry, no alcohol on this trip."

Erik turned back around and closed his eyes. He reviewed the last couple of months. AIT had been more intense than basic training. Learning to fire the M-16 was like shooting a Mattel toy. It had little recoil because of a spring and plunger built into the hard plastic stock, and it was light and easy to carry. Erik knew he was headed for the Nam, so he paid attention to his instructors, all of whom had been in combat, some just a few months before.

Those who had been in a lot of intense, extended combat had an aloofness about them that said nothing could bother them anymore. The ones who acted jumpy and emotionally keyed up sought attention and approval, but they probably hadn't seen the elephant.

How nice it was to be at home with the snow around Christmas after five months in Louisiana. He appreciated all the conveniences such as newspapers delivered to the door, a refrigerator with lots of food, and sleeping in the morning. He had to be careful about his language. "Pass the fucking butter" wouldn't have gone over very well.

Marie seemed introspective about relationships with her children. Erik said that he might not come back alive, but his mother assured him that he would. She knew little about war, except what the Christian Science practitioner had her read in the tenth chapter of Samuel. Harold went about his business, walking to campus early and back in the late afternoon.

Erik was glad that Helen was there. "So, you're going off to defend the republic," Helen said.

"Yeah, can you believe it? Call me Cincinnatus, the citizen soldier," Erik said. "How is Berkley?"

"Bernie and I are leaving Berkley. We're going to live in a commune down by Santa Cruz."

Harold emphatically crushed the newspaper he was reading. "You're what?"

"Going to live in a commune. Bernie and I are dropping out of this warmongering police state to be with people we love and who love us."

Marie looked ill. "Is this the free-love business that I read about with, with hippies? Oh, Helen, please."

"What will you live on?" her father demanded.

"Oh we'll make do with subsistence farming and cultivating herbal teas for some cash. Bernie has his doctorate in philosophy, you know. His family is quite well-off. We have thought it all out. We all pooled our money and bought a piece of land."

"With a degree in philosophy and yours in English, you both should have better sense," Harold said.

"That's your materialistic opinion. Don't worry, you won't have to burden yourself with me anymore," Helen said.

Erik wondered if his father caught the irony of that. He couldn't think about Helen right then. He had to escape.

Reading, as always, helped Erik lose himself. He read *The Young Lions* by Irwin Shaw, about World War II. In that war the whole country was swept up in support of its boys in uniform. He thought how his imagination for those times helped him get through basic and AIT. Soldiering in battle was about to become the real thing, but he was amazed at how the Vietnam conflict did not really affect life in America, except as a reason for students to tweak the nose of the establishment. If there hadn't been a Vietnam, it would be something else. When he traveled in uniform, Erik realized, he was not admired. He felt he and other soldiers were looked down on as very uncool suckers. His stream of consciousness was interrupted with, "Would you like coffee, a soda, or milk with your dinner?"

"Let's see," Erik said, pencil and notebook in hand, "there are five hundred thousand guys in Nam right now. I read somewhere that only about 20 percent have a combat MOS, you know, military occupation specialty, and the rest are in support. Twenty percent of five hundred thousand is one hundred thousand. So, as an 11B20 we will most likely be in combat. Now, say there's a casualty rate of 20 percent, and I think that's high, but a casualty rate of 20 percent would mean that twenty thousand guys will be wounded or killed. Usually KIAs, killed in action, are just one fourth of the casualties, which means that five thousand guys are going to die out of the five hundred thousand in a one-year tour. If this damn thing goes on for ten years, that'll be fifty thousand lives." He did some more figuring. "We of the fighting one hundred thousand have a 20 percent chance of getting wounded, and a 5 percent chance of making the ultimate sacrifice, as they say. Or, looked at another way, we have a 95 percent chance of going back alive on a freedom bird, not counting being wounded. If we were a chairborne ranger—a clerk or some support guy—we would have only about a 1 percent chance of being killed." Erik glanced at the guy he was explaining this to. He looked as if he was about to fall asleep.

"Yeah, I see. Uh, so, say there are two hundred guys on this plane. How many are going to be killed?"

"Hey, good question. I hadn't thought of that." Erik put pencil to paper. "I heard these 707s seat one hundred eighty passengers. If 20 percent on this plane have a combat MOS, it looks like one point eight of us will not be flying back alive. If you factor in the deaths of non-combatants on the plane, three point two would be flying back in a plane-load of caskets. If we're all 11B20s that would mean that nine of us would go home in a flag-draped coffin."

Erik gulped. What would I be dying for? he asked himself. Isn't Ho Chi Minh Vietnam's George Washington? To change the subject he said, "Where'd you go for basic and AIT? What's your name, by the way? I'm Erik."

"Michael, and Fort Dix for both," he replied. "You?"

"Fort Polk. What's your home town?"

"Upstate New York. Lake Placid," Michael said.

"No kidding? I've heard of that. They had the Winter Olympics there once, didn't they?"

"Yeah, 1932. My dad's a maintenance guy for the ice skating rink left over from that."

"You skate?"

Michael brightened. "Oh, yeah. Hockey is my thing."

Erik smiled, leaned back, closed his eyes, and pictured a cold, sunny day in November when he was 7 years old. Playing it over in his mind brought him to a deep sleep.

The plane banked. Erik looked down at the green expanse of land and a lazy, meandering river. It didn't look as if a war was going on. He saw some pencil-thin columns of wispy, white smoke rising straight into the shimmering sunlight. Absolutely no wind, just heat, he concluded.

The pilot got on the intercom and said dryly, "This is your captain. We're approaching Bien Hoa Air Base, so please fasten your seat belts. The temperature outside is ninety-four degrees. We should be landing in about ten minutes. We hope you enjoy your stay in Vietnam and thank you for flying Pan Am."

This is weird, Erik said to himself. He thought there would be some reaction to this absurdity, but everyone remained silent.

Erik wondered where Terry and John were. They had been with him at the Oakland Army Base for the few days it took the army to process them. They were issued five sets of jungle fatigues, which were green nylon for easier drying, and the blouse was loose-fitting and not tucked in. Both pants and top had a lot of pockets. And then there were the formations twice a day to hear flight lists for Travis Air Force Base. They slept in a big armory or played ping-pong in a game area at one end. Terry and John left on an earlier flight. "What can they do, send us to Nam?" Erik said. "Is exactly what the army could do, and did."

Chapter Sixteen

When Erik got off the plane at Bien Hoa airfield, he was enveloped by a wave of heat and humidity. The plane-load of new arrivals walked past the tanned faces of GIs who were going to get on the same plane and fly home. It looked as if they were more anxious than happy, and probably would be until they took off. None of the departing soldiers yelled out cat-calls to give the new guys a hard time.

Soon Erik was on a shuttle bus taking his group to the Ninetieth Replacement Battalion at Long Binh Army Base. Bien Hoa and Long Binh were two of the many satellite towns around Saigon that looked just the same—urban, crowded, and teeming with motorbikes and bicycles. Narrow concrete open-air structures lined the streets for mile after mile. They appeared to be combination living quarters and shops. It was humming with activity and exotic. Erik had the feeling that the war was a big deal to the Americans but way down the list of importance to this country that could easily swallow up a half-million foreign devils.

At Long Binh, the largest army base in the world, personnel clerks matched up an MOS with replacement needs of the divisions that were scattered over the length and breadth of South Vietnam. If the Twenty-fifth Division needed fifty bodies with an 11B20 MOS, the processors created a block of new arrivals and gave them to the non-com reading off names at the twice-daily formations.

Erik spent a night in a transient barracks. He made it to the 0900 formation after a breakfast in one of the mess halls manned by some unlucky KPs. The formation got quiet as a sergeant addressed them.

"The following personnel will fall out to the Twenty-fifth Division right over there, to the sergeant holding the Tropic Lightning insignia. Alberts, Leonard; Andreeson, Terrence; Borsch, John; Cummings, Randall ..."

Erik strained to hear the names. He didn't want to stand too close to the front because anybody left over would get grabbed for KP. "Levy, David; Stennis, Richard; Towne, Douglas; Thorvald, Erik; Troon, Jacob; Weber, John …"

Here we go, Erik said to himself. He had heard of the Twenty-fifth Division. They had seen a lot of heavy fighting in the Pacific Theater in World War II, starting with Guadalcanal.

He grabbed his duffel bag and headed for the subdued black-on-green battle insignia of a lightning bolt on a strawberry-shaped background, the symbol for what was called the Tropic Lightning Division. Stateside colors were a gold lightning bolt on a red fig leaf trimmed in gold. Some guys called it the Electric Strawberry. In Vietnam, all the insignia of rank, such as stripes on the sleeves or bars on the collars of officers, or CIBs, or division patches, were black embroidery on a patch of green.

As the new guys clustered around the non-com, nobody said anything except for one private who couldn't stand still. "Where is the Twenty-fifth based, anyway?"

The avuncular sergeant calmly replied, "It's at Cu Chi, which is about forty miles from here. It's actually only about thirty miles northwest of Saigon."

His answer surprised Erik because it was the first time since he'd entered the army that a sergeant didn't shout an answer if some recruit was stupid enough to ask a question. It seemed that he was now in a unit and had an identity.

When the formation was over and no more stragglers appeared, First Sergeant Bolton said, "Okay, guys, I gotta see if y'all are here, so listen up while I call out names." He read off the list on his orders and checked them off. Everybody was present. "Now, here's the deal. We're going to meet over there by those two deuce-and-a-halfs. Throw your shit in the back and find a seat. We'll be driving through Saigon and then on to our base at Cu Chi. The whole trip is about two hours."

As they pulled out of Long Binh, Erik wondered if the other guys were thinking that this couldn't be so bad, being so close to Saigon. He was sitting next to a guy with longer hair than those who just got out of AIT. It seemed as though he wasn't all that new to Vietnam and anxious to see everything. Erik looked out at the throng of motorbikes driven by all manner of people, some carrying baskets of goods strapped on the back. "Have you been here before?" Erik said.

"Oh, yeah. I'm on my second tour."

"What'd you do before?"

"I was on mobile radar equipment."

"How did that work?"

"At a forward fire-base near the Cambodian border, which is only about twenty miles beyond where we're going, we aimed radar toward the Ho Chi Minh Trail and watched insurgents moving down the trail free as you please."

"What happened then?" Erik was all ears about anything he could learn.

"We could call in arty, but it didn't do no good. It was impossible to do it for every little blip on the radar, and then they would disappear like they was goin' into tunnels."

Forget about being safer near Saigon, thought Erik. It seemed that this area is just a funnel for the North Vietnamese to attack Saigon, like last year's Tet. Tet of 1968 created a huge reaction in the United States, Erik remembered. The shock of enemy forces having the run of the place turned many against this war of attrition. Regular NVA and Viet Cong guerillas had infiltrated Saigon and other population centers. They coordinated an offensive during the main holiday of Vietnam around the lunar new year in late January when the South's guard was down.

"So why did you have to come back?"

"I re-upped so I *could* come back."

Erik looked at him to see if he was joking. His eyes were closed. "I've got a little mama-san in Cu Chi. I stay with her whenever I can. I buy her things and then we fucky-fuck our brains out. I keep my stash with her." He opened his eyes. "You can buy a pack of twenty cigarettes that some gook has taken out the tobacco and replaced it with top-of-the-line, grade-A cannabis. It's good shit, and I get it for one—count it—one dollar!"

Erik was amazed. Back in college he remembered it was five bucks for just one joint, the few times he had smoked it.

"So what's your MOS?" asked the radar guy.

"Eleven-B twenty."

"Ouch. Too bad."

"Got any advice?"

"Yeah. It don't mean nothin'."

Erik kicked that around. Like Jimmy Durante said, everyone is trying to get into the act, or in this case, everybody's a philosopher, mostly existentialists.

The guy next to Erik on the right hadn't said a word to anybody the whole time since formation. He was writing in a notebook.

The urban squalor gave way to countryside. Vietnamese on bicycles and motor scooters scowled at the truck that had forced them aside with honking, reckless driving. "Outa the way, you fuckin' slope," was the driver's constant refrain.

Erik thought of their indoctrinations in AIT, where they were told about how the U.S. Army was a savior to the Vietnamese and how they loved Americans. "Yeah, right," he said aloud.

After two hours of bouncing and swaying, the truck came to a stop. Erik heard some back and forth in English. When the truck moved forward, some MPs closed the gate behind them. "Welcome to the Cu Chi Army Base," said the guy on his left, "home of the Twenty-fifth Division."

Chapter Seventeen

A middle-aged sergeant addressed the new arrivals after noon mess. "First you're gonna get your name and the division patch on your combat fatigues. That's the PX right over there. Also, get your ranks sewn on. If you're right out of AIT, you've been promoted to private first class E-three, with one stripe and a rocker by virtue of arriving in Nam. You also get 120 more dollars a month for being in a war zone. Your 201 file will be forwarded to your unit's HQ. Pay is in MPC, which stands for military payment certificate. It's about the size of Monopoly money, only with fancier printing. You have to pay for the sewing, but it's cheap. We got gooks doing it."

Erik looked around at the huge post. Unpainted two-story wooden barracks occupied a space about the size of a football field. Some beautiful Vietnamese ladies in their *ao dais* were walking through the gate, reporting to work, apparently, in the headquarters offices. Erik was surprised at all the Vietnamese nationals working inside the camp.

At one of several mess halls, where they had lunch, all the KPs were young Vietnamese. In the officers' section, good-looking Vietnamese females waited on tables and endured a lot of joking and flirtatious innuendo. They seemed to take it in stride but, if too coarse, would huff in indignation and say, "You *dinky-dao*." It reminded Erik of the cultural charade depicted in Orwell's *Burmese Days*, in which the colonials thought they were splendid examples of humanity, and the natives had to endure the idiotic foreigners.

"Next," the first sergeant continued, "you'll go to charm school, which is three days of orientation to teach you the ropes before you get fucked up for doing something stupid. But first you'll be assigned to a unit so you'll have a place to sleep."

Erik's gaze wandered to the perimeter of barbed wire, concrete bunkers, and occasional guard towers. "Holy shit, it must be ten miles around this place," Erik said to the quiet guy writing in his notebook.

He got a simple "Yeah" in response.

Erik took a longer look at him. He had dark hair that looked as though it would be curly if grown out. The guy had tried to be inconspicuous, but his recruiting-poster looks drew attention. He was about six feet tall, a couple of inches taller than Erik. Erik wanted to blend in with the background, too, which was not a problem since there was nothing special about him.

"Didja ever see anything so flat?" Erik said, trying to continue the conversation.

Notebook guy looked up. "Yeah, that's why the Twenty-fifth picked this spot back in 1966. They cleared off a mile-wide swath around the perimeter and called it a kill zone."

"How'd you know about that?"

"I was talking to an army recruiter about it. He was in the Twenty-fifth back when this whole thing got started."

"You were talking to an army recruiter?" Erik said, incredulously.

"Yeah, I signed up. I'm regular army."

"What the hell for?"

"I wanted to see what this was all about from a grunt's perspective and then write about it."

"D'jou go to college?" Erik said.

"Are you casting aspersions about a Jew going to college? What am I, chopped liver?"

Erik interjected quickly, "No, I said, 'Did you go to—'" He realized he was being kidded when the guy laughed.

Closing his notebook and still smiling, the guy said, "I'm David Levy, and I *am* Jewish."

"Erik Thorvald." They shook hands.

"Are you from Minne-soooo-ta?" David asked, drawing out the *oh* in the middle.

"Close. I'm from Iowa, the next state south, but my dad's from there." They were walking, now, following the sergeant. "Sounds like you've been there, but your accent says you're from New Yawk."

"Yeah, I'm from Brooklyn, but I had some friends who went to the University of Minnesota. I've been there a few times."

"*Uff da*, then, you know, I s'pose," Erik said.

David laughed.

"Where'd you go to school?" Erik said.

"Brown."

"Brown University?" Erik tried to sound cool about the Ivy League school.

"Yeah."

After a pause, Erik said, "Must have been Providence."

David groaned. "Spare me, oh God, from inane puns. Where'd you go?"

"The University of Wyoming."

"What did you study, besides skiing?"

"You got that right. Otherwise, I was a history major."

"Huh. Me, too," David said. "What do you know about Vietnam?"

"Hmm … Well, I studied that information brochure the army gave us about phrases in Vietnamese in order to relate to our hosts. *Duroc bao quanh ngoi lang cua ban.*"

"What does that mean?"

"Your village is surrounded."

Levy broke up with laughter.

David, Erik, and five other 11B20s in the group wound up in B Company, Third Battalion, Twelfth Infantry Regiment, Twenty-fifth Infantry Division. Their first night with the Electric Strawberry was in a barracks, or what the sergeant called a hootch, that the Third Battalion used when anybody came through Cu Chi for company business, R and R, or DEROS, which Erik learned soon enough stood for "date estimated return from overseas."

The transients in the hootch where Erik and his group entered had longer hair, some bordering on Afros, and mostly wore green T-shirts, fatigue pants, and flip-flops. One of the guys playing cards said barely within earshot, "FNGs." The other players laughed. David and Erik grabbed a bunk in the middle and another PFC took the one next to them.

"How's it going? My name's Erik. Where are you from?"

"Tom Madsen from Blue Island, Illinois. How about you guys?"

They all shook hands and established where the three of them were from. They talked about how they came to be in the army.

"I was a journeyman electrician apprentice and got a draft notice," Madsen said. "I couldn't believe it. I was all set to get married."

"The good old draft—a great leveler," Erik said.

"Unlike the reserves and National Guard, which are white and affluent," David said.

At the far end of the hootch some brothers listened to soul music on a tape player. They all wore sunglasses, one with heart-shaped lenses. Just like in basic and AIT, Erik thought. The urban black guys congregate and listen to their music, and the rural white guys listen to country.

Fortunately, nobody was playing country music or Erik figured there would be trouble. He leaned over from the top bunk and asked David, "What's an FNG, anyway?"

"Damned if I know," David replied.

A supine soldier across the aisle said without looking away from his paperback, "It's a fucking new guy."

"Oh."

Erik thought about the Cu Chi Army Base they had just toured. It had all the comforts of home: a hospital, an airstrip, a swimming pool, laundry, horseshoe pits, outdoor basketball courts, showers, an open-air theater, and several clubs that sold mixed drinks and beer. He counted one officers' club, two for non-coms, and one EM club for the lowly enlisted men. Young Vietnamese females worked in them. Some units had their own place for drinking, such as the Sixty-fifth Engineers. It looked very similar to stateside duty. An artillery battery was having a cookout with T-bone steaks on grills made from fifty-gallon drums cut in half lengthwise. This is probably better than back in the States, Erik thought.

The top sergeant had said, "As you can see, gentlemen, this duty is not too bad. I want to give you the opportunity of being posted right here for the entire year. You know where my office is, right next to the big white wall where we show movies, and, ahem, we've been known to show a few skin flicks after the main feature if the chaplain ain't around. But seriously, gentlemen, you know where to find me, and I want you to stop in if you would like to re-up for another year. If that should be the case, you get a five-thousand-dollar signing bonus, and you wouldn't be out in the boonies humpin' your ruck or poundin' the paddies. You'd be right here helping us get along. So think about it and come and see me."

Erik remembered how a couple of young newbies who were born to be a casualty exchanged glances. Some are going to do it, Erik thought. David wrote something in his notebook as he shook his head.

"Man, this is bullshit," Erik said sotto voce. Being honest with himself, he had to admit he thought about it for a second. Then he realized that these would be the guys who guard the perimeter. He knew that looking at that flat emptiness every night would drive him up a wall. No way would he sign for another year.

After breakfast in the mess hall, the new guys went to the quartermaster as directed to draw equipment. The supply clerk behind a counter talked about what was coming up at the end of January. "Tet is the only holiday they've got in Vietnam, so all the gook relatives git together an' have a big wing-ding. Man, ah was heah for the last Tet, you know, in January sixty-eight. Theyah was some serious shit goin' on, like, you know, the

84

American Embassy in Saigon was overrun. Buku GIs got killed. Right heah in Cu Chi, I mean the town of Cu Chi, some hard-core NVA swept through and three GIs in the Arizona Bar got zapped, all for a little boom-boom."

The spec-four passed out rucksacks, helmets, flak jackets, ponchos, sleeping bags, mosquito netting, tent halves, and web gear as he spoke. "This place was on high alert. We was locked up tight and outa sight. Man, we had our shit together. Ah get to *didi* before this yeah's Tet since ah DEROS twenty Jan. Where you fucking new guys headin'?"

Madsen said, "The sarge told us that we're going up to War Zone C in Tay Ninh province. There used to be seven of us, but that kid from Nebraska re-upped along with that other guy from who knows where, so they'll be staying here."

"That's how ah got this job," the spec-four drawled. "Now ah'm thinkin' of being a lifer. You know ah could retar in twenty yeahs and go fishin', but no fucking way ah was gonna go out in the boonies. This is Charlie's backyard, and he kin have it. Besides, theyah's animals out theyah—you know, snakes and bugs and tigers. Ah hate animals."

"Didn't you ever have a dog?" Erik said.

"A dog ain't no animal," he drawled. "Okay, heyah's your M-16s. You gotta sign for 'em. You lose your weapon, you owe the army one hunert an' twenty-six bucks."

The five grunts walked down the blacktop street, an M-16 strapped over one shoulder and a duffel bag full of gear over the other. David wrote in his notebook as he spoke in a southern drawl, "A … dog … ain't … no … animal."

Madsen said, "I'm glad we're in the dry season. A buddy of mine told me this camp looks like rice paddies during the monsoon, but hell if I know when that is."

"In the southern half of South Vietnam, in which we presently find ourselves," Erik said, professorially, reciting some of what he had learned from his father before he left, "the rainy season of the monsoon climate begins in March and lasts through August, more or less. Meanwhile, the northern latitudes have the opposite weather pattern, so right now our brothers-in-arms of the Central Highlands are enduring the hardships of intermittent monsoon rains. In two months there will be a reversal of weather, if not fortune."

"Jesus Christ! Ask a simple question …" David said, and laughed with the others.

They approached the helicopter pads of the Twenty-fifth Aviation Battalion. A Huey pilot said, "Are you the grunts going to Tay Ninh?"

"Yup," Madsen said.

"Put your gear in that slick and have a seat. I've got to pick up a red bag of mail. I'll be right back."

Erik and the others put on their helmet liners and steel pots. They threw their duffel bags onto the floor, held their M-16s, and sat on the aluminum frame webbed with nylon straps.

The warrant officer returned and threw the mail bag onto their gear and signaled the co-pilot to wind it up, his hand in the air making a circular motion. Erik, sitting next to the open door, asked the pilot, "Where is Tay Ninh?"

"The American base is just west of Tay Ninh City, so it's called Tay Ninh West. It's in Injun country north of the Parrot's Beak and about a dozen miles from the Cambodian border. You can see Nui Ba Dinh about ten miles to the north."

The UH1's engine started whining loudly.

"What's Nui Ba Dinh?" Erik shouted.

The warrant officer yelled, "You'll know it when you see it," as he moved to the pilot's door.

The helicopter flew over terrain that Erik thought was even flatter than around Gainesboro. They looked down on a large area of dormant rice paddies. After a few miles they were above a vast forest. One of the door gunners yelled something and pointed downward. Erik thought he said "Hobo Woods." Tall trees surrounded by a thick jumble of lower vegetation suddenly gave way to a rank and file of singular trees, naked of any underbrush, stretching to the horizon in rows so straight that it looked like a painting drawn with a ruler. The sight prompted Erik to think: rubber-tree plantation, Michelin, weird, awesome.

Tay Ninh West was good-sized, but not as big as Cu Chi. The five replacements went looking for B Company in the Third Battalion area. Like Cu Chi, Erik saw Vietnamese ladies in black silk pajama-type clothes working around the barracks, sweeping, doing laundry by hand, and polishing boots. After he dumped his gear, Erik went looking for a latrine.

"Bodine! I don't believe it!" Erik cried, recognizing his fellow squad leader from basic training.

"Hey, Erik, you scum bag! You finally made it."

"Yeah, there wasn't much I could do about it. Wow, you're a sergeant already?"

"Yeah, I've been over here for a month and a half. I was a real hot-shot in AIT, and I made specialist-four right after that. When I got here the company commander saw my Texas A and M experience and made me an acting buck-sergeant and a squad leader."

"How'd you get here so fast?"

"I volunteered to forego my thirty-day leave and get over here right away."

"Man, you are crazy," Erik said.

"Well, I figure the army owes me thirty days, and I thought I'd rather take it while I'm over here and see something exotic. Plus, I get R and R, too. Hey, I'll make sure you're in my squad."

"Could you get David Levy, too? He's a good guy."

"Yeah, no problem. You're now in third squad, first platoon. We're a reconnaissance platoon. Go over to first platoon's hootch and find an empty cot and hang your shit on the wall pegs next to it. Tell Levy, too. We've got a formation at 1600."

"I'll try and be there," Erik deadpanned.

Bodine laughed. "Fuckin' A!"

SFC Anderson saluted Lieutenant Cushman and said, "All present and accounted for, including the FNGs."

Lieutenant Cushman laughed, returned a relaxed salute and said, "At ease. Welcome to the Nam, gentlemen. As for the rest of you assholes, I don't care how short you are, don't be a bad influence on our new arrivals. Don't be telling them the best thing they can do in an ambush is to duck their heads … and kiss their ass goodbye."

The grunts laughed. They appeared to like their lieutenant, or as they called him, "El-tee," the army's abbreviation for the rank of lieutenant. Erik heard he was a West Pointer. That automatically put him a step above the OCS and ROTC officers. The lieutenant had a quiet confidence about him that impressed Erik right away.

Lieutenant Cushman said, "Now for the bad news. As recon platoon, it's about time we got off our ass and earned our pay. At 0700 hours tomorrow, we're going to *didi mau*, that's Vietnamese for 'haul ass,' up the road toward Nui Ba Den." Cushman looked around and lowered his voice. "There are too many fucking Vietnamese around here," he said. "It makes you wonder if we can function without them. This is just like a French colony, which I didn't sign up for. I mean, goddammit, do we have to have all these hootch cunts around here? The fucking REMFs could be pulling the KP and cleaning the barracks."

Erik and David exchanged puzzled looks, which Cushman must have noticed.

"REMFs. Rear echelon motherfuckers. Even though this post is in War Zone C, the guys in it, like signal, company clerks, supply clerks, and cooks, are still rear echelon." He shook his head. "I'm sorry. Don't get me started, but there have been too many times when I think the VC know what we're going to do before we do it."

His captive audience nodded in agreement. One of them leered suggestively. "Hey, Lieutenant. Maybe we could have the hootch ladies do more than sweep the floors and clean boots, if you know what I mean."

"That'll be the day. Even if they wanted to, which they don't, you're going to have to go off post and pay for it with MPC and a case of the clap, like everybody else."

When the laughter died down, one of the guys said, "What about you, El-tee?"

"I'm saving myself for my wife on R and R, which is in about two months." He kept quiet while the last of the hootch ladies walked toward the gate to check out for the evening. "You know what, gentlemen? They *are* inscrutable, especially when you can't see their faces underneath those pointy straw hats. You can bet they're gathering intelligence." He sighed. "We're fighting a losing battle here, mah fellow Amuhricans. A half-million soldiers and/or marines aren't going to defeat eighty million Vietnamese."

This is why they liked their lieutenant, Erik figured, he talked straight with them.

Fred Sawyer, the lieutenant's RTO, said, "You ain't just a-whoofin', El-tee. You know last month when we got hit, it was no big deal, but during the day all the gooks in the whole camp was asking to borrow money."

Erik got the point. If a GI was owed money, anybody who borrowed from him didn't have to pay it back if he was dead.

The lieutenant said, "Anyway, gather around nice and close." When the platoon formed a tight circle, he said, "Okay, we're going to move out to the dirt road that heads north towards Nui Ba Den, the Black Virgin Mountain, at 0700 tomorrow. Get a good breakfast under your belts. After about three klicks—you know a klick is a thousand meters—we're going to turn west and melt into the enchanted forest. We'll look for any infiltration and build-up for Tet. As you know, Tay Ninh province is a main terminus of the Ho Chi Minh Trail, and if we're worth a shit, we can't just hole up in this fucking Tay Ninh West."

Erik had two thoughts. One, now he knew what Nui Ba Den was as he looked at the mountain rising in the distance out of nothing but flat plains. It looked about three thousand feet high. Two, even though his knees shook and his stomach was in knots, he was in this for all he had. The lose-your-life epiphany echoed in his mind. He thought how quickly things were happening. Ten days before, he was reading by a warm fire and it was snowing outside.

Chapter Eighteen

When Erik caught up with the platoon after burying the three mortar rounds they were gathered around the NVA communication wire. Nguyen carried wire cutters and connectors to tap into communication lines. He made a splice and listened. He said, "No talk, Ar-tee." He kept the earphone to his ear. Lieutenant Cushman sent a post up the trail and one down. The rest of the platoon lighted cigarettes and lay around as though waiting for a bus.

Mason turned off his pocket radio. "Hey, Thorvald. You're from Minnesota, right?"

"Well, sort of."

"Djou hear about the guy in Minneapolis who wanted to take a bus to Duluth?"

"No."

"He says to the bus driver, 'Does this bus go to Duluth?' And the bus driver says, 'No, it goes beep, beep.'"

Erik laughed along with everybody, and tried to shake the pall of dead bodies just down the trail. "Where you from, again?" Erik asked knowing the answer.

"Birmingfuckingham, Alagotdambama. Do you know how many Alabamans it takes to eat a squirrel?"

Hosmer said, "No, tell us."

"Two. One to hold a knife and fork and the other to watch for cars."

The platoon cracked up.

Mason was on roll. "Hey, Lieutenant, I know how to clean up this war in no time and we could all go home."

"How's that?"

"You put a couple of divisions of Koreans up at the DMZ and all the PXs in Vietnam at Cam Mau down on the delta and say 'Go to it, boys,' why they'd kick ass through the length of Nam in no time just to get to that giant PX. I have never seen such a bunch of horse traders in my life."

"Yeah, they're pretty acquisitive, er, they like baubles and grown-up toys, that's for sure," Cushman said.

Nguyen held up his hand. "They talk," he said. He listened with a blank stare, then smiled. "He say, 'Four comrade not here. When leave tunnel?' Girl, she say, 'Four leave tunnel at three.' He say, 'Something hahpen. I need order. What you know about order?' She say, 'I caw you baa.'"

The lieutenant said, "Thanks, Nguyen. Keep listening." To his platoon sergeant: "I'd like to know what those orders are."

Anderson said, "That paper in the gook's pocket was probably his orders. Too bad Nguyen couldn't read more than the 3rd NVA Division, but at least we know who we're up against—the Yellow Star Division."

When he filled sandbags the night before, Erik overheard Mason and Snake talking about Anderson. They said he was a lifer who planned to retire in about five years. They had heard Anderson say that he was too old for this, but he loved the drinking life in clubs all over Vietnam on American bases. Erik supposed the camaraderie was a good excuse to drink to excess and tell war stories. "Cheap drunks, too," Mason said, "fifty cents for a double Wild Turkey."

"Here's what I think," Lieutenant Cushman said. "That company of NVA from the 3rd Division was walking last night from a tunnel complex and laying down commo wire as they went along the trail, probably going to another tunnel. They're setting up a base camp as close as they can get to Tay Ninh without detection. They've set up a cache of rockets and mortar rounds. The CO of said company is waiting for orders, like time and place to attack Tay Ninh West and maybe occupy Tay Ninh City during Tet. Other companies in their regiment will probably hook up with them. They'll send out a search party to see if they can find the four VC that were heading their way. What do you think, Andy?"

"I think you've nailed it, Lieutenant. We should probably have a squad waiting for the search party."

"That's what I'm thinking, too," Cushman said. He turned to the platoon. "Gentlemen, I need six volunteers to set up an ambush on the other side of the four dead gooks."

David said, "I'll go, sir."

Erik knew he was going to do that, and he was ready. "I'll go, too, sir."

"Bodine, where in hell did you get these gung-ho FNGs? I haven't been called sir since I was back at Fort Lewis. What are these guys trying to prove, anyway? Well, hell, you might as well take your people for the ambush since almost half your squad just volunteered."

"Roger that, El-tee," Bodine said with resignation as he gave Levy and Thorvald a baleful look. "Okay, third squad, let's go."

Lieutenant Cushman said, "Sergeant Bodine, we're going to be setting up an NDP about a hundred meters off the trail on an azimuth due west. If you don't see anybody by 1500, get your asses back where we are. Give a whistle when you get near us. Got it?"

"Got it, El-tee."

Bodine and his squad walked around the dead VC. "We're going a ways down the trail. No way am I gonna be near this stench," Bodine announced. "And by the way, thanks a lot, Levy and Thorvald. Hey, Thorvald, your name is too fucking awkward. Every time I say it I sound like I'm in a fucking Ingmar Bergman movie and Liv Ullman's gonna pop out of the jungle like a wet dream. Fucking Swede."

"It's Norwegian," Erik said.

"Same-same. From now on we're going to call you um … uh … Shrapnel, since you like to pick it up or attract it, or somethin' *dinky-dao* like that."

Levy said, "Sorry about volunteering, Bo, I just want to see everything."

"Yeah? Well, put this down in your fucking notebook: Ambushes suck."

Erik and the six other grunts moved on about two hundred meters where they set up two claymores facing the trail. They strung the detonator cords into the foliage down trail from where they sat in a line. They opened a few *C* rations and waited.

Bodine said, "These guys we're fighting, I gotta admit, are some highly-motivated, hard-fighting dudes. They can live on a ball of rice per day. They're lean and mean and can take a lot more than we can. So many get greased, but they don't give up. It's their country, so what are we doing here?"

Erik mulled this over. "Good question, Bo. There's nothing like being here to learn what it's like." He fought an urge to sleep and saw that some of the squad did nod off. For two hours they waited, and nothing happened.

Bodine looked at his watch. "Okay, it's 1500. We've got to *didi*. Pick up the claymores, and let's get the hell out of here."

Everyone held their noses as they stepped around the hideous scene of four dead VC. Erik hoped he could erase it from his memory. If he hadn't been in such a hurry, he might have given some thought to an uneasy feeling of what, being followed? Bodine didn't say anything about it, and Erik didn't think to ask him. When they got to where the rest of the platoon had left the trail, they ducked into the dim world of massive trees that dwarfed their intrusion. About a hundred meters in, Bodine gave a whistle. He heard one in return. They made their way into the new NDP.

Chapter Nineteen

The platoon was digging in more than usual.

"The lieutenant wants us to put in some overhead tonight," Mason said. "We could be in for a long night. The shit could hit the fan."

Everybody scrounged up dead logs and hacked down small trees to make a ceiling over the holes they dug between two fighting positions. Four guys could dive in if they got mortared. On top of the logs they put a couple of layers of sandbags. Erik stood in the middle of the perimeter. They were on a slight rise in a rough clearing.

"Hey, El-tee, what happened with the wire?" Bodine said.

"Some Vietnamese woman told the other guy to be ready by January twenty-seventh with all their materiel and await further orders. After that we cut the wire and dug in here."

"That's in the middle of Tet."

"You got that right," the lieutenant said. He turned his attention to SFC Anderson, who was putting finishing touches on the CP. "So, Andy, we're getting some good intel out of this little foray. Looks like Tay Ninh City or Tay Ninh West are in the 3rd Division's crosshairs for a Tet offensive."

"Once again, Lieutenant, the Roadrunner has foiled Wile E. Coyote's elaborate, but half-baked plans," Anderson said.

The lieutenant laughed. "We'll see." He got Clemons on the radio and told him to start setting up some defensive concentrations. "Three, one. I've got numbered def cons starting with thirteen, which is easier to understand over the radio; that's our pos at eight one five three two niner for illumination. Over."

The lieutenant listened to a reply, and then, "Three, one. Def con fourteen. Eight one six three two eight. Send one whiskey papa to def con fourteen, over."

Soon a white phosphorous round was on its way. It landed fifty meters outside their perimeter with an impact not much louder than a truck backfire. He adjusted from the white smoke, coming ever closer to the perimeter.

Erik could hear the lieutenant repeating this technique for about an hour. Bodine explained that he was aiming all twelve howitzers at designated spots around the perimeter so he didn't have to call them in later. "The lieutenant must be jumpy about tonight," Erik said.

"He's not the only one," Levy said. "Can't you feel it? Even the trees are just standing there, observing our impending doom."

Erik gazed at a palisade of towering trees. Their large trunks devoid of lower branches reminded him of Easter Island statues. They looked omniscient and, as David implied, menacing in their silence. "They're just trees, for chrissake," Erik said. "You must be reading about Caesar and the Druids, who communed with trees."

"Yeah, I am, actually. I was just thinking that warriors have prepared for battle for thousands of years and were inclined to be superstitious. You think I'm into my reading too much?"

Erik laughed. "Yeah, for sure. Do you think there will always be wars?"

"Given mankind's stupidity, and throw in a little paranoia, probably so, until the big one. You see one thermonuclear war; you've seen 'em all."

"Ha, ha. Good one. If I ever get out of this I feel like finding a beautiful woman and, well, screwing all night long."

"Yeah, me too," David said. "It must be a primal reaction to the proposition of dying. You know, perpetuating the genes."

"Maybe the sex drive and fear drive are on equal footing," Erik said. "Our military leaders fear an enemy getting the upper hand. Fear extrapolates into killing the threat, ergo war. It's an urge to survive just as strong as the impulse to, as you say, perpetuate the genes."

"Or, maybe it's just wanting to get laid. I was just putting out some shit for the sake of argument. Too bad you didn't go to Brown. We could have had some great discussions. Some classes were a dozen guys, gals too, sitting around a table, giving reports, and debating."

Erik thought he indeed would have liked that. He could never have similar polemics with his father. If he disagreed with him, his father would look disgusted and not deign to continue.

Erik found a spot within the perimeter and dug a hole about a foot square. "Auuuuughghghg!" he yelled into it and filled it in with dirt. He tamped it down hard with his entrenching tool.

"What the fuck was that all about?" David said.

"Call me *dinky-dao*, but I've got this gnawing fear in the pit of my stomach. I just buried it in that hole. Fuck it! I'm going forward," Erik said.

David smiled as though he understood and had his own ways of dealing with sheer terror.

They sat and ate a can of beans and franks and one of peaches. A shrill cry made them jump. "Where the hell is that bird?" Erik said.

A lizard screamed again, claiming a sandbag right in front of them. "That's a fucking *lizard?*" David said.

"Yeah, who would have thought? You learn something every day if you're not careful," Erik said, trying to sound calm, but the sudden shriek of the gecko sounded like a warning. "I have this weird feeling that we're being sized up." His qualms were allayed somewhat by the relaxed conversations in the NDP and a radio playing Crosby, Stills, and Nash.

David was very still, eyes wide. He and Erik stared silently, breathing slowly, straining to hear anything. David whispered, "Shhhhh. Did you hear that?"

"What?"

"The clink of metal against metal. Think we should tell whoever's got the radio to turn it the fuck off?" David said.

"Wait till this song's over."

When it finished, the lieutenant said to kill the radio. Erik couldn't get over the incongruity of top-forty music on the radio no matter where they were. He thought about easy chairs, electric lights, air conditioning, real beds with clean sheets, and refrigerators that most Americans in Vietnam were enjoying right then. "Maybe I should have re-upped."

"Yeah, maybe," David said.

Erik peered into the hazy dusk and listened. No breeze disturbed a single leaf. All was quiet. The still air seemed to bode malevolence. From a ways off, he heard what his mind wanted to think was a benign popping of a paper bag, as if he was at the movies in Gainesboro.

"Oh, shit. That's gonna be incoming," Snake said from his foxhole.

In about twenty seconds they heard the slight rushing of air past the aluminum fins of a mortar round as it dropped almost straight down. It detonated not more than thirty meters in front of them. Spent shrapnel fell on foliage like rain drops.

Another pop. The next round impacted about the same distance on the other side of the perimeter.

"They've got us bracketed," David said, his voice taut. "They know right where we are."

Erik locked and loaded his M-16. He peered into nearly total darkness. He flipped the safety to automatic.

Shrill, accented voices erupted from all directions. "What you do now, GI? What you do now, GI?"

Erik felt the hairs on the back of his neck stand straight out. He slapped himself to make sure he wasn't dreaming. "Be cool. Be brave. Be here."

"What the fuck!" David whispered.

"What you do now, GI?—" The taunting stopped at the sound of distant artillery.

In a moment an illumination round screamed its intervention as a small explosion six hundred feet above the canopy ejected a brilliant magnesium ball of flame suspended from a parachute. It swayed to and fro as it drifted down, painting the scene in a brown hue that looked like a daguerreotype. The shadows of the trees did a slow dance, back and forth. Erik saw no one, but the mocking started again. "What you do now, GI?"

Four tell-tale reports from a mortar punctuated the chanting. Everybody scrambled under sandbagged cover. They waited for the incoming. Crunching explosions close by sent a gust of air through the cramped space. Their loose chin straps rose and fell in its wake.

"Man, am I glad we dug in. Sounds like nobody got hit," David said.

Erik said, "I wonder how many we're up against."

"I don't know. El-tee's gotta be calling in some arty," Mason said.

As if in perfect timing, four muffled blasts of 105s answered. The disembodied voices stopped abruptly. The crackle of artillery ended in a volley of concussive impacts about two hundred meters away.

They heard no more from the mortar. "Maybe the lieutenant had their number and blew their shit away," Erik said.

"*Xin loi*, Charles," David said, as they scuttled back to their fighting positions.

Despite his pounding heart, Erik laughed at David's ridiculous sarcasm at an enemy that had them surrounded. He saw something move inside the perimeter. "Goddamn, that's Bodine. What's he doing?"

Bodine held an M-79 grenade launcher. He put the stock under his armpit and aimed the 40mm barrel at a forty-five-degree angle. "What you do now, slopehead?" he yelled. He pulled the trigger. *Thunk.* The fat little golden grenade flew into the darkness. As soon as he fired, Bodine hit the ground as AK-47s instantly opened up on the muzzle flash. The grenade struck something and the explosion added to the cacophony of the AKs.

Erik's shaking hands managed to unsnap a hand grenade from his web gear. Anger at being taunted overcame a desire to hug the ground and stay there. You're in it for all you've got, he cajoled himself. He gripped the smooth metal casing of the grenade and pulled the pin, but kept his fingers on the aluminum tail that followed the contour of the grenade.

He raised his head slightly, looked for muzzle flashes, and heaved it. The aluminum piece flew off, releasing the little pointed hammer to set off the slow-burning core, which took four and a half seconds to reach the plastic charge. A shattering explosion sent bits of coiled steel wire into what he hoped was a cluster of NVA.

David was unsnapping all his hand grenades from his web gear to do likewise as other grenades exploded all around the perimeter. "Sounds like everybody's doing that. They must not want to give away their positions," David yelled.

The firing stopped. "You guys okay?" It was Ellis, the medic.

Erik said, "Yeah, we're okay. What do you think they're up to?"

"They're probably fixin' to make a probe or let all hell break loose and rush us from all sides. I don't think they like moving on our claymores."

Erik said, "Goddamn! No wonder they're called spooks. I have seen nada, zilch, nobody. Have you, Levy?"

"No. Maybe they're gonna *didi*. They don't want to mess with us."

"Our shit's together, maybe so," Erik said wishfully, squinting into the eerie half-light.

David said, "It's so fucking quiet. What are they doing?"

Another illumination round popped overhead.

Mist and smoke hung in the air. Erik thought how no one could paint this hellish scene and do it justice. Just as he thought he had seen the worst of the night, a bugle call ended any hope of a break in contact.

"Oh, no," Erik groaned. He had read Bernard Fall and knew it meant "no quarter." The Viet Minh had used it against the French when they moved in for the kill. He shivered in the warm tropical night.

"Goddammit. Let 'em come!" Lieutenant Cushman shouted from the command post. "Enough of this shit. Don't let them get inside your head. Hang in there. Arty is on the way."

Erik stared at a low bush that seemed to be inching forward. He suddenly realized those were leaves in a pith helmet. "God, give me strength, and forgive me," he whispered.

Charging NVA fired rocket-propelled grenades. Several swooshed across the clearing and disappeared. One hit right in front of Erik which rang his ears into deafness. He depressed the lever on his hand-held detonator, sending an electrical charge through the wire to a claymore. A flash of light from a blast which he couldn't hear made a hole in a wave of NVA.

David blew a claymore, grabbed his M-16, and raked his field of fire with a full magazine.

Erik squeezed off four-round bursts. His magazine emptied in about ten seconds. He clicked it out and inserted another twenty-rounder. He kept firing.

AK-47 rounds cracked overhead like hail on a tin roof. A single NVA made it into the perimeter and ran towards the CP with a smoking satchel charge. Erik had him in his sights and pulled the trigger. *Click.* "Damn!" He was empty. Cushman saw him and fired his forty-five. The large-caliber bullet drove the sapper backward, still clutching the bag, which exploded a second later. It left a hole in the dense grass amid bloody flesh and severed arms. Erik gulped back bile rising in his throat.

Just as Erik got a new magazine clicked home, three NVA rose out of the grass and ran straight at him. He emptied a full magazine into them. They fell to the ground. He shoved in a new magazine and drew a bead on another group. They disappeared in a red flash. Erik's jaw dropped at the horrific sight of a 105 round blowing up sinewy young men into a scattered mess. Other HE impacted around the perimeter in random patterns. It was an awesome spectacle which Erik figured had to boost the morale of the surrounded platoon.

The reckless onslaught continued, but in small clusters of youthful soldiers. The unremitting artillery not only ripped through charging NVA but tore up vegetation all around the perimeter and made for clearer fields of fire. The ground shook continuously in the clamor of battle. Erik's hearing was back.

Gray-clad NVA faded back into the darkness dragging wounded and dead comrades with them. Lieutenant Cushman yelled, "Check fire." The shooting stopped. Was it all over, or would they attack again? Either way, Erik felt a tremendous weight lifted from his shoulders. He had held up, but at what cost? He knew he would always see visions of this night, yet he was elated that he was whole and alive. He had killed many young men who shouldn't have had to die. What madness!

He hoped he would never know such fear again. He felt completely spent, but had to talk just to make sure he was alive. "You know the three requirements for defending an NDP?" Erik managed to ask David, whose eyes were wide and showing white all around. Erik guessed he looked the same.

"No," David said, absurdly playing the straight man. "What are the three things?"

"Preparation, preparation, and, uh … uh …" Erik strained to get the third word out, "preparation."

SFC Anderson called out, "Anybody hit?"

"Yo. I can't see out of my left eye." It was Hosmer.

Bodine shouted, "Sanborn caught some flak on his shoulder from a mortar round. Doc got him patched up."

Somebody called out, "I have a bruised psyche."

Erik chuckled in spite of the enervating tension. "That was Mason," he said to David.

"Fuckin' comedian," David said.

Robertson yelled, "I think the Okies bought it."

"Better them than me," Snake said in a low voice.

Erik and David lined up magazines and grenades. The illumination continued. It could go on till daylight if they wanted. Such was the seemingly endless supplies of the Americans.

No more happened that night. At dawn the exhausted GIs did a body count, the main score sheet for the Vietnam conflict. Lieutenant Cushman thought that maybe sixty of the enemy were killed or wounded. It was only a wild guess given the NVA's always taking their casualties with them, thus enhancing their ghostly reputation. Nevertheless, the GIs counted thirty-eight dead bodies around the perimeter. Some of the count was an estimate, given the remains of body parts strewn about.

SFC Anderson came up to Lieutenant Cushman. "Downs is tangled up with a dink, both dead. The dink must have gotten through with a chicom grenade and it blew while they were fighting over it. Flattum caught three across the chest when he stood up for some reason, probably to help Downs."

Doc Ellis said Casper got it right between the eyes.

Erik didn't even know Casper's real name. He remembered some guys kidding him back at base camp. He got his nickname because he was real quiet and all of a sudden out of nowhere he'd be standing right next to them. "That Casper," they said, "wouldn't say shit if he had a mouthful."

Lieutenant Cushman called for a dust-off for Casper, Downs, Flattum, and the half-blind Hosmer, who caught some splinters in his eye when an AK round hit a log right in front of him. Sanborn refused to go, saying he would walk out with the rest of the platoon.

The three KIAs were laid out and covered with ponchos. Erik pictured an Oklahoma town having a funeral for Downs and Flattum, which would, no doubt, morph into a patriotic celebration about dying for your country.

We are the Romans, Erik thought, the new imperialists. Of course we need a strong army with career men, like Lieutenant Cushman, who would come back with his shield, or on it, in our country's defense. But, goddammit, we can't go around the world attacking other countries on the whims of misguided old men.

When the dust-off corkscrewed into the clearing, Erik knelt by the three bodies and kept the ponchos from blowing off. He didn't want to see their young faces.

Chapter Twenty

Lieutenant Cushman called for a rendezvous with two battalion deuce-and-a-half trucks from Tay Ninh West at a rubber-tree plantation next to Highway 13. The platoon got there in mid afternoon without further contact. The trucks had not arrived, so the platoon lay among the rows of rubber trees. Nobody talked. A waft of marijuana reminded Erik of burning leaves in Gainesboro.

David broke into the hushed cloud that had enveloped the subdued recon patrol. "Did you ever see anything like it?" David said to anybody who might be listening.

"What's that, Levy?" Lieutenant Cushman said. He had shed his web gear and sat near David and Erik.

"Look at these rows of rubber trees," David said. "It's kind of mind-blowing how they're in perfect lines that come together at a vanishing point." His eyes had that thousand-mile stare.

Lieutenant Cushman looked down the rows. "You're thinking too much, Levy. How long you been out in the field, three days? What're you going to be like when you've been here a year?"

"Yeah, I know. It worries me, too. But guess what, Lieutenant, too many recons like this and I won't have to worry about being here a year."

"This one was unusual, so hang in there. I just had a funny feeling about last night," the lieutenant reflected. "Of course, a feeling of foreboding is not an overactive imagination around here. You go a klick in any direction from our bases and highways and Charlie is likely to pop up anywhere, what with his network of tunnels. We were lucky last night."

Last night, Erik thought. He sat in silence. He looked around. The lack of banter among the platoon was conspicuous. If they were like him they were sorting things out in intricate processes of delusion that allowed them to hold on to their sanity.

David was quiet now. Erik figured he had to get his mind off blown-up bodies and the metallic smell of dried blood on the rainforest's exposed dirt, too.

Erik wanted to jump off the runaway train of gloomy thoughts. Think of something, he told himself. Think of tomorrow. What are you going to do tomorrow? What are you going to do? What are you going to do … what you do now… what you do now, GI? Stop! He had to decompress from last night. Decompress, decompress, decompress all the way, he sang silently to the tune of "Jingle Bells."

"So, where you guys from?" Lieutenant Cushman said.

Erik could tell that the lieutenant was trying to get their minds focused on something. He was surprised at his coolness. They probably taught him how to deal with killing at the Point in military psych 101, he reckoned. Erik tried to answer but couldn't seem to concentrate. David was still looking down a row of rubber trees.

"Gentlemen, we're going to continue this stimulating conversation over some beers after Tet," Lieutenant Cushman said with a touch of sarcasm. "Here come the trucks."

Chapter Twenty-one

For the next three days all units were on high alert during Tet. Some NVA forces probed Tay Ninh West and occupied part of Tay Ninh City, but not in great strength. The GIs hunkered down and let some ARVN units deal with them. From everything Erik gathered, Marvin the ARVN wasn't worth much as a fighter. His heart wasn't in it like his counterpart from the North.

Erik read in *Stars and Stripes* that Nixon wanted more South Vietnamese participation in the fighting. Everyone at Tay Ninh West thought it laughable to think that the ARVN would hold up if the Americans pulled out. Erik heard rumors about secret B-52 strikes in Cambodia while the bombing on North Vietnam increased. He wondered how, exactly, was Nixon's "peace with honor" going to come about.

Lieutenant Cushman called a formation of his reconnaissance platoon at 0900. "The old man is putting you guys in for a unit citation," he said. "I think this post and Tay Ninh City was the 3rd Division's target and their attack didn't amount to much. It's possible we hurt them, and it took the wind out of their sails. They thought we were going to be easy meat, but we hung tough.

"We've been sitting on our ass the last few days, so we're going to have a forced march, meaning we will jog and walk, jog and walk around the base, twice, with full packs. Then you can celebrate the end of Tet. Last guy in has to buy the first round. Shrap and Levy, I'll see you guys at the Sixty-fifth Engineers' club this afternoon at 1400."

The juke box in the EM club was playing Jefferson Airplane about as loud as an airplane taking off. Erik and David were talking as best they could above the music with Mason. Erik said, "What's your full name?"

"Robert Emerson Lee Mason," Mason yelled. "Yeah, I'm a Southern military brat. Robert E. Lee Mason."

The three of them were standing in the middle of the packed bar with a cigarette in one hand and can of beer in the other. David said, "Are you going to follow in the footsteps?"

"Nah. I want to play guitar in a band like this one." He waved his beer in a circle. "I love music."

After a couple of beers the three of them swayed to tracks from *Surrealistic Pillow* with silly grins on their faces.

After "Embryonic Journey" David said, "What's your old man think of you being in a band?"

"He wanted me to enlist, but I didn't want to and I got drafted. I had long hair, too, which he wasn't wild about."

Erik said, "At least you know what your dad wants. I can't figure my old man out."

"You have my sympathy. My dad at least wants me to be happy, but he was worried about my future. He thought being in the army was a rewarding career with security. That's a laugh, but his heart was in the right place. Anyway, maybe you ought to tell your dad how you feel."

"Yeah, maybe I will. I should do that. We'll see."

The Beatles' "Roll Over Beethoven" started playing. David hollered, "You wanna go talk to El-tee over at the engineers' club?"

"Nah, that's too quiet. I'm going to get anesthetized and groove on the music."

Erik said, "See ya. Don't re-up or anything. Take care of that bruised psyche."

Mason laughed.

The Sixty-fifth Engineers knew how to rig up a club. They cut a hole in the wall of the Quonset hut to accommodate a large-capacity air conditioner. David and Erik walked in and let their eyes adjust to the dim interior even though strings of miniature lights created an idea of a ceiling and abated total darkness. "They just wouldn't believe this at home," David said as they savored the drop in temperature.

"There's the lieutenant," Erik said when he could see past the bar on his right and into an area of tables with chairs, a few slot machines, and a jukebox.

A middle-aged Vietnamese waitress stood by the bar. She wore black silk pants and a loose-fitting long-sleeved purple blouse buttoned at the top. She was matronly and probably not subject to the constant GI flirting, except Erik figured a few old engineers would try. "How about three beers?" Erik said.

"I got the first round," Cushman said, and slapped down two dollars in MPC when the mama-san brought three cans of Carling Black Label. "Keep the change."

They sat quietly.

Erik thought how they were members of a small fraternity that had witnessed the terrifying confusion of combat. Anybody who experienced it would not want to relive the feeling of having every nerve in their whole body exposed. He suddenly realized that if they were back in the world, people would think this long silence was odd. Cushman examined the details of the label on his beer can. David focused on a slot machine against the wall. Erik noticed this when he wasn't staring at a ceiling fan turning around, and around, and around, like the dust-off that came for the KIAs.

After a while David lifted his beer in a toast. "I heard the colonel is putting you up for a Silver Star, Lieutenant."

"That's the rumor, but I don't know," Cushman said. "Like I said, Lady Luck was with us and our artillery was our ace in the hole." His West Point ring sparkled in the soft light of the simple but homey bar.

They had another round. One of the three other customers played "Hey Jude" on the juke box.

When it was over, Cushman said, "Levy, I hear you graduated from Brown and then signed up to see the real thing," Cushman said. "Now I suppose you're going to write about it."

"That's part of it."

"What other reasons?" Erik said. He had learned that Levy didn't volunteer much about himself. He hoped the beer would loosen him up.

David said, "I came from Brooklyn. I lived in a Jewish neighborhood with a lot of relatives close by. My dad came to America from Germany when he was a young man before Hitler came to power. His brother, my uncle Oskar, stayed in denial. He even rowed on a crew in the '36 Olympics, unusual for a Jew. Somehow he survived the war. Afterward, my dad sponsored his coming to New York.

"Uncle Oskar never said much at get-togethers. He had some tattooed numbers on the inside of his arm. I asked my dad about them. He told me that Uncle Oskar had been interned at Auschwitz and survived. He feels guilty. He doesn't want anybody to know about it.

"Like other good physical specimens—he had been a professional soccer player—Oskar was allowed to work for the Nazis. I guess, basically, he was a collaborator so he could survive. There's no other way to look at it. He helped calm the new arrivals, you know, 'Put your luggage over here. This way to the showers. You can come back for your things later.'

"I asked my dad why Uncle Oskar didn't fight the Nazis. He said, 'I don't know. I wasn't there.' As I grew older I studied German history and learned about the 'final solution.' It became clear that Hitler only wanted to conquer Europe so he could kill more Jews. It was all in Hitler's book *Mein Kampf*. There was no reason not to know about that. There should have been an uprising. There should have been individual courage, like I may die, but I'm going to take one Nazi bastard with me. But instead we had collaborators in hundreds of concentration camps.

"Nobody talked about this if they survived. At different times, although rare, I would notice the tattoos on a few other people, women, too. They wore what happened to them on the inside of their forearm, not on their sleeve.

"A *cause celebre* grew about the Jewish victimhood and the Holocaust. I wish the world didn't talk about a time when the Jews were victims but a time when they revolted and overthrew the Nazi regime even before Hitler invaded Poland.

"Would King David have stood by? I don't think so. He would have led a resistance starting with five smooth stones. I think a lot of good Germans would have joined them. There might not have been a war in Europe. If not before the war there sure as hell should have been revolts in the concentration camps instead of people being led to slaughter like sheep.

"Anyway, I wanted to test my courage. I wondered if there was something in me that was not brave."

Cushman cleared his throat and said, "Let's get another round. Hey, mama-san, three more." Then to David he said, "That's, uh, interesting, Levy. I wasn't aware of this perspective."

"There are damn few of us."

"Most of the world knows there's nothing cowardly about Israel," Cushman said. "They're surrounded by Arab countries that want to wipe them off the map. Israel cleaned their clocks in six days in '67."

"Yeah, I know," David replied. "Israel is trying to prove something, too."

Erik said, "David, ol' buddy, did you ever think of running for political office?"

David smiled. "I also wanted to get my ticket punched by serving in the military because I want to run for Congress. In our society, like it or not, we are in a cult of militarism. Anybody who's been in combat has more credibility when speaking out against senseless war."

Lieutenant Cushman tapped his West Point ring on the table, apparently absentmindedly. "I've got to go get some shut-eye," he said. "I've got officer-on-duty tonight. You guys be good."

Erik and David had another round.

David said, "I've got to get laid."

Erik was thinking the same thing. "Yeah, me too, but how?"

"I've been asking around. There's a cook in the mess hall who will sneak in some lovely ladies of the evening for a reasonable fee."

Erik asked, "How much?" Not that it mattered. He would have gladly paid the hundred dollars in MPC he had on him to lie with smooth, feminine softness and warmth.

"Ten bucks to the cook and the same for the women."

"I'm totally in." Erik weighed the situation. He was about to participate in a corruption of the people they were supposedly sent to save. Having survived the intensity of battle only by a stroke of luck and kill or be killed, he concluded that life has no moral compass. Sure, there are no atheists in foxholes, but faith can't change the course of a bullet that has your name on it. If our leaders prayed for wisdom and had an ounce of morality, they never would have gotten us into this. What hypocrites, he thought, backing a corrupt regime in Vietnam and raining death and destruction on people who just want to grow rice and be left alone. No, God is not here. One might as well enjoy hedonistic pleasures, like fornication. That's why there's so much of that parallel activity since wars began.

"What are you thinking?" David said.

"I was just doing some mental acrobatics."

"In that case, shut the fuck up."

The Vietnamese cook was happy to make the arrangements for that evening. He had to get fresh vegetables and pick up the night shift on the KP truck. He told David and Erik that business had been bad during Tet. This was his first deal in the new year.

When it was dark, Erik and David went to the back end of the truck with its contraband.

Erik called softly, "Hellooo."

The ladies walked forward, their white teeth reflecting light from the mess hall.

Erik helped the first one down. Oh, my God, Erik thought, she's beautiful. Her lustrous black hair was parted in the middle and pulled back into a bun. She wore a sheer light-blue blouse that showed her bra underneath and a tight, black knee-length skirt that revealed no nylons. She had sandals on her feet. "See ya," he said to David.

Erik and his prostitute walked toward the post chapel, their arms around each other's waists. Erik slid his hand down to a diminutive, rounded, and nicely protruding posterior. He grew more aroused with every step. He stopped and faced her and ran his hands slowly up and down her bare arms. Oh, how smooth! Why did her skin feel like silk? Is it because Vietnamese women have tiny pores that constantly effuse invisible beads of sweat in the tropical heat? Her thin arms felt cool and sensuous. He asked her name.

"Kim."

"That's nice. Mine's Erik."

Kim looked to be 19 or 20 years old. Her smile was beautiful. Erik put his lips to her lovely mouth. Despite what he'd heard about prostitutes and kissing, she pulled him close, one arm around his neck and the other around his waist, and kissed him sensuously. Her breath was sweet.

They went into the deserted chapel. The chaplain's desk was in the back, with a chair next to it. On the chair was a cushion, which Erik grabbed and laid on the floor. With his knees on it he unzipped Kim's skirt, which fell easily to the floor. The removal of each article of clothing slowly revealed her lovely body. He stood and held her close for several minutes. Tears ran down his cheeks. He massaged the small of her back and caressed her exquisite skin. Despite all the alcohol he was ready and in ecstasy to be alive. He loved her for offering herself even if it was for money.

Feet crunched on the gravel outside, getting louder. "Quick! Under the bench!" Erik tossed his shirt and her clothes to Kim as she rolled under the next row of benches. Thankful that he never took his boots off, and that he had his OD T-shirt on. He buttoned his pants and zipped up as he knelt on the cushion. He folded his hands, and leaned on the back bench as though deep in prayer. The screen door creaked open.

Somebody bumped into the desk and clicked on a lamp. Erik turned around. He saw a man with the white collar of a priest under a jungle-fatigue top like Erik's, except it had the insignia of a chaplain on the collar.

The chaplain looked startled when he saw Erik. "Wha—who are you?"

"Hello, Father," Erik said. "I was just praying. Sorry about using your cushion. There weren't any—"

"That's fine, my son, fine. I'm glad you are kneeling in prayer." The priest frowned. "Is there anything of great concern to you right now?" He took a few unsteady steps toward Erik.

Still kneeling, Erik turned to the front. He could barely see the wooden cross at the altar, and he was relieved that he couldn't see Kim. The chaplain placed a hand on his shoulder. He smelled of alcohol. "I'm worried," Erik said. "I have seen death stalking me," which wasn't a lie.

"Be not afraid, my son. Jesus said, 'He who believeth in me shall have everlasting life.'"

"I'd be happy with just the next twelve months," Erik said. "After that I'll take my chances."

The chaplain let out a long, wheezy laugh. "Humor in the face of danger will help sustain you in your mission," he said.

Erik didn't want to prolong this conversation, but asked, "What is the mission, Father?"

"Why, it's to fight the good fight like Saint Peter and bring our Lord and Savior to the godless communists."

Erik waited for a while, as though in thought, then said, "I feel better now. Thank you, Father."

"You are fighting for a good cause, my son. There is a special place in heaven for those who die for liberty." The chaplain careened toward his desk and took something out of a drawer that could have been a pack of cigarettes. "Now I must get back to those in need at the officers' club. Stay as long as you want, my son."

"Thank you, Father." The screen door clapped shut, and the sound of the chaplain's footsteps faded. Thank goodness for the army's use of gravel around the post, he thought, and breathed easier.

Kim came out smiling. "Who that?" she asked.

"A shill for Mars." Kim looked puzzled. "Never mind. Let's put your clothes on and get out of here." He suddenly felt very tired. "I'm sorry. I need to go lie down."

On the way back to the truck Erik learned that Kim supported her mother and father and had succumbed to their urging that she earn money from the rich Americans. Her father had worked as a share-cropper for a wealthy landowner and was conscripted into the South Vietnamese Army. He lost a leg to a land mine. They lived in a rude shack made of flattened aluminum beer cans. Erik gave her $100 in MPC and said that he hoped she didn't have to sell herself for a while.

Kim said, "I suh-leep in truck tonight. Thank you. Thank you. You nice man. Maybe I find other work. I don't know. Thank you."

"Goodbye, Kim. Take care of yourself."

Chapter Twenty-two

Erik and David didn't talk about where they had gone for privacy that night. In the meantime they went on some more recon patrols with Lieutenant Cushman and the platoon. They had a few scrapes with fire fights to cover a withdrawal, but nothing like being surrounded by a company of hard-driving NVA.

They came across defoliated jungles and large areas of pockmarked, barren land caused by B-52 air strikes and Agent Orange. It reminded Erik of what Tacitus said about Roman conquests: "They make a desert and call it peace."

One day they hunkered down in one of the rubber-tree plantations.

Erik said, "Can you imagine the manpower it took to lay out this plantation? That's what the French did, just exploited the hell out of the Vietnamese and paid them so little they might as well have been slaves. They were never allowed to develop a commercial class. Being on this Michelin plantation is like on a slave ship—bad karma."

Lieutenant Cushman said, "Yeah, and if we're here thinking this, you can imagine what the Vietnamese feel when they see this symbol of colonialism. You know," he went on, "the old man was pleased with the body count I gave him that time we were surrounded, but it won't make a bit of difference. Every year there must be two million boys coming of age in North Vietnam. Do the math. We cannot kill them fast enough. They won't give up until every fucking foreigner is off their fucking land."

"It's pointless for us to be here," David said. "We could salt their soil, so to speak, like the Romans did to Carthage at the end of the third Punic War to destroy their civilization. With us it would be to use atomic weapons. If we did that, we could forget about ever having a positive influence again. We already dropped two atomic bombs on Asian people. I don't think this half of the world would look very kindly on a third."

The Viet Cong and North Vietnamese Army seemed to be biding their time, too. They still caused casualties with land mines and booby traps. Erik learned never to pick up anything off the ground that could be taken as a souvenir. *Do they think the Americans will grow weary of spilling blood for no apparent reason? They are probably right,* Erik concluded.

Life magazine published the pictures of 241 Americans killed in one week of fighting. Erik thought, *what a waste,* and they were probably mostly draftees. He suddenly wanted to feast his eyes on beauty and goodness to get his mind off the obscenity of war. *No more prostitutes,* though. He had always escaped with books. *Maybe there are books for sale in Tay Ninh City.* He thought he might get a Vietnamese/English dictionary to learn about the language.

Since they were not on duty Lieutenant Cushman said he could get a jeep and drive to Tay Ninh City. He wanted to take some pictures before he rotated out. Erik and David could come along.

The lieutenant parked on the town square in front of a post office. Its pastel-yellow facade was obviously a leftover from the French. *If the streets weren't so dusty and blighted with trash,* Erik thought, *it would be as pretty as Storm Lake.* The oppressive heat and humidity made it even less appealing.

Across the square was a store-front with the word "Fahasa." It looked like a book store. "Okay if we meet at the jeep in an hour?" Erik said to Lieutenant Cushman. "I'm going to that book store and then walk around."

Erik walked through the open door. He asked a clerk if they had any Vietnamese-to-English dictionaries. The clerk looked at him, blankly. When the manager heard him he hollered up the open stairway to the second floor, "Thuy!" Erik supposed she was the only employee who spoke English.

Thuy came down the stairs dressed in the traditional Vietnamese *ao dai*—silk pants underneath a full-length skirt with slits up the two sides, a tight bodice, long sleeves, and an upright collar. The whole ensemble was a mother-of-pearl color. She smiled when she saw him.

Erik stared at the exotic and beautiful vision before him. He recovered enough to say, "Hello. My name is Erik." He put out his hand.

Shaking hands, Thuy said, "Hello, my name Thuy."

"Do you have any dictionaries?"

"Yes, we hap many."

They walked to that section of the store, where he made a selection. Erik asked, "Do you have any English books?" He wanted to stay with her as long as possible. She looked to be just over five feet tall and very cute with a lithe figure. Erik guessed that she was 22 years old. She showed him some American books. He bought Salinger's *Nine Stories*.

Erik felt Thuy was interested in him, too. He told her the one sentence he learned at Tay Ninh West on AFVN-TV. "*Viet Nam ca hai mua, mua mua va mua nang*," which meant Vietnam has two seasons, rainy and dry. Thuy laughed with delight. She smiled so sweetly that Erik fairly melted. He had to be with her more. "Do you think we could go out on the square and talk?"

"Yes. We go now. I tell manager you from army newspaper and want to write about Vietnam culture."

They sat on a bench. Erik looked at the heavy traffic of men and women on bicycles and motorbikes, some balancing precarious loads of conical hats, mangoes, or other items for market, he assumed. Down one of the side streets, GIs in jungle fatigues were enticed into bars with Vietnamese women in heavy make-up and wearing skimpy Western clothes. Again, Erik felt that he was part of a temporary plague that the Vietnamese would wait out and eventually overcome while they went about making a living. In the meantime, he thought, the Americans were turning a large segment of their women into prostitutes.

"I from Hoi Nhon on ocean. My father fisherman, die in storm. My mother work very hard in fields to send me to university. I study very hard in Vietnam literature and Engrish. I graduate and Fahasa give me job. I work same twenty-five dollar in month."

"Where do you live?"

"I live in pagoda. It have temple with wall around big area and gate closed at night. We have gardens where everybody grow food. I suh-leep in bare room with four other Vietnam women. We hap mats on floor for bed."

Erik was surprised at the depth of typical Vietnamese poverty. The more he learned about Thuy, the more he respected her. "Do you pay money to live at the pagoda?" he asked.

"I pay same ten dollar in month, but we hap a kitchen where Vietnam women cook for everybody in pagoda. It not a lot. I get hungry, but I don't need much. Sometime I meditate at shrine of Buddha."

Erik nodded.

"I no hap boyfriend. Vietnam men want woman not go to university. Want obedient wife. I twenty-four. Too old for Vietnam man to marry."

Erik moved closer to put his hand on hers. "I'm the same age."

"No! Cannot touch with many people to see," Thuy said emphatically. Her voice was like music. Is it conceivable to be in love so quickly? "Is there someplace we can go to be alone?" Erik asked.

"No. It impossible in pagoda."

"I care about you very much. Maybe I can get jeep and come take you someplace," Erik said. He wrote his army address on a piece of paper. "Here is my address. Could you write address of book store? I could send you a letter. I will come see you as soon as I can."

"I will miss you. There are many stories about Vietnam women who wait for soldier. They sad and lonely, but I will wait for you."

Erik ached with desire, and his heart leaped for joy at her words. What will come of this? He jettisoned any rational thoughts about the difficulties of marrying into the Vietnamese culture.

Chapter Twenty-three

The lieutenant who took Cushman's place didn't want to do much about going out in the field, especially when the rainy season started in April. He led some patrols beyond the kill zone of the post during the day and went to the officers' club at night. Erik figured this was in keeping with the company commander's apparent attitude of not looking for trouble. Erik heard on the grapevine that, since Hamburger Hill, a directive came down from division that all units should just maintain the status quo and reduce the maximum pressure they had ordered before.

A story about Hamburger Hill in the Central Highlands appeared in a June issue of *Stars and Stripes*. Erik read that 72 Americans were killed and 354 were wounded in the taking of hill 937. It got its name as a meat-grinder operation for the high ground that the 101st Airborne finally won after ten days of frontal assaults up a steep grade. Five days later, the Americans left, and soon after, the NVA retook hill 937 unopposed.

This is ridiculous, Erik said to himself. There is no overall strategy besides attrition. Controlling South Vietnam would take hundreds of divisions beyond the twenty infantry divisions we have now. The army is resorting to Orwellian newspeak to explain some of their failures. In a press conference, an officer said of Ben Tre, "We had to destroy the village in order to save it."

When Erik's platoon went on operations, the more experienced grunts counseled the new ROTC lieutenant as much as they could. He was open to advice, apparently not hung up on always being in command. To be laid back was cool with the guys who just wanted to survive and go home.

In November, Erik read about a massacre in a place called My Lai. It was reported that some GIs in a platoon from Charlie Company of the Americal Division had fired point-blank into villagers, mostly women and children, killing about five hundred.

Erik talked to David about it. "This happened in 1968. Can you believe it was a secret for so long? Of course we've heard a lot of rumors about GIs doing bad shit in free-fire zones around here, which seems to be a license to kill civilians."

"We're becoming more and more like the enemies we defeated in World War II," David said. "I read that the platoon leader at My Lai, a Lieutenant Calley, was as new as everybody in the company since they had recently come over as a unit from Schofield Barracks in Hawaii."

This was unusual, Erik knew. Practically every unit in Vietnam had new guys and old guys constantly rotating through the year. Erik had seen how the new ones learned a lot from the old guys.

"They were all so green," Erik said. "Nobody kept that fucking lieutenant from getting carried away. Okay, so they lost a man to a booby trap. Did the big bad enemy turn them into animals? If we can't fight a war without committing atrocities, maybe we're in the wrong war."

"What we have heah," David drawled like the warden in *Cool Hand Luke*, "is failure to communicate." He added, "And failure of leadership."

"You guys have no idea," Canelli said. Antonio Canelli, from San Francisco, had been listening to the conversation. He was with the Ninth Division in the Mekong Delta before they became the first unit to rotate out in Nixon's Vietnamization program in August. Canelli didn't have enough time in-country so was transferred to the Twenty-fifth Division.

"Do tell," David said.

"Our division commander down in the delta was absolutely crazy for body counts in Operation Speedy Express. It trickled down to everybody being pressed to kill anything that moved."

"Who was that?" Erik asked.

"General Julian Ewell, the butcher of the delta," Canelli said. "I was in the Ninth's Sixtieth Infantry and artillery was used like you wouldn't believe. If a village was anywhere near, say a sniper, or something, our platoon leader would call in a strike and obliterate it. It was a slaughter which upped the body count. The officers were under that much pressure. You talk about My Lai. There was same-same My Lai about every month for six months when I was down there."

Erik recalled other stories in *Stars and Stripes* since he arrived in 1969. The ones that stood out were Chappaquiddick, Charles Manson, the moon landing, and Woodstock.

Sometimes the platoon lounged around Tay Ninh West for a week at a time, drinking beer at night and watching Hollywood movies in the outdoor theater. During these downtimes platoon relations eroded, especially between blacks and whites. When a southern boy nailed a Confederate flag above his cot, he was confronted by a black guy from Chicago. The two guys did some pushing and shoving until others in the platoon intervened. SFC Bodine made the white guy take down the flag.

The machinations David and Erik went through to line up Vietnamese women early in the year became passé. By September they could have a woman any time they wanted. Prostitutes gathered outside the gates of Tay Ninh West every night. GIs, including officers, made a selection and their choices were allowed in.

All Erik wanted was to be with Thuy. His admiration for her grew as she showed him pictures of her austere upbringing in a concrete house with open windows on a red-dirt path among similar houses in a grove of palm trees.

When he wasn't with Thuy, Erik could picture every detail about her. Her obsidian eyes shimmered with intelligence and took in a great deal as she gazed at whatever caught her attention. Sometimes her long eyelashes fluttered, which Erik found extremely attractive. He tried to give her money, but she wouldn't take any. She said she could earn it herself.

Erik managed to go to Tay Ninh City a few times and meet Thuy at her friend's small apartment. Their love-making was sweet and unselfish as they found joy in each other's pleasure. They exchanged letters. Erik always kept this one with him:

> Dear Erik,
>
> How are you? I have just finish work and write to you a letter at 11 p.m. This is first time I write a letter and I send to you a couple of pictures. I hope you like it. That is picture when I work at new bookstore in Da Nang province one month. My company have bookstore anywhere in Viet Nam.
>
> I miss you so much. I only know I love you, and I want marry with you. I want you live with me forever and don't leave me. I will love you all my life. I want you understand that.
>
> I dream about you everynight and can't sleep. I very lucky when I meet you. I think that is fate. I wish we can meet early. I hope you will live in Viet Nam. Goodbye,
>
> Thuy.

Erik and David began counting the days when they had two months left of their year-long tour. They went to different places for R and R. David went to Hong Kong and ordered several tailor-made suits, sport coats and trousers to send home.

Erik went to Hawaii to see Pearl Harbor and to feel closer to home. He called his parents long distance, and they sounded thrilled to hear his voice for the first time in about nine months.

"Hello, Mom. It's Erik."

She screamed. Away from the mouthpiece she cried, "Harold, get on the phone. It's Erik." Into the receiver she said, "How are you, my dear? We've missed you so much. You're too far away. We can never visit you. This is too hard."

"Hello, son," Harold said. "How's it going?"

"Hi, Dad. Fine, fine. Yes, Mom, it *is* hard, but it will be over soon. Thank you for your letters. And, Dad, thanks for your letters about the weather, and monsoons, and stuff. Oh, and the Southern Cross constellation, that was very interesting."

"Can you see it?"

"Yes, during the dry season I saw it every night. How's Helen?"

Silence.

Marie said, "Well, she's doing some camping out in California."

"Mom, she's living in a commune in Santa Cruz. I got a letter from her. I was just wondering if there was anything new."

Harold said, "My guess is she's pregnant. Helen has always marched to the beat of a different drummer. I'm just glad she got a college education before she went off on this tangent."

"I'd like to go see her on the way home," Erik said. "I can't talk long, but just wanted to hear your voices. How have you been?"

"We're fine," Marie said.

They talked for a little while longer and then said goodbye. Erik thought his mother's voice sounded strained. He figured she was probably worried about Helen. No doubt she's anxious about what to say when she goes to bridge club. Erik felt she should be honest and blasé about what her friends thought. So Helen lives in a commune. See the humor in it. Make light of it. What's so bad? He wished he could see his mother and talk to her. He hoped she would find comfort in the daily lessons of *Science and Health*, the Christian Science publication.

Although Helen's letter was a little heavy on the pure love that everyone has for one another, she'd get tired of it, Erik was sure. It's just a stage in her quest for … for what, perfect ice? A moment when she basked in fatherly love?

A lot of the short-timers in the platoon tried to finagle their way out of anything that was unusual. This conflicted with Erik's and David's early axiom about proactive survival skills. Such were the problems of low morale in army units. David had to walk a fine line when he became a sergeant and a squad leader, balancing initiative with risk.

Somehow Erik and David never succumbed to using marijuana, unlike most of the draftees, who developed a habit that followed them back to the States. Not being a dope-head was part of the reason that, soon after David, Erik was promoted to sergeant, too. He kept his nose clean and learned a lot, which he imparted to new guys in his squad to better the odds of surviving.

Erik and David often talked about history. Both agreed that there was nothing noble about what they were doing for Vietnam in contrast to the "good" war of World War II.

"They were in it for the duration in that war," David said. "And then they came home and went on with their lives."

"From what I saw in Hawaii," Erik said, "Vietnam vets are loud and obnoxious. They seemed to want attention. They did the 'I don't want to talk about it' bit, but then went on to tell war stories, and, I think, exaggerate their experiences. They know in their hearts we're fucking up this country and want approval to assuage their guilt. The Vietnamese people know who the good guys are, and it ain't us."

One day in December, first platoon was in a blocking position for a company operation about six miles west of base camp near the Cambodian border. The four other platoons made a sweep, with weapons platoon giving them mortar support.

Bodine, who was now the platoon sergeant, told everyone to settle in but to be ready for any activity to their front, which was perpendicular to the direction of the sweep. In theory, NVA units would move past them heading for Cambodia to escape the advancing company-size force of Americans.

After noon chow, the platoon leader, Lieutenant Hilliard, called a meeting with Bodine and the squad leaders. "I got a transmission from Captain Murray. They're getting slowed up by a ville. They found some weapons and a couple of suspected VC, which they'll have to deal with. We're just going to hold our position."

"Christ!" Bodine said. "It starts getting dark around six o'clock. I hope they hurry the fuck up."

Erik looked at the dormant rice paddy they were in. He cursed under his breath. He didn't relish having to spend the night where they were. He looked down the row of GIs in position along a raised pathway. The ground they faced was absolutely flat for a couple of miles.

"Do you think we should site in some artillery?" Hilliard asked Bodine.

"Nah, it would just give a heads-up to any gooks heading this way that we're here. Anyway, squad leaders, have your people relax, but designate at least one guy to keep an eye to the front for any movement."

This should be routine, Erik thought, as he walked back to his squad. Nothing's going to happen. But, goddammit, stay away, darkness. I'm too short for this, he told himself.

"Okay, second squad, write letters, line up your magazines, take a crap, or whatever, but stay low and watch the front. Take turns right down the line," Erik said.

"Hey, Sarge, can I jack off?" It was the new guy, Miller.

Erik said, "Way to go, Miller. We were wondering what to call you."

Mason called out, "Squirt, Jack the Zipper, Hand-job. Take your pick." Everybody laughed.

"Anyway, we might be in for a long wait. The company got delayed. Keep your shit together," Erik called out.

At least the sun isn't beating down, Erik thought, as first platoon languished in the overcast afternoon until dusk. They ate some cold Cs. All too soon it was totally dark.

Suddenly, about a half-klick to their left, small arms opened up like a string of firecrackers on the Fourth of July. Erik cursed that the company had run up against something.

Bodine had a starlight scope and would give the order to fire if he saw movement to their front.

In about ten minutes Bodine yelled, "Open up. They're out there." The sound of about thirty M-16s firing into the blackness was deafening. It was met with a fury of AKs returning fire.

Their aim, marked by green tracer rounds, was high as usual for AKs, but cracked menacingly close to their heads. "Stay down!" Erik shouted. "Return fire, but stay low!"

A sharp *clink* told Erik that a round had found somebody's helmet. Mason fell on his face and didn't move. "Goddammit. No!" Erik cried in helpless frustration.

The enemy's firing stopped as quickly as it had started. After a minute, Bodine called out, "Check fire! Check fire!"

Erik crawled to Mason. He called out, "Medic!" He feared nothing could be done. He took off Mason's helmet and blood poured out. A neat little hole in his temple looked so benign, but the other side of his head was blown open with part of his brains sticking out. A wire from an earphone had been yanked from a pocket radio, which was playing "Ob-La-Di, Ob-La-Da" by the Beatles. "Mason! Mason! You Alagotdambama sonofabitch!" Erik shouted in anguish, tears stinging his eyes. "What were you doing?"

117

Chapter Twenty-four

Erik lay on his cot looking up at the bare wooden rafters of the barracks. The same movie kept playing in his mind. Green tracers, like laser beams, hit him right between the eyes. Fade to black. The end.

He ran over the events of the previous night. Mason must not have heard him yell to stay down. He was sleeping or lost in some reverie of rock and roll. He didn't hear Bodine. He was confused at the sudden firefight and raised his head to look around. That's when he caught the round that went through his steel pot like it was cheap plastic.

Erik realized that his anger directed at Mason was misguided. It was an obvious attempt to relieve his own guilt for not taking care of his men. He should have known Mason was listening to the radio. He should have told him to knock it off.

But, no, you were just worried about your own ass because your days in the Nam were winding down, he chastised himself. Even thinking about Thuy didn't take his mind off Mason lying there through the night covered with a poncho and his jungle boots sticking out.

At daybreak, Bodine called in a dust-off for Mason and another KIA. The company hiked back to Tay Ninh West. Erik thought they would find some bodies from the firefight, but they saw none. The North Vietnamese or Viet Cong had disappeared, probably heading to Cambodia, taking any dead or wounded with them.

"Shrap." It was Typo, the company clerk.

"Yeah?" Erik said, still staring at the ceiling.

"The CO wants to see you."

Erik stood in front of Captain Murray's desk and saluted. He waited numbly to hear what the CO had to say.

Captain Murray returned the salute and said, "Have a seat, Sergeant Thorvald." He shuffled some papers. The *wup, wup, wup* of a helicopter beat a path overhead. "I'm afraid I have bad news for you. The old man just called me from brigade in Cu Chi and said the Red Cross contacted him last night. I've been asked to relay the message that your mother died of an apparent heart attack yesterday. I am very sorry."

Erik looked out the window. A single tear spilled out of his right eye. He would not be able to talk to his mother at least one more time. He surprised himself by how badly he had wanted to see her and could hardly wait for DEROS. Now, he could never say he loved her as he should have done many times. "I'll miss you," she used to say when he went off to school. He realized the captain was waiting quietly during the few minutes he was alone with his thoughts. He hauled himself to his feet. "Thank you, Captain Murray, for your concern."

"You'll need to get down to Cu Chi for some transportation to Tan Son Nhut and then home. Typo will get your orders cut." Captain Murray smiled weakly. "Despite his nickname, he's a pretty good company clerk. How much time do you have left?"

"Twenty-seven and a wake-up."

"Well, with less than a month you won't have to come back. You'll get thirty days bereavement leave stateside. If you show plans for going to school, you could probably get an early out. Or, depending on your home situation, you might be able to get a hardship discharge."

"I appreciate the information. You've been very kind. I won't take up any more of your time."

"No problem, Erik. You've done a good job here. You will be missed."

"Thank you, sir, but I know I could have done better."

As Erik went back to his hootch, his thoughts turned to Thuy and Levy. He decided to write a letter to Thuy and find David before he caught a slick to Cu Chi.

> Dear Thuy,
>
> I have bad news. My mother just died. I must go home. I don't know what the future will bring, but I will not forget you. I have never loved anyone as much as I love you. I hope you won't forget me. We are from different cultures, but our love can overcome that. I will write again, soon.
>
> Love,
>
> Erik

Erik found Levy in the mess hall and told him what happened. After expressing his sympathy, David said, "I guess I'll have to solve the world's problems without you, Shrap. At least we got a couple of things figured out, like My Lai and the returning Vietnam veterans."

"You know it. Well, I've got to *didi*, so keep your head down for the next thirty days. I can't save your ass anymore." Erik threw a mock punch at Levy's gut. "Thanks, man, for everything. You've been a good friend."

"Don't mean nothin'," David said, using a grunt's response to just about everything. "I guess I should start speaking the king's English. It won't be long and I'll be out of here, too."

"I look forward to reading your book. If you ever need help with your political campaign, let me know."

"You can count on it."

"See ya."

"So long."

They shook hands, which turned into a back-slapping hug. Erik turned away and headed for the helicopter pad, an M-16 over one shoulder and a full duffel bag over the other.

Chapter Twenty-five

The College Square Interdenominational Church was crowded with people attending the funeral. Many of Marie's friends came up to Erik and expressed their shock at his mother's early death at fifty-eight. "We didn't know. She seemed so healthy," they said.

Erik replied several times, "Mother didn't know, either. She never went to a doctor. She was a Christian Scientist. Thank you for coming."

"She was very proud, as we are, of your service. I suppose you were very much in harm's way," they said.

"A little," he said. He wanted to say "It don't mean nothin'," but mumbled, "Thank you."

In a few days the relatives were gone, the neighbors stopped bringing food, and mourning evolved into acceptance. Erik recalled the Hindu saying: The cause of death was birth.

He sat alone in the living room of his father's house. A warm fire crackled in the hearth. It was the unexpected death before his mother transitioned into old age that was hard to take. He wondered if Helen's going off and becoming a hippie had any impact on his mother's health. And now Helen was pregnant and not married. Stress does affect the heart, certainly, but his mother had ignored any symptoms she may have had. "Thank you, Mary Baker Eddie," he said, quietly.

"Talking to yourself, Erik?"

Erik jumped. His father came in, followed by Helen and Bernie. "Yeah, I guess so," he said.

He stood up and hugged Helen. "Are you okay?" she said.

"Yes, I'm fine." He looked at his sister. She wore a long flannel skirt in autumn colors and a loose-fitting, dark wool cardigan over a peasant blouse. She was beginning to show. Her face looked serene.

"Did that capitalist war get you down?" Bernie said, stroking his beard. He was tall and thin. His sandy-colored hair was tied back in a ponytail.

"Not as far down as those guys who came back in a metal casket," Erik said. "Anyway, don't you mean the running-dog imperialists? I think that's the usual party line."

Bernie sniffed. "If the foo shits …"

"Look, getting involved in Vietnam is a huge mistake, but it's not an indictment of our democracy, because we'll learn from this."

Harold sat looking into the fire. He said to Erik, "How was it over there fighting Nixon's war?"

"It was a learning experience," Erik replied.

Harold said, "I'm surprised Johnson dropped out and didn't run for a second term. He went through so much to become president."

"What do you mean?" Erik said.

"Well, his involvement with the Kennedy assassination. He had so much to gain."

Erik looked askance at his father. "You're kidding, right? You don't actually believe that, do you?"

"Yes, I do," Harold said, still gazing into the flames.

Helen and Bernie's eyes widened a little but looked as though they were maintaining their cool, because everybody's got to do their own thing.

"Far out." Erik had decided in Vietnam not to be judgmental about his father. He was going to do his part to improve relations. Maybe a question or two. "Where's the evidence?" Erik said. "That was six years ago. A conspiracy that large would leak out."

Harold shrugged. "Lyndon couldn't stand to be second fiddle."

"That's all you've got? I remember a long time ago you said Roosevelt was probably involved with Pearl Harbor because he had so much to gain. It's interesting you would entertain two, kind of, well, half-baked ideas."

Harold gave Erik a withering look.

Erik said, "You look disgusted. Why?"

Harold looked surprised. "No, I'm not disgusted."

The phone rang. Harold got up and went into his study.

"So, what are your plans, Erik?" Helen asked.

"I don't know yet. I'm just going to try to get acclimated in the next couple of weeks. I could use the GI Bill to go to graduate school. If I want to do that, I can get an early out. How about you two?"

Bernie said, "We're getting by. We don't need much. Our herbal tea business is taking off and pays for essentials and some food. We grow some things ourselves and do odd jobs, too. I'm reading a lot of philosophy, and I plan to do some writing."

Erik asked if there were any downsides to living in a commune.

Helen said, "Sometimes everybody doesn't do their fair share. That leads to some bickering, but then we stop and think about our love for each other and all is well." She glanced at Bernie. "Living in a tent gets old." She was becoming more voluble. "So did the multiple, um, bedmates, which also led to some ruffled feathers and hurt feelings. Bernie and I made a new commitment, and we're quite sure that the baby is our child."

Bernie looked at Helen with what appeared to be relief. Maybe Helen had given voice to some of his feelings. Erik figured six months and they'd be out of there.

Harold walked in, smiling. "That was Doris Monnae. We're going out for dinner tonight, so I'll be gone."

Helen and Erik exchanged surprised glances.

"Who's Doris Monnae?" Erik said.

"She works at the library. She lost her husband to a brain tumor last year. She was at the funeral."

Erik remembered her, only because she seemed a little intrusive in a circle of relatives as she rubbed Harold's arm when saying condolences.

Helen said, "Oh. That's nice. So, Father, have you been busy getting back in the groove at work? Has it been difficult?"

"Now that the college became a university, and I'm the Dean of Instruction, I'm busier than ever."

A couple of weeks later, Harold brought Doris home with him after dining out. They had been seeing a lot of each other. She looked to be in her mid fifties. She wore dark, expensive clothes, which helped minimize her ample figure.

"Oh, I'm so happy to meet you all," Doris exclaimed, very sweetly. "Harold has told me so much about you."

"I hope we can get along anyway," Erik said.

Doris giggled. "Oh, you card. How is the conquering hero?"

"Fine."

"And, Helen, what exciting news for you and Bernie," she gushed. "When is it due?"

Helen beamed. "In March, the result of our summer of love." She squeezed Bernie's arm and smiled beatifically. "Boy or girl, we'll love it so much, our little love child."

Let's see, Erik calculated, that's three times Helen has used the word *love* in two sentences. He wished she would take off the rose-colored glasses and get back into the real world.

"How was it in Vietnam, Erik?" Doris asked.

"Well, it's a huge mistake to be there. We're propping up a regime that's rotten to the core. Every time Thieu has an election, he wins by 99 percent. I read an article in *The New York Times* about how our ambassador advised Thieu to win by 60 percent so it looks more believable. But, no, he's got to win by 99 percent."

"Did you see any action?"

"Some."

"What was that like?" Doris asked.

"It was all probability. You had to have your shi … your wits about you, but you had to let the dice fly."

"Was it really horrible?" Doris said.

Erik looked out the window. "Well, it had its moments."

"Did you ever have to shoot anybody?"

"Look, I'd rather not …" He turned back to the window. "Hmm, it looks like it's going to snow."

"Did you lose any—"

Erik sprang to his feet and glared at her. "What the fuck do you want, blood and gore? Do you want to know how many young men I blew away? Do you want to hear how I could have helped one of my squad survive, but instead I had to wash his blood and brains off my hands with a canteen? War is not a romantic rite of passage. It is brutal and obscene, period."

Nobody said a word. Erik walked to a tall window and stared at the falling snow. Where is the green? he wondered. This is all too sudden.

"I'm sorry," Doris said. "I just wanted to learn about this very controversial subject that is tearing us apart."

No more battles, Erik thought. "I'm sorry, too. I didn't need to do that. I need no special treatment." He ached to see Thuy. They had been corresponding regularly and he loved her more than ever. Would she wait for him?

Chapter Twenty-six

Erik was accepted into graduate school at the University of Iowa on an MBA program in international business. He moved to Iowa City for the spring semester and rented a room a couple of blocks from the university. It was a lot bigger than Sturgis State. The campus spilled into the business district which had a lot of restaurants. He washed dishes at one of them when he wasn't attending classes or studying. Harold let him use his mother's car, but he didn't drive it much. He was on a mission to earn a master's degree as quickly as possible. He wrote a letter to Thuy every week, and she did the same. The missives were filled with longing and promises. He hardly glanced at the beautiful co-eds in jeans and T-shirts without bras, although he looked a little longer at the ones with long, blonde hair. How different that was.

After Helen and Bernie left, Erik gave his father a call. He wanted to give him his phone number and more or less reach out to him like Mason had suggested. He thought it would honor his memory.

"Hi, Dad. How's it going?"

"Fine, Erik. How are you?"

"Great. Grad school is going well. It's amazing what a little studying can do. I wanted to give you my phone number and just tell you that, well, I love you."

"Well, that's nice."

"I thought about you a lot when I was in Vietnam. There were many fond memories. You gave Helen and me a good home."

"You certainly helped with the upkeep and I appreciate that."

"Uh, sometimes I guess you were pretty busy, but I wondered if you ever resented me for anything, because sometimes I felt that you, well, sort of disapproved of my goals or something," Erik said.

"Give me some specifics."

"What?"

"Tell me a time when I did that. Give me some specifics."

"I don't want to list specifics. It was just a general question. I had a lot of time to think when I was over there, staring into blackness night after night, and resolved to, well, I want to understand you, and communicate with you more." This is not going well, Erik thought, but no more battles. "Let's be closer. Same with Helen. She's going to be all right, but, you know, keep her close. She needs us."

"I can't relate to this commune business."

"Well, I just wanted to see how you're doing without Mom and everything. Give me a call sometime, or Helen, too. After all, we're family," Erik said.

"I'm getting along okay, Erik, it's tough, but thanks for the call," Harold said.

Erik hung up. "Aaaauuugh! Same-same," he said aloud.

At the end of term, Erik drove up to Sturgis to visit some old friends. He had called his dad to say he was coming. When he pulled in he walked to the Square and stopped at his favorite bookstore.

Mrs. Hastings was just walking out. "Oh, Erik, hello. I'm so glad you came back in one piece."

"Hi, Mrs. Hastings. How are you and Dr. Hastings?"

"We're fine, thank you. That's great news about your father!"

"What?"

"That he's getting married, silly."

"Oh, that. Yes. Well, he's moving kind of fast, I guess, but what the heck?"

"Trevor and I are just so happy he and Doris found each other."

"Yes, I suppose. Well, I'm going to see what the bookstore has to offer. Good to see you."

Holy shit, Erik thought, he didn't wait long. Shouldn't a father tell his son about a marriage? But what do I know, he said to himself.

When his father came home after walking from the campus, as usual, Erik said, "So, Dad, I heard you and Doris are getting married. Is that true?"

Through clenched teeth he said, "Yes, we are."

Gritted teeth? What the fuck? "Well, congratulations, but I'll be honest, I'm surprised. Don't you think you might have told me before I heard it from somebody else?"

Harold shrugged.

"I'm doing my best to understand you and you're not helping."

Harold looked surprised. "I want you to be my best man."

Erik laughed. "That's funny. You just snarled at me and then you want me to be your best man. This is totally fucked. Have you no idea how you come across to your children sometimes? I can only think that maybe you thought I was going to be critical of you since there was not a very long mourning period. That might explain it, but why are you so keen on marrying Doris? She practically got whiplash when she threw herself at you. You're quite a catch, being a dean and all."

Harold looked very pleased at that suggestion, but didn't deign to continue the conversation.

Are you for real? Erik wondered. *If you don't have a good father, you must invent one.* "I will be your best man, but let's make this a start to a better relationship."

"Okay, Erik," Harold said as he looked at his watch. "I'm going over to have dinner with Doris. Have fun seeing some of your old friends."

A month later, Erik received a phone call from his father telling him the date of the August wedding. "I'm glad you're going to be my best man. Oh, and we're not going on a honeymoon right away because there's an all-school reunion in Gainesboro a week after the wedding. They invited me to attend since I was a superintendent. I thought you'd like to go since you loved Gainesboro so much," Harold said.

"It's possible. Summer school will be over. I might go."

The wedding was at the church on the Square. Extolling the marriage of two older people who had lost their mates was the main theme of the conversations among the guests, mostly faculty and their spouses. One of the religion professors joined Harold and Doris in holy matrimony.

The reception was held at the faculty dining room in the union. Walking across campus Erik came upon a peace rally of students carrying signs reading "Stop the War in Vietnam," "Get out of Vietnam," and "Hell No, We Won't Go." On the steps of the library a guy with a guitar was singing "One, two, three, four, what are we fighting for?" covering Country Joe and the Fish.

Good, Erik thought. Bring it to all the campuses. The war is insane. He considered asking if he could talk to them about what it was like to be drafted and fight a war eight thousand miles away. But he kept walking. He didn't want to relive that any more than he had to.

Arriving at the reception he was surprised to see a dozen tables loaded with wedding gifts. His stomach churned with disgust. Obviously he and Doris had not written "No gifts, please" on the invitation. "Whiskey tango foxtrot?" he whispered.

Doris stood by one of the tables and practically swooned at the haul. Erik turned away. He thought how it's not as if Harold and Doris were a young couple just starting off and needed any of that stuff. To 99 percent of the families in Vietnam, this would be luxury beyond their wildest dreams. Does anyone else find this whole thing repulsive? he wondered with amazement. There must be something wrong with me because I do, he thought.

Erik wanted to get drunk, but not here, not now. During the dancing after dinner, he excused himself and headed back across campus. The peace rally was still going strong. He stopped and sang with them, "All we are saying, is give peace a chance," over and over, and confronted his guilt about Mason as tears rolled down his cheeks. Mason would want him to let it go. *Ob-La-Di, Ob-La-Da, life goes on.*

Chapter Twenty-seven

Erik looked forward to seeing Gainesboro again. He wished Thuy was with him. He would tell her stories about growing up in a small Midwestern town. In the boom years after World War II, all the families were able to buy a car and a few appliances, but the box with the hypnotic screen wasn't one of them, thankfully. It seemed like kids were playing all the time and he couldn't remember any of them being fat. Even the adults socialized more.

Growing up in Gainesboro was fabulously rich and comfortable compared to how Thuy lived. He ached to see her again. Now that it was August, he thought how she would be sleeping on a straw mat. A mattress was too hot. The differences in their lifestyles reminded Erik of the time when a rebellious British leader was captured by Roman legions and brought back to imperial Rome. Seeing the unimaginable wealth and architecture of his captors, he said, "What do you want with our mud huts?" Indeed, what does the United States want with Vietnam?

Summer school was behind him. He would have his master's degree in one more semester. He hoped it would lead to a job in Vietnam. Maybe he could parlay it into a position with the U.S. State Department. He had to get to Vietnam. Thuy would not wait forever, although her letters said she would. He missed her lively eyes and sweet voice. His hands held a memory of her silky body.

Even with Erik's cheerful thoughts he had a funny feeling that his father would disappoint him in some way. But he resolved to think positively and try to be understanding of a hard-working father who had the respect of his colleagues and community. Maybe, he thought, Gainesboro would strike a harmonious chord and his father would be the way he remembered.

He thought how his father hadn't jumped into action when Doug Torgerson was getting pounded by that biker in front of Heglan's store. He had admired his father and that didn't fit the picture. Now he was more understanding of him. He had seen good soldiers freeze in Vietnam. Nobody is brave all the time.

As for Doris, he promised himself to look for her good side. Nobody's perfect, but goddammit, he had never known anyone so materialistic. She was ambitious, that's for sure. She was not well off. Erik had heard his father say she was a preacher's kid who had grown up in the Depression, probably in austere circumstances. Maybe that explained her fascination with shiny objects. This is not emphasizing her better qualities, nor does it matter what he thinks, Erik reminded himself.

He turned off the main highway to the paved road that became Gainesboro's Main Street a mile away. A wave of nostalgia swept over him as he saw all the landmarks of his youth. There's the park, but the band shell is gone. The movie house looks just the same, except the door is boarded up. The hotel had no sign of life, let alone a restaurant. Erik figured if there wasn't a reunion going on, you could fire grapeshot through the downtown and not hit anybody. But this Saturday it was as it used to be. All the diagonal parking spaces were filled. A lot of people strolled along the sidewalks, but there were no shops to go into.

The reunion program was at Our Savior Lutheran Church. Gainesboro's ivied school had succumbed to the erosion of time and weather, and, with no one to care for it, was torn down. The halls that had once echoed with youthful voices were no more. They had faded away because of the demise of the small farms and the great migration to larger cities.

Like everyone else, Erik covered Gainesboro with a leisurely walk. Everybody ended up in the church listening to an alumnae band that played many of the Sousa marches that used to serenade shoppers on warm Saturday nights from the band shell in the park.

Erik saw his father and stepmother sitting in a pew and found a seat right behind them. "Hello, folks."

"Oh, hi, Erik," they chimed. "Did you just get in?" Harold said.

"No, I've been walking around town."

"It's too bad about the school where your dad was superintendent," Doris said.

"Oh, was he superintendent?" Erik said, thinking it was always about status with her. "Yes, the small schools are gone. They used to be what gave the towns their identity. When Gainesboro played Mondalia in basketball or baseball, it was a big deal."

"Did you see our house?" Harold said.

"Definitely. I even sat on the cistern where Mom took my picture in every season."

Doris cleared her throat and folded her arms.

Harold turned to Doris and said, "Well, are you getting hungry? Let's head down to the basement and get in line."

"Oh, let's. I'm starving!" Doris exclaimed.

Harold and Doris got up and walked up the aisle heading for the cafeteria.

That's odd? thought Erik. Not a word. He decided to wait and sit at a different table.

Balancing a dessert plate on his arm while carrying a paper plate laden with fried chicken, green beans, and potato salad in one hand and a cup of coffee in the other, Erik made his way across the crowded room to an empty spot at a table.

A sound system had been set up in the front of the room. Paul Ostby, from the class of '59, warmed up as master of ceremonies while most of the people were finishing their desserts. "Well, I wanna tell ya," he announced, "this town has gotten so small that you have to go out in the country to change your mind." A few chuckles indicated that some people were listening. "Hey, wasn't that band great? I love those marches. Let's hear it for the alumnae band."

People put down their forks, or ended their conversations, and applauded enthusiastically.

"And now," Paul continued, "I'm going to call upon you to come up and tell us about your lives since you left good ol' Gainesboro High. What's the oldest class we have here? Anybody?" Erik looked around.

A little voice in the back said, "Eighteen." Nobody else spoke up.

"Well, I guess the class of 1918 has the honors. Come on up, whoever you are."

A blue-haired lady emerged from the audience. She blew on the microphone. *Whoosh*! "I guess it's working," she said with an impish smile. "You know me—Agnes Nelson. I've had a good life as a farmer's wife. Hiram and I had three children. One of our boys took over the farm. Greg and Margaret are with me. Stand up you two." They stood up and gave a wave. "Our daughter, Margaret, became a lawyer in Des Moines, but I don't know what she does, exactly." Her listeners smiled. "My other son, Karl, is a fireman in Denison and couldn't come. I've got seven wonderful grandchildren.

"I lost Hiram last year to a heart attack. You remember Hiram. He didn't go to Gainesboro, but went to Fonda. I never held it against him, though." A few chuckled about this perennial sports rivalry.

"I'll never forget Gainesboro High. It gave me a good start. Thank you. It's good to see some of you again. Well, that's it." She handed the microphone back to the MC and returned to her seat.

A man from the class of 1943 came up and talked about his grown-up children. He finished by telling about getting drafted when he graduated and taking part in the D-Day landing. He received a rousing ovation.

When Paul got the microphone back he said, "I gotta tell you this story. Of course, you all know Richard Peterson, the basketball star that almost took us to state for the first time in Gainesboro's history. And you're probably aware that he went on to play at Drake University, and then was a sports writer for the *Des Moines Register* for what, forty years?" He looked at Richard, who gave him a nod.

"For twenty of those years he had his own column called 'Rich's Rebounds', so he was fairly well known throughout the state. It seems that Richard was driving through Storm Lake to get up here and he stopped at an antique store to look for an icebox to convert to a liquor cabinet. Lo and behold he found one. The owner had seen people of all kinds come into his store over the last fifty years. He didn't take credit cards, so Rich asked if he could write a check. The antique dealer said that he guessed it would be okay. Rich wrote out a check, but wanted to let the guy find out who he was, so he asked him, 'Do you know whose name that is on the check?' The antique dealer, without batting an eye, says, 'I was kind of hoping it was yours.'" The crowd erupted in whoops of laughter at the joke on Richard.

Richard came up and regaled the audience with a few sports anecdotes and talked about his two boys and three grandchildren. He finished by thanking his wife for putting up with him, and handed the microphone to Paul.

Paul said, "Okay, who else? I see Dr. Thorvald, a former superintendent. I understand that Dr. Thorvald earned a doctorate when he left here and became a professor over at Sturgis State. Now he's one of the deans. So, Dr. Thorvald, do you want to come up and say a few words?"

Erik looked across the room. His father modestly waved, as though to let it go at that, but Doris and other folks around the table coaxed him into saying something. Looking as if he was deep in thought, he threaded his way to the front and took the microphone. Erik felt a moment of pride, but something in his inner self told him that whatever happens, it don't mean nothin'.

Harold took a moment to look at the friendly audience, many of whom he had known when he lived in Gainesboro. "It's certainly nice to be here. My wife, Doris, and I got married recently. When I retire from Sturgis State, we're going to build a home in Arkansas on a lake. We'll travel to a lot of scenic and interesting places, like Norway. So, Doris has some very exciting plans for our retirement. I have great memories of when I started my career in Gainesboro. Everyone was so friendly, and hard-working. You were all very supportive of the school. I guess that's about it, and thanks for having us. We've enjoyed the reunion." He handed the microphone to Paul and returned to his seat while the alumnae and friends clapped politely.

Erik's jaw dropped. He wrestled with anger, frustration, shock, and disappointment in a tag-team of emotions. That's it? After everybody else had spoken of their children and grandchildren and spouses, he couldn't acknowledge his son sitting across the room? His father didn't mention Marie, his wife of thirty-five years, loved by all, who passed away about a year ago? What about Helen, an excellent student at Gainesboro's school, of whom his father could be proud—not a word? Erik smiled ruefully about his premonition of a big disappointment.

The MC invited others to share their lives with the group. Erik heard none of it. He looked at Harold, who was listening to other speakers. What has he become? Doris, sitting next to him, was all smiles. If she had an ounce of decency, Erik thought, wouldn't she have given him a sign to say something about his family that was so connected to Gainesboro?

"So, is there anybody else that would like to say a few words?" Paul said. "We've got plenty of time. Anybody?"

You're not a potted plant, Erik said to himself, get off your ass and talk. He felt himself rising and said, "Hello, could I share a couple of things?"

"Yes, please do. Come on up."

Erik walked to the front and took the microphone. "Hi, I'm Erik, one of the other Thorvalds who lived here." Several heads turned to make a quick glance at Harold. "Gainesboro has a place in my heart forever. I was just a little kid, but I took in a lot and learned. I saw how Orville Johnson kept the school neat as a pin and took pride in his domain down by the furnace. I'm thinking, whatever your job is, do it well.

"Remember Iva Rasch, the school secretary, who saw the humor in her name when she married Anthony Rasch? She laughed right along with everybody when one of the teachers played a joke on her with a dribble glass? It's hard for kids to grasp, but if a joke is played on them or they're teased, it works best to laugh with it. That's what I learned, anyway.

"Speaking of kids, oh my gosh! Gainesboro was crawling with them. Nobody had TVs so we played outdoors a lot. It was so much fun, and parents weren't hovering. There was no bullying or fighting. We learned to get along. You probably don't want to hear some of the mischief we did.

"Oh, we worked, too. We learned all about that, but I remember the autumns were especially fun when raking leaves as a group. Our reward was gathering around a bonfire and roasting hotdogs, and stuff. That cooperative working experience stayed with me.

"One Saturday morning downtown, I saw an average middle-aged guy have the courage to stand up to a motorcycle gang because it was the right thing to do. I think the bikers knew it too, and left. Don't fold, be bold became my motto along with what can they do … er, never mind. That's a different story.

"This Gainesboro, a town my mother, Marie, loved as well. She acted in school plays because townspeople often fulfilled needed roles, and revealed that to give of yourself is to get out of yourself, a sublime way to live. I'm sorry to report that Mother passed away nine months ago." Again, there were subtle looks toward Harold.

"My sister, Helen, read just about every book in the town library. Fortunately, her attraction to the world of books rubbed off on me.

"And finally, Dad took Helen and me ice skating on a bright and very cold Sunday afternoon in November before it snowed. The ice was perfect. Never saw it again, but I'll always remember that day. It proved the adage that the best things in life are free. But more than that, it was, how do I put it? It was sharing happiness that rose above what one person can feel. What is that extra measure of joy? Call it love. You can't reach it by yourself.

"Starting life in this town and learning what is truly valuable was the best thing that ever happened to me. Thank you." Erik returned to his seat.

After warm-hearted applause, Paul said, "Thank you, Erik. I think your words struck a responsive chord. Now, would anybody else like to say anything? Anybody? Nobody? Okay, with that, then, the street dance should be getting underway. Emma's Bar and Grill will be open, she tells me, so throw some business her way if you want some liquid refreshment. Thanks for coming, and hopefully we can do this again sometime." Paul smiled amid clapping as the gathering broke up.

A few people stayed, chatting with friends. Erik hugged Babs and Arthur Heglan, laughing about old times. They asked about Helen. Erik told them that she couldn't come since she lived in California and was expecting a baby. Erik's father and Doris stood nearby. Erik said to them, "Hi. Could we go outside and talk?" His heart pounded as he walked up the stairs thinking hard about what to say.

In front of Our Savior Lutheran music drifted along the tree-lined street. Daylight was fading, but the sultry air held the heat of the afternoon, just as Erik remembered Gainesboro in the summertime.

Erik channeled David. He asked his father, "What am I, chopped liver?"

Harold said, "What do you mean?"

"I was sitting across the room and you didn't even acknowledge me when everybody else talked about their families. You didn't mention Mother or Helen, either."

Harold looked surprised. He thought a moment. "That is quite self-centered."

Erik felt relieved, but thought again. "What, of me, or you?"

"You," Harold said.

"Oh, yes, I'm way out of line," Erik said.

"Look, if you're going to be critical you can go peddle your papers elsewhere."

"No, I've got papers to peddle right here. Extra! Extra! Absent-minded professor forgets family."

Harold fumed. "What's wrong with you? Why are you attacking me? You had a good home."

"You're right. It's foolish to think I could get through to you. You can do whatever you want, but goddammit, how could you not acknowledge Mother? If you ever mention her you won't get any?"

"Don't be coarse," Harold said.

Doris said. "I think you're upset because you want to dwell in the past and your father wants to move on."

"Obviously. I can live with that. I won't have to watch your act anymore. Last winter a mink coat? Really? That didn't take long. My mother would never, ever have wanted one." He turned to Harold. "What happened to you? I know where you came from, Father, and you should know better."

"And I suppose you are the ultimate arbiter of what's right," Harold said.

"Don't parse it. It's a feeling. Something didn't click with you. Your belief in those crackpot conspiracies reveals a cynical heart where a soul should be. I can't believe you were played so easily and then didn't mention Mother who was part of your life and connected to this town. Everybody's thinking 'what the hell?'"

Harold looked around and seemed satisfied that no one was close enough to take any notice of their conversation. He lowered his voice and scowled, "Judge not."

"I don't know a lot, but I do know a little about character. You've never been in the grips of a crushing fear and soldiered on anyway. If you had you'd know more about what's truly valuable. It's love, family, friendship, courage—not material things and accolades from sycophants and gold diggers."

Harold scoffed. "Don't lecture me. If you ever attain what I have through hard work you might have room to say something."

Doris wrapped her arm around Harold's. "You should just be quiet. Your father was a great provider. We know what we can do." Doris said.

"Oh, really, Doris. What, pray tell, would that be? Hmm, let me work on that. Oh, wait. Here's a flash. There's nothing you can do that would have the slightest interest to me."

Harold said, "Don't count on any support from me with your attitude."

"It's funny how you don't know me. You think that's important to me." He remembered the philosopher. "I'm going to do what Nietzsche said about fathers."

"What's that?" Harold said.

"If you didn't have a good father you must invent one."

"What is that supposed to mean?" Harold said.

"I think he meant that a son shouldn't depend on a father for an identity. You think for yourself and invent one so that you are not forever tied to a bad father as an excuse to fail for the rest of your life. It's tough, but it's called growing up. You take the good with the bad, and the bad is a teacher, too. I swore not to be like you."

Harold's face froze. The three of them stood there, eyes flashing anger mixed with disgust.

Erik took in a deep breath and exhaled slowly as though relieved of a burden. He said, "No more battles. Life's too short. I will always remember you and skating that one beautiful autumn day with Helen. You used to be a good father."

Harold took out a handkerchief, wiped his brow, and looked to the night sky as though trying to make sense of a math equation. Doris stroked his arm.

"Anyway, I'm out of your life, which seems to be the way you want it," Erik said. "I'm leaving. This is goodbye."

"Where are you going?" Harold said grimly.

"Back to Vietnam to marry someone I love and who loves me. Who knows, Dad? Maybe we'll have a third act someday." He hugged his father until Harold awkwardly returned the gesture. Taking hold of Doris' hand before she could resist, he smiled and said, "Sorry." Doris looked perplexed and opened her mouth to speak, but no words came out.

Erik turned away, headed for the lights and the music, and didn't look back.

Chapter Twenty-eight

It took six months before Thuy and Erik could be married. Engagements were drawn-out affairs in Vietnam. To move things along, Erik had to pay provincial officials money to get to the next step. Steeped in tradition from Confucian and Buddhist influence, a date was finally set. Thuy wore a beautifully embroidered *ao dai* and Erik wore a Western suit and tie. Standing next to her he knew he had made no mistake about leaving a comfortable life back in the States. Her black hair framed a delicate chin, a cute nose, lively eyes, and a serene beauty that belied a passionate loving intimacy. She laughed easily, like a wind chime, and Erik loved her more every day.

While Thuy kept her job with Fahasa Books in Tay Ninh, Erik set up an apartment in Qui Nhon during the engagement. He had gotten a job with the Coronel Coffee Company after availing himself to the services of the economic development division at the American Embassy in Saigon. Qui Nhon was on the coast but near the Central Highlands on Route 19 that led to Pleiku in the interior. He was given the job of buying land for expanding farther north. The company had a plantation in the mountains at Buon Me Thuot that grew the more bitter robusta bean, but they were studying the feasibility of growing the milder and fuller flavor of the arabica bean. Consequently, Erik was in the field a lot testing soils and climatic conditions.

Another reason Erik and Thuy set up a home in Qui Nhon was that it was only forty miles from Hoi Nhon, a village north of them where Thuy's mother lived. Erik was shocked at the impoverished conditions in which she lived. Her house was poured concrete with open windows and shutters that could be closed during storms from the nearby South China Sea. It had five rooms in which the family of six slept on straw mats. Thuy's father had been a fisherman but was lost at sea during a storm.

This neighborhood had no streets but dirt paths. Everyone used a little knoll of palm trees for going to the bathroom. Thuy's mother was a proud woman who only reluctantly accepted a little money from Erik to augment working in the rice paddies for one of the absentee landowners.

Stars and Stripes, which Erik often picked up at an American hospital in Qui Nhon, had a headline that read: "Disaster in Quang Tri." This was a battle that was supposed to show how an ARVN force could stand up to NVA units with minimum American backing after most of its divisions had rotated back to the States by 1972. The rag-tag Southern units had retreated to the walled city of the fourteenth-century Nguyen Dynasty. The Americans rained B-52 airstrikes on the northern forces that besieged the moated redoubt in a fairly populated area. Erik knew the Americans put too much faith in bombing. The ARVN soon enough turned tail in a rout anyway.

"We can't win this way," Erik said. "Everybody hates the Americans. The handwriting is on the wall."

"Everybody alway know North would win sometime," Thuy said. "We just didn't know when."

"Do you want to leave? Do you want to move to the United States?" Erik knew the answer but asked anyway.

"No, I cannot leave my mudder. She do everything for me. She work hard and send me to university. I will never go away from her," Thuy said.

"Well, you know I would never leave without you. How bad can it be? We'll work it out." He gulped down the last of his coffee. "I've got to go to Pleiku today and meet with the province chief. Have a good day at Fahasa." Thuy had been able to transfer to the Qui Nhon branch.

"You be careful. I miss you," Thuy said and gave Erik a kiss.

As he drove up Route 19 in the company car through the Mang Yang Pass he sensed déjà vu from 1954. He had read that during the closing weeks of the siege at Dien Bien Phu it was clear that the French were going to be defeated. It was then that a French force stationed at Anh Khe decided to make a break for a larger post in Pleiku, combine their strengths, and hold out a last hope against the Viet Minh. This *Force Mobile* was armed to the teeth in trucks and armored cars. When they got to the Mang Yang Pass about five thousand Viet Minh charged out of the hills, AK-47s blazing, and overwhelmed the strung-out French convoy. It was a slaughter. When it was all over the French KIAs were so many that the Viet Minh buried them standing up in mass graves near the road. Erik shuddered involuntarily as he drove by the very spot. He wondered if there ever would be peace in this country.

* * *

When he arrived at the provincial headquarters he asked the secretary if he could see Mr. Tien.

"He not here," she said. "He coming from Anh Khe."

"You mean he doesn't even live in his province?"

"Oh, no, he live in military compound."

My God, Erik thought, South Vietnam is not really a country. It's inhabited by so-called leaders that are in it for themselves, getting what they can before the take-over by the North.

A black Ford with tinted windows pulled up. The driver hopped out and opened the back door. Out stepped Mr. Tien in dark aviator glasses and a semi-military uniform with two gaudy medals on his chest. His trousers were tucked into black leather airborne boots. He was topped off with a peaked cap with some gold brocade on the bill.

"Hello, Mr. Tien. I'm Erik Thorvald from the Coronel Coffee Company and I would like to take some soil samples and look at some of the plants in your province."

Mr. Tien grunted. "Follow me."

They walked into his office, bare except for a desk and a couple of chairs. Mr. Tien put his feet up on the desk and slapped his boots with a swagger stick.

Christ, even a swagger stick, Erik thought. He said, "We are checking the area for the possibility of growing coffee on the mountain slopes of Pleiku."

Mr. Tien nodded his head. He looked to the door and saw nobody watching. He held out his hand. Erik was expecting this.

"You know we could be creating a lot of jobs for your people."

Mr. Tien slapped his palm with his swagger stick and smiled.

"How much," Erik asked.

"One hundred U.S. dollar or two million piasters."

By the time he left, Erik had whittled the payoff down to fifty dollars, which was all he was authorized to grease wheels in the usual practice of doing business in South Vietnam. He parked his car on a back road near one of the taller mountains and began hiking up a slope with a southern exposure. He took several soil samples. Too much acidity and they could forget it even if it had cooler temperatures and lots of sun. He cut some branches from the natural vegetation that looked similar to coffee bushes. He was working up a sweat. Did he ever dream he would be back here humping the boonies? Now he was humping a beautiful wife. Erik! Don't be crude! But it was the love of Thuy that brought him back, he knew, and he didn't regret it.

He heard a buzzing noise. What the hell is that? A bees' nest, he guessed. He got closer; it was now more of a grinding sound. He crept closer and parted some branches. He saw a pair of arms working handles in a circular motion. He realized it was a hand-powered generator. He felt cold steel on the nape of his neck.

"*Nam nuhm!*"

Erik started to comply and somebody grabbed his knapsack and shoved him down. He lay prone and put his face in the ground. He felt hands probe him all over. Somebody yanked out the billfold from his back pocket. He heard laughter and exclamations. He turned his head slightly and glanced at a pair of feet in sandals made of tire treads.

"*O tren.*"

Erik got up slowly and saw he was in the middle of four gray-clad NVA complete with pith helmets and AK-47s, which were held at the hip and pointed at him. One motioned him to follow the one who had strapped his weapon and was making his way through low branches on the steep slope toward the noise of the generator.

The lead guy broke through to a piece of fairly level ground in which the vegetation had been cleared away. Six NVA looked up casually. When they saw Erik, jaws dropped in surprise as everyone jumped to their feet.

Erik tried to maintain an air of innocence and not show he was afraid. Be brave, get out of yourself, let the dice fly, he cajoled himself. He did not want them to know he spoke any Vietnamese. He raised a hand and smiled. "Hello, everyone!" Two of the squad were young women. One actually gave a hint of a smile back at him.

The man in charge, a captain, who couldn't have been more than twenty-five and was the oldest, came up to him and said, "What hap we here?"

Erik couldn't hide his surprise and wondered if this was going to be like the WWII movies in which the clever enemy discloses he was a student at UCRA and learned all about America. "Greetings. My name is Erik. I'm from the Coronel Coffee Company."

"I know abow it. It French plantation that exploit Vietnam worker, as you capitalists do. They down Buon Me Thuot. What you do here?"

"We're thinking of expanding farther north." Erik was surprised at how close these guys were to the Pleiku military base, now mostly ARVN. Mao said to grab the enemy by the belt. "Where did you learn English?"

"I ask question. You my prisoner."

"What for? I'm a non-combatant. What good am I?" His concern was growing. His car was left on the road. Thuy would be worried.

"When Reunification come we hap many American prisoner. Your country will give food aid for them. We give much food to people who suffer your war," the captain said with a knowing smile.

"What are you doing here?" Erik asked as friendly as he could.

The captain frowned and wagged his finger at him. "You no ask question."

Erik concluded that they were gathering intelligence by listening to radio traffic and the generator was their power source. Batteries don't last long in the tropics. Pleiku was fairly close to the Ho Chi Minh Trail and they were planning an assault on this outpost when the final push came.

The captain gave Erik a shove and said, "You sit."

Everybody sat around and pulled out tin cups and a ball of rice encased in oil cloth from their packs. Lunch time. Erik heard a cargo plane lazily approach the airstrip and caught a glimpse of it through the trees. One of the NVA, with a yellow star on a patch of red on each epaulette, pulled out a brick of plastique explosive, C-4, no doubt extracted from a claymore mine. The man with the C-4 tore off a piece of the white putty and put it in front of him and did one for the cute girl next to him in pigtails who looked uncannily like Gina Lollabrigida. One could imagine a similar figure underneath the loose-fitting trousers and top. Lolla smiled demurely at Plastic Man as he passed the C-4 to the other girl to do herself. Everybody did likewise as it was passed around. In the tin cups they poured water from their canteens. One of them pulled out a butane lighter and lit up his bit of plastique. It flamed into an intense heat for about thirty seconds over which he held the cup for hot water. He finished by dunking an overworked tea bag a couple of times and put it back in his pack. Butane passed around the lighter and the ritual was repeated as the patrol seemed to savor this break and munched slowly on their rice.

Erik looked at the captain, whom Erik designated as Doc, because for all he knew he was a PhD like Giap, their esteemed leader second only to the late Ho Chi Minh, who had died a couple of years ago. With his wire-rimmed glasses and diffident nature Doc seemed too intellectual for a soldier in command, although his thick hair was cut short in a military style. Take Plastic Man, Erik observed; his vanity was plain to see as he often ran a hand through his lustrous black hair as if to show it off.

Doc kept glancing at Lolla. Then his eyes fell on Erik and all the AKs lying around. He said something to the other girl, plainer and stockier than Lolla, who retrieved some green cord and tied Erik's elbows together in the back.

After lunch some of the men got out stubby cigarettes for a couple of puffs. Others stretched out for a nap. Doc told one of the boys, who looked half-awake, probably dreaming of home and his water buffalo, to stand guard. "Meet Sleepy," Erik said in a whisper.

He lay back and rested as best he could, but his mind was racing. He watched Plastic Man speaking to Lolla and getting an occasional giggle from her. The C-4 was lying not two feet from him. He looked at Sleepy cradling his AK-47, who, true to his name, was nodding off. Plastic Man and Lolla had lain back. He could hear Doc talking on the radio somewhere, probably for a better signal. The rest were dozing off in the hottest time of the day. Erik inched his way closer until he dug his fingernails into the lethal play dough and pulled off a handful. He slowly slid back and put the glob of C-4 in his pocket.

Chapter Twenty-nine

The squad of NVA broke camp about three o'clock in the afternoon. Erik could only guess because one of them had taken his watch. Stocky, the girl who had tied him up in the back, undid him and circulation in his arms relieved the cramped pain that had set in. Under a watchful eye from Butane, he was allowed to step away and relieve himself.

When he returned, Doc and several others were waiting with a green nylon cord, probably standard issue for making tents between trees, Erik figured. They put his knapsack on his back, empty except for his sweatshirt. On top of that they placed the disassembled generator. Doc motioned for Erik to extend his arms. He tied his parallel, but separated wrists, with a convoluted knot allowing some play with his hands.

They set out in a brisk walk down the mountain trail. Butane was in the lead. Third in line was Plastic Man who seemed to be berating the guy in front of him. Erik figured he was some sort of political commissar who was along to make sure everyone was a good little communist. The third person behind Plastic Man was Lolla, whose swaying hips and convex rear were evident under her austere uniform and made Erik ache for Thuy. Doc followed Erik.

"Where are we going?" Erik asked.

Surprisingly Doc seemed to welcome conversation. "We go to secret camp in Lao across Ho Chi Minh Trail. You will be with other Americans. You will be interrogated. You will be out of our hands."

"Where did you learn English?"

"At London School of Economics."

Erik turned back to see if he was serious. Doc was looking at Lolla who was three people ahead of Erik. Erik said, "She's pretty isn't she?"

Doc blushed. "You walk. Be quiet."

Erik continued, anyway. "Why don't you talk to her? Tell her how you feel?"

Doc didn't say anything. Erik thought, so much for that. Then Doc said quietly, "I don't know what to say."

They reached level ground and proceeded through thick forest. A jet screamed overhead. The column stopped and looked up. They heard a distant explosion.

Doc said, "You Americans think jets and bombs stop us. We sometimes laugh. They usually miss. They only guess where we are."

They took a break. Some smoked. Erik was sitting next to Doc, who was watching Lolla talking to Stocky. He said, "I think she likes you. She often looks at you when you do things," which wasn't a total lie. Doc was a lean young man with fine features.

Doc's eyes lit up. "You tell me true?"

"Yes, for sure. Do Vietnam people like poetry?"

"I too busy student to learn poetry," Doc said.

Erik said, "I can help you. Um … do I ever get something to eat?"

"We stop in village. Get rice."

They came to the edge of a rice paddy at dusk and waited. An ARVN compound loomed about five hundred feet to their left. They watched as the compound's perimeter lights blinked on, resembling a diamond necklace. When it was dark the squad of NVA and their prisoner trotted across the flooded expanse on a raised dike. Half way to a tree line a mortar popped from the direction of the compound. Doc shoved Erik down as everyone hugged the ground. A flare directly above burst open and lit up the valley. The rice paddies became a mirror of light. When the illumination round burned out, the squad jumped up as one, including Erik, and moved on at a faster pace.

They reached a grove of palm trees that held simple houses with thatched roofs. As they walked along a dirt path Erik looked through open-air windows at families eating by candlelight in front of tiny cooking fires. Villagers they met didn't seem surprised at a squad of NVA walking among them. In fact they smiled and gave words of encouragement. Doc went up to a house and whistled. An old woman came out and got close enough to recognize Doc. "Sister," he said in Vietnamese, "we have a prisoner …" Erik couldn't understand the rest of it but picked out a few words about giving and Reunification. She disappeared and came out with a stack of flat sheets of dried rice.

Erik noticed a barrel of rain water at the corner of the house and indicated getting a drink to Doc, who nodded an okay. Erik drank his fill from a gourd dipped into the cool water, which slaked his thirst. He ate one of the sheets of dried rice which reminded him of lefse back in

Minnesota. People from the village gathered around in the dim light to watch the American eat with his hands tied, not that easy.

When he finished, one of his captors tied a nylon rope around Erik's neck, ran it under his crotch, and tied it to his wrist bindings, thereby making it impossible to chew his way to freedom. To the rope behind him somebody tethered another line high on a palm tree. All of this was the evening's entertainment by torchlight for the onlookers. Erik had to admit it was a lovely village, his discomfort and situation notwithstanding. Butane tossed him his knapsack. Erik lay on wooden boards under a thatched porch roof after taking out his sweatshirt and removing the generator. He put on the sweatshirt over both arms and lay his head on the bunched-up knapsack. Okay, he thought, food and sleep is good. The rest of the squad divided up into various homes. He was curious if Plastic Man and Lolla paired up.

Despite his exhaustion he thought of many things at breakaway speed. Slow down, don't panic, one at a time, he said calmly to himself with a deep breath. What was Thuy doing? She'll be all right until I get back, he assured himself. He pictured her giving him a poke in the stomach and that musical laugh when she teased him about his attempts at speaking Vietnamese. Get back? Just how was he going to accomplish that? He had to do something before he got to this camp that Doc alluded to, but what? He thought about his father and Doris. He wondered if they did it a lot. He had a vision of Doris naked in her mink coat and opening up her chubby little legs to a randy Harold. What you think of sometimes, Erik, he scolded. He must address why he's so critical of them sometime. He had written them a letter about volunteering on a hospital ship for passage to Vietnam. Of course, he had some help to get that arranged from Alex Cushman, now a lieutenant colonel. Apparently Alex was in the fast track at the Pentagon and could pull some strings. Erik felt that Harold would write back, but it would take some time in regular mail. Erik recalled staying with Helen, Bernie, and their daughter in a little flat above a bakery in Berkley before the ship left. Helen was totally involved with being a mother. Bernie had put aside his revolutionary zeal and enjoyed his role as resident philosopher at a junior college. Helen did not want to talk about their father, which was okay by Erik. Dreams of Thuy helped him make it through the night.

Chapter Thirty

Erik awoke to half-light, which told him it was about 6:00 a.m. It had rained during the night so he was glad they let him sleep on the porch. He urinated along a rickety fence made of sticks. He ached all over from the dampness and his teeth were mossy, but he had to get his mind on track for learning opportunities. The palm trees above looked so peaceful and pretty that he forgot his misery for a brief moment. This village, he thought, shouldn't have to be touched by war if America had just stayed the hell out, and he wouldn't be in this predicament. But then he never would have met Thuy, a state of being he could not imagine. His life would be a series of empty events. Why did he love her so? He concluded it was her intelligence, humor and selfless expressions of love when they were alone, unlike her very proper behavior in public. Her love was deep and true and not for show.

He drifted back to sleep despite his self-talk about facing the day. He was awakened by somebody kicking his buttocks. He turned to see Butane standing over him. Erik got up and Butane untied the rope around his neck and wrists, but left the nylon handcuffs. While Butane untethered the rope to the palm tree, Erik drank water from the rain barrel. He ate some dried rice, which he now kept in his backpack, and understood to eat sparingly because that was all he would get for a while. The rest of the squad emerged from various homes. He noticed that Lolla and Stocky came out from the house next door.

Doc pulled out a packet from his side bag and laid it on a roughly hewn wooden table. He pulled out maps, compass, and a magnifying glass. Magnifying glass! Of course, a magnifying glass! Erik had an idea that depended on getting hold of that little round lens with attached handle. Plastic Man pointed out something on one of the maps and told Doc something, who nodded. Erik wondered if the rest of the squad

146

saw that Doc's body language spoke a good deal about his disdain for Plastic Man.

Through the trees Erik saw a dot on the horizon. It grew to an F-16 approaching fast but silently as it raced the speed of sound. Nobody else saw it. So quiet he thought, barely skimming above the palm trees. They didn't hear the roar until the plane was directly overhead. Everyone instinctively hit the ground, except Erik who grabbed the magnifying glass and put it in his pocket. The jet with its afterburners glowing disappeared over the northern horizon.

The villagers and soldiers alike sheepishly got up and wiped red mud from their uniforms, laughing in relief and exclaiming about the surprise. Plastic Man went over to Lolla. Grinning, he put his hands on her shoulders and said something. Lolla didn't look all that happy about his attention. Maybe he had tried to put some moves on her last night. She glanced at Doc who was putting his maps back in the case, apparently not thinking about something missing.

The squad bade farewell to their hosts and set out. Erik raised both hands and wagged his fingers and smiled at the children as if he were an uncle waving goodbye. They howled and waved in delight at the improbable sight of a tied-up American prisoner doing such a thing. Erik couldn't help but laugh out loud. He hoped he wasn't losing his mind. He noticed Doc looking down, shaking his head from side to side and smiling very slightly.

They hiked without incident for hours. The terrain was becoming less hospitable as they climbed hills and descended into uninhabited valleys. From one of the high points Erik looked westward into untamed country of endless mountains and ravines with patches of blue water in a vast green expanse. Is this the end of the earth? No, he answered, it's the land of the legendary Ho Chi Minh Trail. Erik figured this desolate, remote corner of the world would make the Hindu Kush seem like rush hour in Chicago. How easily it could absorb traffic from the North without detection, frustrating the can-do Americans and their advanced technology.

A trickle of water at the base of a cliff provided a good stopping place for lunch. The patrol filled their canteens. The Central Highlands was draining the waters of the winter monsoon so the streams were full. Now, in April, days of sunshine were becoming more frequent, and although not directly overhead, the sun was high and made for hot afternoons.

Erik walked over and put his mouth under the waterfall and drank his fill. He was being watched, but it seemed not so closely. There was no way he could take off at an opportune moment and get very far with his hands tied. His captors had become accustomed to his unthreatening manner. He good-naturedly took everything they dished out, whether it was the arduous pace with his hands bound or being the subject of jokes. He laughed right along with them when they thought it was funny how he tried to brush his teeth with the frayed end of a stick under the little stream, getting wet in the process.

Erik sat behind Doc during the lunch ritual. He asked Doc if he could get his notebook and pen back. Doc reached in his side pouch and gave them to him.

Lolla was not sitting by Plastic Man, who sat asserting his authority by talking animatedly to four of the guys about something. Was he performing his party-hack duties for the benefit of Lolla? Stocky was talking to Lolla. She was very pretty, that Lolla, Erik thought. Her chin and mouth formed an exquisite heart beneath her pert nose, a sign of beauty when more pointed. Her high cheek bones between girlish pigtails and hints at a voluptuous figure probably had most of the guys falling in love with her. Erik imagined a poster of her with rich black hair under a pith helmet in a size-two uniform. The North would be up to their keister in new recruits, Erik supposed, including the southern boys. As to Stocky, Erik figured she could play halfback for a Division II football team. Erik began writing in his notebook.

"Captain," Erik said to Doc in a low voice during siesta time, "I have written some words that you might say to, to—"

"Mai," Doc said. "Her name, Mai."

"Yes, Mai. Anyway, if you can get her alone in the moonlight sometime you could make sweet talk."

Doc hesitated but couldn't resist looking at the words.

"You could sort of translate it into Vietnamese, or just say them in English like poetry. Mai will get the idea."

Erik looked at the words over Doc's shoulder:

> Around the world I've searched for you. I've traveled on when
>   hope was gone to keep a rendezvous.

> I know sometime, somewhere, somehow, I'll look at you and I will
>   see the smile you're smiling now.

> It might have been in Ha Noi town, or in Da Nang, or in Sai Gon,
>   or even London town, no more will I go all around the world,
>   for I have found my world in you.

A smile crept over Doc's face, but quickly changed to a serious expression. He tore out the page with the words, folded it, and put it in his pocket. He handed back the notebook without a word.

Erik retreated and lay on his back. They soon packed up and headed out.

This routine went on for two more days. After untying Erik from his night-time fettering the patrol and captive set out on trails that traversed high slopes or along streams in deep ravines. Erik was aware they had turned north. It was cooler at night, but the afternoons were hot. Erik's T-shirt, denim shirt, and khaki pants were getting ripe. He sweated more than his captors, but their loose sailcloth outfits didn't exactly smell like a meadow of clover, either.

Plastic Man appeared to grow more frustrated about a lack of attention paid him by Lolla, so he took it out on petty complaints to his underlings. He did a slow burn when he saw Lolla and Doc practically bump heads when they bent down to pick up a pair of binoculars that fell to the ground. Their hands touched and eyes met. Lolla's long lashes fluttered. Doc quickly straightened up, cleared his throat and looked through the binoculars.

"Look here, American," Doc said, still peering at something in the distance. "See flat mountain. That place of Khe Sanh battle of Tet in 1968. Many brave comrades surround marines. Kill many. Marines leave Ho Chi Minh Trail." He handed the binoculars to Erik.

Erik looked where Doc was pointing. A curiously flat-topped rise was an anomaly among jagged green mountains surrounding it. Erik knew combat engineers had carved a landing strip on this remote mesa a few miles from Laos. C-130s supplied the operation to interdict supplies on the Ho Chi Minh Trail, but the marines were soon surrounded by about 45,000 crack NVA. The siege lasted four months until April when General Creighton Abrams decided it was too costly to maintain this outpost, named for the nearby village of Khe Sanh, and withdrew, but not before inflicting heavy casualties with B-52 airstrikes. "Yes, we lost almost three hundred marines, but many more of your army were killed—maybe ten thousand. Your leaders were willing to send your comrades into a valley of death trying to overrun the outpost. Americans never understood how they could do that. It was thirty losses for every one of ours. We value our soldiers and marines more."

Doc said, "Nothing is more important than independence. We are willing to lose many, many people. We wear you down. Same we do with China for thousand years."

They camped on some high ground by a rocky outcropping devoid of trees. It presented a breathtaking view of a full moon rising over serrated mountains. Its radiance on this clear night brushed the valley below with a silver patina. A river glowed like mercury. The rocks on which they stood were still warm from the heat of the day. All was quiet. Erik was in awe of the untouched primeval beauty in this far-flung country. Ten North Vietnamese and one American, it seemed, forgot themselves for a moment.

"Listen!" Doc said. "Our brave fighters of the Reunification are crossing river at night."

Erik scanned the valley floor and heard a low rumbling. He finally could barely make out a column of trucks emerging from a canopied road and slowly crossing the river, which looked to be incredibly shallow. Then he realized the trucks were traversing a rocky causeway just below the waterline. "Clever fellows," Erik said.

Doc smiled. "Too clever for rich Americans with everything."

Some of the squad drifted back to their bedrolls. Lolla sat down with her feet dangling over a craggy ledge. Doc sat down beside her. Lolla didn't look at him but appeared to have expected him to join her.

Plastic Man grabbed Erik by the arm and yanked him back among the trees. He roughly tied the rope around Erik's neck. Erik bent down and brought the dangling end up between his legs which Plastic Man tied to the wrist bindings as he spat out some angry words that were too fast for Erik to understand.

"*Xin loi*," Erik said.

"*Cut di!*" Plastic Man said. He pushed Erik down, secured him to a high tree branch, and stormed off to his pack and wrote something in a notebook.

Erik weighed his possibilities for escape as he watched Plastic Man in the moonlight. He was sure there'd be hell to pay for anyone who crossed Plastic Man when they reached wherever they were going. Too bad he wouldn't be with them, he resolved, and that will really piss some people off.

Chapter Thirty-one

By noon the next day they came to a tree line that gave way to a wide expanse of bleached rocks that resembled a cobblestone street running alongside a swollen stream. Even though it was early spring, Erik was surprised at the sun's intensity when it beat down on exposed skin. He guessed they were level with the de-militarized zone between North and South Vietnam, which was at seventeen degrees north latitude.

After everyone munched on dried rice and sipped tea in the shade, Lolla and Stocky decided they would go upstream to wash their uniforms and dry them on the rocks. Visions of Lolla without her austere loose-fitting outfit, and perhaps sans underwear, flashed in Erik's imagination. Naturally, Erik knew, the entire male contingent was thinking the same thing. It occurred to him that maybe Stocky wouldn't mind it either.

That morning Erik noticed longing glances exchanged by Doc and Lolla, and the tension between Doc and Plastic Man was palpable. Of course it was like pouring gasoline on a fire when Erik told Doc that sometimes he noticed Plastic Man making disparaging faces behind his back followed by a look to Lolla as if to say Doc was a *thang ngoc*. He actually hadn't seen that, and Lolla obviously didn't think Doc was an idiot, but oh, well, Erik said to himself, all's fair in what they were in right now—love and war. Doc's face had turned red with rising anger.

This might be the time, Erik thought. Things are looking up. Stocky, whose plain oval face seemed happy about doing some laundry, shouldered her AK and followed Lolla as they gingerly, in sandals on a bumpy traverse, made their way around a bend. Doc was on the radio in the shade with Butane cranking the generator. Sleepy, as usual, was assigned to watch Erik, but lacked enthusiasm. His eyes were focused upriver.

Erik began an animated fascination for the rocks he was standing on, picking some up and examining them with feigned interest. Funny how they looked like ostrich eggs, he thought. He moved a little farther downstream one rock at a time. He sat with his back to the others and inspected one up close. Still holding the rock to his face, he chanced a look back. Sleepy had moved for a better angle, craning his neck for a glimpse of the girls. Plastic Man and the others sat in the shade smoking.

Erik began to work the C-4 in his pocket upward where he could reach it. He got it in his left hand. With his other he strained for the magnifying glass, which was difficult with his bound wrists. He stretched his leg out and worked the glass up and tried again. Yes! He had it and put the handle in his mouth. He turned to his left and saw Plastic Man and the others saunter down to the river's edge. They made a show of skipping a few rocks but obviously their interests were more prurient. "Now or never," Erik said in a whisper. With his fingers he kneaded the C-4 into an elongated glob and let it slide down to the cat's cradle which held fast his wrists. He leaned forward and focused sunshine in a bright little dot on the plastic explosive.

He heard an angry shout from Doc. Oh, no! his mind screamed. Then he heard Plastic Man defiantly yell something, presumably back at Doc. This is it Erik, thought. They're going to have it out.

He continued his task in desperation. "Come on! Come on!" he said through gritted teeth. Suddenly the C-4 burst into flame and disintegrated the nylon rope instantly. He could feel his skin blistering, but he was free. He slowly looked back. Doc and Plastic Man were toe to toe while the rest gathered around. Sleepy stood alone watching the developing confrontation. Doc said something that must have really gotten to Plastic Man because he looked apoplectic and started to unstrap his weapon. Everybody grabbed for Plastic Man's AK before he got it off his shoulder. The shouting reached a shrill dissonance.

Erik bolted. Had he not made a splash, Sleepy no doubt would still be watching the altercation, but looking back as the current carried him away, Erik saw him run to the river's edge wielding his AK. He fired wildly on full automatic and stitched a seam that was close enough. Erik dove. He broke to the surface out of range, laughing maniacally.

Chapter Thirty-two

"Yeehaaaaaah!" Erik screeched and yelled "Yes. Yes. Yes!" as he floated downstream. He had a vision of Plastic Man, Doc, and the others frozen in place, mouths agape, and still clutching each other's tunics when Sleepy fired a burst at something in the river. "Wait! Where's the American?" they must have said, dreading the answer they already knew.

Erik made his way to the right bank. He didn't know what lay ahead. Maybe a waterfall. Maybe a dam. He was pretty sure this river headed for Quang Tri or joined one that did and eventually emptied into the major Ben Hai River which formed part of the DMZ border. He had to think and dry his clothes, or maybe find something to float on, or start walking.

Let's see, he thought, Quang Tri was on Highway 1. If he could get there he could hitch a ride all the way to Qui Nhon and home to Thuy. It would be a three-day trek if he was lucky. He had no food. What about that? Would he dare stop at a house for food? His frenzied high was beginning to wane. He took a deep breath and brought himself down to calm considerations. He decided to walk for now so he could find some food—probably steal it—because he knew on which side the rural Vietnamese sentiments lay. Then he could look for something to float on. He didn't have the tools to build a raft. Maybe, he thought hopefully, he could find a boat.

He made his way for about an hour through tall thin trees. It was rainforest but not the huge trees he remembered in Tay Ninh province. Probably due to the altitude, he guessed. He paralleled the river so as not to go in circles. The east-flowing river was his compass because one had to dodge and weave if hiking through the forest. At least he wouldn't be thirsty. The water was clear.

He stopped to rest and put his hand on a tree for balance. He felt himself growing weaker by the minute. He looked up into broad leaves with clumps of little nuts. "Hold the phone," he said. "This is a betel nut tree." He had seen a lot of Vietnamese women, mostly the coffee pickers, chewing these nuts wrapped in its broad fronds which acted as some kind of a stimulant. He tried some, enclosing a bunch in a leaf and popping it in his mouth. He started out again chewing and walking. In about fifteen minutes he began to feel a pleasant sensation take over his mind and body. "No wonder they chew this stuff," he said aloud, which had become an unconscious habit.

A roar ahead told him he was wise to have exited the river of his deliverance. He sang "I looked over Jordan and what did I see, coming for to carry me home." "Well, not a band of angels I hope," he said. "There I go again, talking out loud. Gotta stop that. You're not totally bonkers so shut the fuck up." Sure enough, huge boulders formed a waterfall under a misty rainbow. It could have messed up his whole day, he realized, if he had been swept over that twenty-foot drop.

Skirting the falls, he looked down into a wider expanse of shallow water. He spotted a *V* made of nets that pointed to a bamboo cage. "Fish," he said hungrily, and descended the escarpment to the river's lower level. He looked around. Smoke was wafting skyward from a mountain-side to his right. Maybe it's a Montagnard home, he considered. They are friendly to Americans, but you can't know for sure.

He waded toward the fish trap, scanning the slopes that bordered the river. Nobody around. He found four fish in the trap. He grabbed one and banged it on an exposed rock and put it in one of his pockets. He did the same with another, clutched a third, and walked downstream.

He stopped at a sharp rock and began scraping off the scales and fins of his catch. It's funny how he felt he was being watched, and, just to appease himself, he looked to the bank on his right. Standing not twenty feet from the water's edge was a dark-skinned man with black hair holding a bow and arrow. He was barefooted and wore a loin cloth. Erik had the strange sensation that he had somehow gone back in time to about AD 1000. This is what being alone in this wilderness does to you, he thought. You talk to yourself and have weird fantasies. On closer inspection he could see the guy, whom Erik was sure was a Montagnard, was wearing an olive-drab T-shirt that was army issue. Erik contritely made a gesture of giving him the fish.

The man waved his hand sideways and pointed to Erik, as if to say "you need it more than me." Erik figured he was a pitiful sight with scraggly beard, ragged clothes and emaciated. Now the Montagnard was flailing his hand at him several times, which to Westerners meant go away, but to Vietnamese the gesture signifies "please come here." Erik knew that to them, crooking an arm toward oneself with a come hither motion was too demanding and impolite.

Holding his fish, Erik walked toward the river bank. By the time he clambered onto dry land, the Montagnard had gathered sticks into a pile. From his rude quiver he pulled out a longish piece of dried bamboo that was split down the middle forming a trough. He unsheathed a knife and proceeded to scrape fine threads of bamboo into a clump. He looped the bowstring around a stick about the size of an arrow and stuck it in a tight hole in the bamboo. Pushing and pulling the bow for about a minute, he created enough friction for the entwined stick to smolder at its base and form a tiny ember. When he blew on it ever so slightly the clump of bamboo filament next to it caught fire. Carefully adding twigs they soon had a fire going. The Montagnard skewered one of the fish with an arrow and handed it to Erik. Erik took it and offered a fish to his benefactor. They silently roasted their fish over the fire. Erik wolfed down his fish and sucked on the bones. The Montagnard looked on with such concern that tears welled up in Erik's eyes. Then he laughed about his good fortune. The Montagnard joined in as he gestured for Erik to have the other fish.

After eating they sat cross-legged and tried to communicate, which was nigh on impossible. They mostly just looked at each other and smiled a lot. Erik plucked at his shirt and then pointed to the Montagnard's T-shirt.

"Ga reen bray," the Montagnard said.

"Green Beret?" Erik said.

The man nodded animatedly and smiled. Erik was aware that Special Forces had made friends with a lot of these folks in the Annamite Mountains whom the French named Montagnards. Much consternation was voiced by the Americans when they began pulling out and abandoning their allies. Some said the North would retaliate for their having helping the Americans. It never should have happened. These people would have been left alone and not bothered by North Vietnamese moving supplies in the back country and Americans trying to stop them.

Erik had to move on, but first wanted to explain how he felt about this kind stranger. He pointed to him and then clasped his hands over his heart. The Montagnard knew immediately what he was trying to say. He did the same thing with his hands after pointing at Erik.

They stood up. Erik gripped the man's forearm with his right hand and the Montagnard did likewise. Erik looked into a pair of eyes of such guileless calm that Erik envied him. "Goodbye," he said.

The Montagnard nodded and smiled.

Erik moved on with new energy, still thankful he didn't have to do this with his hands tied.

Chapter Thirty-three

While the sun was still out, Erik decided to learn exactly which way was due east. Following the river might lengthen his journey. He could cut across country when it meandered from where he wanted to go.

He stuck a long stick straight up into a sandbar and marked the sand at the top of its shadow. He sat and waited for about twenty minutes thinking of what may be the latest in the war. If the North made an offensive across the Demilitarized Zone he could be sitting in enemy territory right now. The peace agreement signed in January was a joke and everybody knew it. Let's see, he thought; the Paris Peace Accords started in 1968, which means that they've been talking for four years. Of course the first year was spent on deciding what shape the table should be. Then the next year had both sides making accusations followed by leaving the table in a huff until the next day. He marked where the tip of the pole's shadow had moved and connected the two marks by scratching a line in the sand. By bisecting that line with a perpendicular, which pointed due north, he formed a compass rose.

He followed the line pointing east and made note of a mountain peak to follow. For now the river traced the right direction, so he forged on.

When darkness fell Erik moved into the woods and stretched out on a bed of leaves. It was comfortable enough, but his stomach growled. Forget about it. Tomorrow is another day. He turned on his side and looked at the wide valley in the light of a waning moon. He felt a crushing loneliness that was only allayed with thoughts of Thuy, the brass ring of the crazy merry-go-round he was on. The gurgling water had a calming effect and he fell asleep.

It was not a constant slumber. He dreamed he heard voices. Maybe it was real. Erik didn't trust his mind any more. Dawn was breaking. He could make out a stag approaching the river and drinking, followed by three deer. Something spooked them and they darted back to the forest, except one stayed too long and was cut off by a stunningly awesome Bengal tiger. Erik whispered William Blake's *Tiger, tiger burning bright, in the forests of the night.* The deer froze while the tiger crouched, ready to spring. The white patches on the back of its ears looked like a pair of hypnotic eyes on a chimera about to devour him. Erik shivered. Be very afraid of the tiger, not a runaway imagination, you idiot, he chided.

What drama, Erik exclaimed to himself. As if this wasn't enough theater, he heard a helicopter following the river and approaching fast. The principals of the riveting scene in front of him heard it too. The tiger looked up and the deer bounded into the river and was swept away in the main channel. When Erik looked back for the tiger it was gone. He couldn't tell where it went. He didn't know whether to shinny up a tree or run into the clearing and try to flag down the helicopter. Desperation to get home won and he ran out yelling like a cheerleader and waving his arms.

He could see the astonishment in the pilot's face, but it turned to circumspection. The Huey with two door gunners continued on. They're just checking things out, Erik hoped, before setting down. "That's okay, take your time," Erik said anxiously, hoping the tiger had *didi maued.*

Erik watched the pilot do a one-eighty and come back, probably to give the co-pilot a look at this bearded apparition. Erik flailed his arms as the tantalizing green machine beat a cautious fly-by. He was close to breaking down completely when his would-be rescuer disappeared around a bend. Above the *whop, whop, whop* of the blades he heard AKs open up followed by a door gunner returning fire. "Oh, no," Erik shouted when he heard the clank of rounds hitting metal.

The chopper suddenly reappeared in a steep bank, its turbojet screaming in protest at the pilot's demands. It landed on a sand bar while Erik churned water to get to it. "Hurry up," the crew exhorted. Erik reached the open side door and flung himself aboard at the very moment the pilot went to full power and lifted off. He impossibly hugged the aluminum floor and gave it a warm kiss. He pulled himself to the edge and looked down at the receding terrain he would have had to cross. To the crew, who couldn't hear him, and whatever, whomever, Lady Luck, or some ineffable entity, he said, "Thank you."

Nobody talked above the noise on the flight back to the coast. With sandy beaches and wide inlets Erik guessed they were at Da Nang. An airfield swathed in several tiers of barbed wire drew closer as they slipped into a slow descent. The pilot maneuvered his ship just above the PSP floor and parked in a spot among a dozen or so helicopters of various types.

"Man, was I glad to see you guys," Erik said after the engine wound down. "What were you doing out there?"

The pilot took off his helmet with TAYLOR printed on it in black letters. He grinned roguishly. "Just gettin' some hours in before this whole thing goes south," he said. "I thought we'd do a little reconnaissance toward Khe Sanh. The bigger question is, what in the hell were you doing out there?"

Erik said, "You got a club around here? I could use a cup of coffee. Man, look at that. I almost caused you guys to slog the boonies, too." He walked over and kissed the rotary boom that had four bullet holes in it. "That wouldn't have been much fun for you. I am in your debt, forever."

Taylor said, "Yeah, I guess they were trying to knock out the rear rotor. We would have had to land and then they could have finished us off or taken us prisoner."

They all headed for a club. Erik felt like doing cartwheels, but didn't have the strength.

The coffee was divine. "It's absolutely the best I've ever had," Erik effused, savoring every sip. The five-man crew looked at him with what appeared to be a mixture of curiosity and sympathy, which gave him an indication of how bad he looked. He went to the latrine and washed up. He did look like hell, he allowed.

When he returned, the co-pilot said, "We didn't know what to think when you came running out of the woods. You looked like a wild man, but possibly an American wild man. We weren't sure if it was a trap. When somebody locked and loaded on us downstream we figured you were legit because if it was a trap they would have been right behind you. So we came back."

"You know I slept right there in the woods and dreamed I heard voices. Maybe some NVA went right by me during the night. And then when the tiger came out ..." Erik stopped. His audience cleared their throats, looked at each other sideways. "No, really, there was this huge golden tiger that had a deer paralyzed in fright by the river right in front of me."

One of the door gunners uttered a drawn-out, "Right."

"You know what guys, I'll get back to you on that, because I don't even know if it was true myself," Erik said, which brought guffaws all around including himself.

The club manager brought out hot cinnamon rolls and a pot of coffee. Erik told the whole story.

"Man, were you lucky," Taylor said when he had finished.

Everybody laughed when one of the door gunners asked, "How can I meet Lolla?"

"Where there's a will there's a way. Maybe you can look her up when this is all over." Erik didn't bring up the tiger again. Something about it bothered him but he couldn't put his finger on it. "So, what's the latest news?" Erik said.

Taylor said, "Nixon keeps talking about peace with honor. I don't know how he got re-elected. He and Kissinger bomb Cambodia secretly for over a year, and now that country is screwed up. The Cambodians are so pissed at us that they're aligning themselves with the Khmer Rouge, which were nothing before we came along. Nixon ordered a pointless bombing raid on North Vietnam just before Christmas. We lost sixteen B-52s. That's a hundred and sixty guys, for what? The peace accord was about to be signed in Paris, and it changed nothing."

Erik nodded at everything and was frankly surprised at this view by someone in the military. They usually talked about how we were stabbed in the back by the press, or our hands were tied. "Did you ever see the details on that Paris document that's supposed to end this war?" Erik said.

The co-pilot, Walters, said, "I think I can field this one. First of all, everybody knows it's just a piece of paper to get us the hell out and doesn't mean much, but here it is: a ceasefire in place, sixty days for all U.S. troops to leave, both sides have to release their prisoners, the South would negotiate with the Provisional Revolutionary Government—the Viet Cong—to decide their own political future, and Reunification would be carried out step by step through peaceful means."

Taylor said, "That's a laugh seeing as how it's being violated by all sides. Now there's some scandal buzzing around the White House which the newspapers are calling 'Watergate' because of a break-in at the Watergate Building by some guys working for Nixon, I guess. Vietnam is no longer on America's front burner. That's a good thing. We're supposed to leave, I mean us guys, in the next day or so."

"My wife, Thuy, and I are going to stick it out come what may. How bad can it be?" Erik said, wondering if he was just whistling past the graveyard.

Chapter Thirty-four

Erik hitched a ride on the last American convoy going to Saigon with equipment from Da Nang. The United States' diminished role in fighting for the South did not reduce the stockpiling of war materiel at sites being turned over to the ARVN. Erik saw rows and rows of neatly parked tanks that had been off-loaded from a cargo ship, giving an impression that this conflict would last for decades until a stalemate was declared. But, as Thuy said, most of the Vietnamese in the South felt an undertow of inevitability that the spartan, austere North would win, more sooner than later.

In the seats of power in Saigon it was all baubles and showy accoutrement to disguise decadence and corruption. That was Erik's gut reaction the last time he was in Saigon and saw the chrome-helmeted cadre that guarded the Presidential Palace. Even the name denoted a bygone era of colonialism. It left a bitter taste in his mouth that America propped up this government that never had an honest election with a cost of over fifty thousand American lives and billions of dollars.

The convoy of deuce-and-a-halfs followed Highway 1, the only lengthwise trans-country route there ever was in Vietnam, and Qui Nhon was on it. Erik kept track of their progress by the occasional concrete kilometer markers left by the French, which resembled gravestones. How prophetic, he thought.

They pulled into Qui Nhon about 3:00 p.m. after an early morning start. Ten hours to go two hundred miles, such was the slow traffic and numerous villages to go through. The U.S. military hospital and airstrip in the heart of Qui Nhon was on the itinerary so it was very convenient for Erik, since it was only a few blocks from home. But first he used a phone at the hospital to call his boss in Saigon.

"Mr. Coronel, this is Erik Thorvald."

"He leeves! What happened to you? *Et, s'il vous plait,* call me Marcel."

"It's a long story, but I was taken prisoner by some NVA outside of Pleiku."

"Yes, we found zee car and had to pay some puffed-up province chief to get it back."

"*Xin loi* for that, Mr. Cor …, I mean, Marcel, but I'm not surprised. I had to pay him, too. It'll be, ahem, on my expense account."

"*Oui, alors*, we are not going to expand farzair nord until zees whole war gets settled one way or zee ozair. So, my turn to say *je regrette* you had some difficulties, but enough about zat. I'm going to open a plant in Bien Hoa to make anstahnt *café*. I need you to go to Australia to check out zee markets for zat and to see if you can find out anysing about making anstahnt *café*."

"Yes, sir. I look forward to it. I'll get down there as soon as possible, probably by train. *Merci beaucoup pour tout.*"

"*Au revoir.*"

Wow, that went well, Erik thought as he hurried to his apartment with growing excitement. He found the key right where it was supposed to be. He was anxious about his appearance, but did the best he could with his shaggy hair and gaunt visage. Of course she won't care, he assured himself. At least he would be shaved and washed.

He found her walking along a dusty, tree-lined street of narrow stores containing family businesses open to the sidewalk. A tea shop with baguettes here, a store offering black-market sodas and cigarettes there, and a smattering of motorbike repair shops was the typical urban fare. Thuy's head was down, apparently oblivious to the bicycles and motorbikes plying the streets and people walking home from market with their purchases for the evening meal.

"Thuy," Erik called gently a few paces ahead of her.

She stopped and looked up. Her face was a study of emotions from shock, to surprise, to joy, to concern. She ran to Erik and, forgetting about not showing affection in public, she embraced him. They rained kisses on each other like some avian mating ritual. Erik held Thuy in his arms while passers-by looked askance and navigated a quick detour around this exhibition.

"Thuy, Thuy, I was afraid I would never see you again," Erik said.

"Wait," she said, putting her hand to his lips, "me too. We go talk."

They walked side by side with arms around each other's waists to their favorite spot of palm trees bordering a public square next to a beachfront promenade with benches that offered a view of the South China Sea. The evening softened the sharp contrast of white sands and sapphire water, which was almost too exquisite to take during the day. At dusk it was a popular place for couples to stroll or sit on a bench and talk of love while spent waves sighed against the shore. Vendors were part of the scene, but not invasive, and sold drinks of crushed sugar cane or ice cream cones under street lights.

"I missed you so much," Thuy said. "I was so worried. What happened?"

"It was quite a deal, but getting back to you kept me going," Erik said. He told her everything—Doc, Plastic Man, Lolla, Stocky—all of it. He told her about the tiger and the white patches on the back of its ears, his fear, and the deer's look of hopeless defeat. "I don't even know if the whole thing was real," he said.

Thuy sat quietly for a while as though searching for the horizon, now indiscernible in the matching shades of ocean and sky. What she said next amazed Erik for her intelligence, her insight, and the depth of her understanding of him. He often wondered what those eyes behind their lovely black eyelashes saw when focused on something in his merely three-dimensional world. "I think tiger not real. It your father, and deer your sister. You say you alway help Helen. Maybe you do more but you afraid. You say you never be like father who not brave, but you not brave and stand up to father for you and Helen. Maybe you leave but too afraid to live without easy life and money from father."

It was Erik's turn for contemplation. This could very well be, he decided. He remembered Helen's relationship with Harold who, in a way, had her paralyzed with feelings of vulnerability. She had no foundation of love that a father should cultivate as if to say, "You're the one, kid." Harold was cold and self-serving, like a tiger on the hunt. Hmm, and he himself, Erik thought, didn't do much to help her aside from silly machinations that boosted his ego as the boy wonder of action. As Thuy said, he was living the comfortable life without the courage to really effect change by talking to his father. He had had a very easy life compared to Thuy's sleeping on a straw mat in a concrete house with open windows. Her neighborhood had no streets but a network of dirt paths, and no running water. She had to squat in a grove of palm trees to go to the bathroom.

Marie, bless her, embraced Christian Science and died too young. Was she searching for something beyond material comfort provided by Harold? This is a lot to chew on for chrissake, Erik said to himself. He could go on peeling layers of his family's psyche like an onion to what end? But he felt a sense of relief as though a little truth can go a long way toward peace of mind.

"You are amazing, darling Thuy," Erik said with his cheek next to hers. "How was I so lucky to meet you?"

She pushed him back. "It was karma, silly boy."

They walked home intertwined, Thuy with her head nestled against Erik and her arm around his back, and he with his head on hers and arm enfolding her shoulder.

Erik thought about what Thuy said and Vietnamese mysticism. Every house he'd ever seen in Vietnam, no matter how simple, had a Buddhist shrine. It was the one spot, in an otherwise stark decor, that had a bit of finery, such as an embroidered cloth, fancy candle holders with large candles, incense burners, pictures of deceased loved ones in ornate frames, and perhaps a likeness of Buddha in a picture or statuette. Thuy's mother's shrine was like that. A picture of Thuy's father lost at sea was in a prominent place.

"What does karma mean?" Erik said.

"It mean action, deed, and work cause thing happen to you in future. Good in heart mean happiness to come. Bad in heart mean sad life and unlucky," Thuy said.

Hmm, Erik thought: *As ye sew, so shall ye reap.* "You are such a deep thinker. I like karma if it meant I found you."

Thuy laughed. "Karma help you escape, too."

"What do you mean?"

"You think abow it sometime. Not now. Think abow kissing me all over and getting in touch with me in the closest way."

"I am, Thuy. Believe me."

Chapter Thirty-five

Thuy and Erik did not want to start a family. The future was too uncertain. Erik told Thuy about the Paris Peace Agreement of January 1973 and how the established government in the South was supposed to work with the Provisional Revolutionary Government for self-determination. Thuy said that nothing would be done with that as long as Thieu was in power. Now in March of 1975 the *merde* of the Nixon and Kissinger intrigues was hitting the *ventilateur*.

Nixon had resigned from office in disgrace last August in the wake of Watergate. Kissinger had accepted a Nobel Peace Prize for his role in bringing an end to the Vietnam War, but it was only a sleight of hand to end the United States' role in a tragic mistake. Le Duc Tho, Kissinger's North Vietnamese counterpart in negotiations, declined to accept the proffered Nobel Prize. As far as Erik was concerned that spoke volumes about the character of both men. Kissinger was enamored with the trappings of power and recognition as a Secretary of State who engaged in realpolitik. His public persona disguised a ruthless disregard for human lives and a consummate liar. At least Le Duc Tho had the honesty to refuse the prestigious and pecuniary award saying there was no peace in Vietnam until the Reunification was completed.

It wasn't as though Erik lived in a cave. He followed the United States and its players on the world stage. He read *The New York Times* foreign editions, watched BBC programs, and had access to books. In the Nixon impeachment hearings, Kissinger's role in the secret bombing of Cambodia came out. It was prima facie evidence of his playing fast and loose with the truth. Through the CIA, he undermined the legitimate government of Allende, the popularly elected president of Chile, until he was overthrown in a military right-wing power grab. He gave the Indonesian president, Suharto, the green light to annex East Timor after a meeting in Hawaii that included President Ford. The result was a bloodbath of innocent East Timorians.

It was on the Ides of March that Erik felt a heightened level of conversation at market. He could make out something about fighting in Buon Me Thuot. He asked Thuy what they were saying. She said Buon Me Thuot was under attack by soldiers from the North and Pleiku was surrounded.

Thuy and Erik walked home and were shocked to see images plastered on the news of South Vietnamese soldiers and their families, loaded down with possessions, scrambling to get on cargo planes taxiing on runways as they left well-known military bases in Da Nang, Hue, and Pleiku. ARVN soldiers in uniform hanging on skids of departing helicopters appeared cowardly and disgusting as the world looked on. This was the side that America had backed with boundless support in lives and money. As though unable to look away from a train wreck, Erik and Thuy sat transfixed at the spectacle. Widespread panic snowballed in front of the North Vietnamese Army's advance in an all-out offensive to take the South. It was not a commendable sight and confirmed the suspected fragility of ARVN resolve.

Thuy looked concerned. Erik said, "Don't worry. What can they do, send us to Nam?"

Thuy laughed if only for a moment. "Oh, Ay-rik. What will they do to you?"

"Who knows? We'll find out soon enough."

"Yes, we'll find out it will be like Hue in 1968."

"No, I don't think so. They'll be reasonable because they are in a position of power. I think the mass killings in Hue were a case of desperation and bad leadership at the lowest Viet Cong level. My Lai was condoned by U.S. officers all the way up to the divisional level. That wasn't the North's policy," Erik said. "Even the Viet Cong disavowed the massacre saying it was done by fanatical young soldiers. I read a report about it. When it was apparent that they couldn't hold Hue, they began killing witnesses to their crimes. Hue, My Lai, and other excesses were inevitable tragedies that go with war."

In a few days they heard a rumbling through Qui Nhon's streets. Erik and Thuy walked toward the airstrip and were not surprised to see NVA tanks setting up a command post. No shots were fired anywhere that they could hear. Erik was stunned at the short time it took for them to arrive from Pleiku, presumably through the Mang Yang Pass on Route 19.

Erik said, "Let's walk to the beach."

Thuy nodded distractedly.

Walking past shops Erik found the business-as-usual atmosphere odd. Most of the army and their families had already left by any means possible. Where would they go? he wondered. Saigon can't accommodate everybody. The activity around him was reminiscent of when he arrived as a callow GI six years ago. It was the feeling that the American War was not primary in the everyday lives of the people, whose main attention was on their children and eking out a living, confident that this blight of foreigners would go away as they always do. The sellers were blasé, as if to say, "Okay, the North has finally won and we will have Reunification. Buy some mangoes."

Thuy said, "You should go to the American Embassy in Saigon. I will wait for you. You go to United States."

"I'm not leaving you. Everything will be okay. No way I'm going to that madhouse in Saigon," Erik said.

By mid-April, Tan Son Nhut airport was swamped with Americans, some with Vietnamese families, for flights to Clarke Air Force Base in the Philippines. It didn't look like a panic, but more of an organized scramble of officials, both American and Vietnamese, who didn't want to face the music if Saigon collapsed. Erik turned to a BBC channel and saw President Thieu waving a piece of paper in front of the Presidential Palace saying that he had a personal guarantee from President Nixon that the United States would support South Vietnam, and ducking back inside. The cameraman panned to the correspondent who said, "Trouble is, Nixon is no longer president, and Congress is not inclined to support the war anymore. President Ford is not showing any indication of committing any military units to prevent this ignominious end."

In subsequent news bulletins soon after, Erik heard that President Thieu, General Nguyen Cao Ky, and others of high rank in the Republic of South Vietnam were leaving the country on flights from Tan Son Nhut, which was practically surrounded by North Vietnamese forces who launched artillery and rocket attacks on the airfield. One such attack killed two U.S. soldiers involved in the evacuation. Erik reflected that these may be the last Americans to die in the Vietnam War.

It was all over. The North declared victory on April 30, 1975. Two days prior, Tan Son Nhut was no longer able to receive planes for all the damage and debris on the runway. That left the helicopter landing pad on top of the American Embassy as the last resort of escape. Panic ensued as Vietnamese who had supported Thieu and the Americans clamored to be allowed into the embassy compound and to eventually climb the exposed staircase to waiting helicopters. Erik watched with dismay at this final image, knowing there was no way to accommodate everyone who wanted to leave.

On April 29, President Ford ordered Ambassador Martin to be evacuated by force, if necessary, by U.S. marines, to the USS *Blue Ridge*, part of the Seventh Fleet cruising off-shore. The final days had helicopters shuttling back and forth continuously, some of which were from ARVN units and shoved overboard to make room for U.S. helicopters. Once on deck, the ambassador wanted to continue with the evacuation, but was ordered by Washington to cease. On the last day of April, NVA tanks broke through the iron gates of the Presidential Palace in downtown Saigon. Just a few blocks away, a flood of humanity inundated the abandoned American Embassy. Most were lower-level bureaucrats desperate to escape. From the BBC reports it seemed the anguish was intense. What did they know, Erik wondered, or was it a bit over the top? The rest of the milling crowd seemed to be curious onlookers to what was inside the impotent fortress America.

Chapter Thirty-six

Erik wondered about his job, but he couldn't get through to Marcel. Thuy went back to work at Fahasa. Three of the four television channels were off the air. The one channel they got ran continuous loops of old footage about the life of Ho Chi Minh and the glorious people's victory over the disloyal and misguided illegal government of South Vietnam. A general of the army made occasional live feeds with announcements, one of which was that henceforth, immediately, Saigon would now be called Ho Chi Minh City.

Erik thought he would write a letter to his father since he didn't know how long he would have the opportunity to do that. But first he read a copy of what he had written several months before.

November 11, 1974

Dear Dad,

As you can see by the date, I'm writing this on Veterans' Day, or Armistice Day, as it used to be called. It was a day to celebrate the end of a terrible war, a war to end all wars. Of course we found out that wasn't the case. WWII was probably justified, but maybe we'll learn lessons from Vietnam about the futility of wars of choice. People will say all those Americans died for nothing, but I say they actually died for a cause, and that is we can't go around the world trying to force our will on countries we have no business being in. It was an expensive lesson, but the sheer enormity of it will leave a lasting impression.

The real reason for this missive is that I've been doing some thinking, with the help of Thuy, for whom my love grows every day. I had an epiphany that I could have done more to build understanding between you, me, and Helen. In my mind I have been overly critical of you and Doris. There's nothing like

168

hypocrisy to foment baseless loathing, the log in my own eye, as it were. I guess for that wisdom and other truths, such as "He who saves his life will lose it; he who loses his life will save it," is why I consider myself a Christian. Even though I don't believe Jesus was divine, I believe in what He said in the two additional commandments about loving God with all your heart, etc., and loving thy neighbor as thyself. That was about self-respect. He was attuned to the power of the mind and the capacity for goodness in humankind that binds us all together. I suppose one could call it God or a holy spirit, to which I prayed for strength and guidance many times. I have no time for those who make a big show of it, but I do believe in the power of prayer.

Nobody is perfect. Not me or you. When I was in the army I had a lot of time looking into darkness. My mind wandered and of course I thought about home. There were many fond memories and some not so good. When I returned I remember saying to you that there were times that I was disappointed in our relationship and that you were, well, reserved in expressing what I think you might have felt for Helen and me. You said, "Name some specifics." Instead of doing that I jumped at the chance to condemn you for being a callous old man. I should have had the goodness in my heart to start right there and have the courage to express feelings and love unconditionally, and to emphasize the good times we had. That would have been the right thing to do. So, sorry for that and please consider this a new start.

Depending on what transpires here, I would hope that you and Doris and Helen and Bernie and their beautiful little girl could come visit Thuy and me. I can tell you one thing: If there is ever a lasting peace here, there is going to be a string of hotels up and down the coast of Vietnam on the fabulous, extensive, white-sand beaches.

Love,

Erik

When his father wrote back, Erik could see that perhaps Doris was a good influence on him. Men should listen to women more, he posited. Throughout the world are backward countries where men treat women as second-class citizens. Take the Arab countries; discrimination against women is instilled in their culture and they're not too far removed from the Middle Ages. In South America, the banana republics should cut back on the machismo a little and let women have a say. Maybe they wouldn't be so poor for all the money they spend on weapons and a decked-out military. Absolutely no women were involved with decisions about Vietnam. If there were, there might have been more brain and less brawn. Male intellectuals with an army at their disposal are a dangerous combination. Erik shelved his ruminations with, "Ah, well, what do I know?" He re-read his father's letter.

November 19, 1974

Dear Erik,

It was very good to hear from you. I have often wondered how you were getting along. How is work? I hear the coffee prices are going up worldwide.

We are getting ready for Thanksgiving. I talked to Helen and literally begged her to come for a big dinner. I sent plane tickets for the three of them so there could be no excuse for not coming. Doris is dying to see our granddaughter, Magdalena, who is now three years old. Hard to believe.

Your letter was very touching. It opened a place that Doris said I should take into consideration, and that is that perhaps I was a little too locked in to my career. It was such a challenge for me—a Minnesota farm boy making his way into an academia populated by Ivy League, erudite émigrés to the hinterlands for enlightening the unwashed hoi polloi. Thank goodness I was a good student, blessed with some intelligence, and infused with a Norwegian work ethic at a very early age.

Be that as it may, you brought to my attention a period of family bliss highlighted by that time we went ice skating. I forgot the balance of work and time with my children, and, I'm afraid, got too involved in the former for reasons stated above. I'm sorry. But as you said, we can go from here. Indeed, we would love to come and see you and Thuy, who I gather is a remarkable woman.

Please tell me if there is anything I can do in what must be a very unstable situation. Take care of yourself and that lovely wife of yours.

Love,

Dad

Erik was still amazed at "I'm sorry" coming from his father. That just wasn't in his make-up. Life is good, he thought, but wished his mother could be part of it. How she would love Thuy.

Hard pounding on the front door interrupted his daydream. What the hell? He opened the door and his jaw dropped. There stood Doc and five NVA with AKs at port arms.

Chapter Thirty-six

"Doc!" Erik exclaimed.

Doc's look of surprise matched Erik's and then turned to puzzlement. "My name Major Tran. Who Doc? Never mind. You must go to re-education camp. *Moi ban di.*"

Erik said, "*Toi khong muon thé,*" meaning "I'd rather not."

Major Tran laughed and pointed his finger at Erik. "You funny, Thor Vald Ay-Rik. I remember you. I still hap your wallet as souvenir in Ha Noi."

"Good. Maybe I can get it back."

"If you come Ha Noi some time I give to you."

Erik looked up and down his street—more of an alley. He saw other soldiers pounding on doors. "I must leave a note for my wife."

"Okay. You get passport, toilet things, and one change of clothes."

Erik went back inside accompanied by an AK-wielding private. Here we go again, he thought. He dashed off a note to Thuy on the pen and paper lying on the table.

> Darling Thuy,
>
> Soldiers are taking me to a re-education camp. I don't know how long or where. Wait for me. I will love you always. Erik.

He threw a change of clothes, toothbrush, and shaving kit in a small duffle bag and found his passport. Stepping outside he said to Major Tran, "Thank you. I see you got promoted."

Tran motioned him to start walking with a very serious expression as if to say, no funny business, Erik supposed, for the benefit of his squad. In a few minutes he said, "Yes. Promoted. Why not? You think I hap trouble when you escape?"

"Well, yes, actually I did. *Xin loi* about that."

"I hap trouble. When we get to big camp in Lao, Comrade Phuc make accusation against me. He say I let you escape. We have a, a, what you say, court martial?"

Erik nodded. They were heading toward the airstrip. He saw a young American in a run-down neighborhood say goodbye to a young Vietnamese girl whose make-up was running with tears. He guessed he was an AWOL soldier who fell in love with a prostitute. "So you had a court martial?"

"Yes, I tell you later. We hap a lot of time. You will be in a camp up to one year," Tran said.

"Shit! For sure? You've got to be kidding."

"I tell you true. You are lucky. Traitors have re-education for five years in jungle prison. All officers in South puppet army from lieutenant on up hap to go. They should never fight against great patriotic war. So, you see, Americans not as bad as anti-revolutionaries who take up arms against own country. Now be quiet. We talk later."

About fifty foreigners were standing on the tarmac when Erik arrived, mostly Americans. Some were ex-pats in business, like himself, but he saw a lot of what were probably ex-GIs who went native for some reason, probably for the women who fawned over them in hopes of getting married and taken to the States. The AWOLs stood out for their immaturity and scared look. Erik figured that's why they bolted in the first place, that and confusing sex-for-hire with the love of a woman.

A U.S. Army deuce-and-a-half pulled up. Erik looked incredulously at the sight. How much stuff did we leave here? he wondered. Americans with hands bound piled out. "There but for the grace of God go I," Erik whispered. These were the POWs and MIAs. The poor bastards, he thought. He could only imagine what they'd been through. The victors of this whole disaster will use them for all they can get.

Another truck pulled up with a load like the Qui Nhon group, probably from Da Nang. Their captors began making chalk marks on the tarmac, five rows of twenty lines. An American jeep pulled up. A colonel stood on the hood. "You stand at line," he shouted. Soldiers began shoving the bewildered foreigners into formation.

When all was quiet the colonel continued. "You must have re-education for wrong thinking. You work or fight on side of corrupt colonial government. Uncle Ho was a forgiving man. We forgive, but you must change bad ideas. You work, too, for damage you do. We go to Bien Hoa. You will be questioned. You will go on truck for long journey south near Ho Chi Minh City."

A young officer stood at the head of the first line and blew a whistle. He pointed to a truck. The men scuffed along the tarmac dejectedly and crawled aboard the back end of the designated deuce-and-a-half. This whole thing is well organized, Erik conceded, what with the arrivals and timing. Not surprising. They wore down a world power and won a war.

Another American-made jeep pulled up. Major Tran was in the back seat. He surveyed Erik's row filing toward a truck. Erik was about to pull himself onto the tailgate when he heard a shout. It was Tran, who motioned him to his jeep. "Sit in back. We talk on way to Ho Chi Minh City."

The convoy started out. Erik said, "Thanks. Small world, isn't it? Who would have thought our paths would cross again."

"Yes, small world, as you say. You marry Vietnamese woman? Does she work?"

"Yes, she went to university. Works in a book store."

Dodging bicycles and motorbikes on Highway 1, the driver didn't yell "Get outa the way you fucking slope." Even with no U.S. military convoys and ubiquitous helicopters, the countryside still looked the same as when Erik arrived in 1969—impoverished Vietnamese people living in simple farmhouses which dotted flat fields of rice. The harvest season was in full swing.

Women and men in the archetypical black pajamas and conical straw hats cut stalks of rice in the adjacent fields and laid them on the side of the blacktopped highway. As Erik rode along he saw the whole process. On the strewn stalks the harvesters walked back and forth until the grains of rice were loosed. Removing the stalks left rice on the blacktop which they neatly spread out for drying in the sun. From a distance it looked like a golden blanket lying right next to the traffic flow.

Erik was aware that part of the North's appeal to the peasants was land reform which allowed them to work for themselves and not an absentee landowner. It appeared again that the emperor's rule ends at the village gates. They only wanted to grow rice so as not to starve until the next growing season, and raise a family. Erik often observed Vietnamese parents' devotion to their children without fawning over them.

The sun-dried rice was put into burlap containers a little bigger than a golf bag. Erik presumed the stalks were used as silage for water buffalo.

Major Tran began talking again. "Court martial of me because comrade Phuc son of Politburo man. He had to be listened to. He have grudge against me."

"I could see that very clearly," Erik said. "He was obviously jealous of you about Mai."

"Yes, well, he say he allow you to escape. I say he lie. So there was court martial and witness talk. My squad no like Phuc. They all support me. They no like Phuc becaw he not real fighter. He never in important battles. He just a party official with too much privilege. Then Mai talk. She say Phuc not good man. He tried to force himself on her when we stay in that village. Trial say I am innocent of wrongdoing. Phuc sent back to Ha Noi to be Politburo underling. Officers glad to be rid of him."

"That was good of Mai to defend you. Whatever happened to her?"

"I married her. We have child."

Erik laughed. "That's nice. I'm happy for you."

"That why I like you. You help me with Mai, even though that your plan. When you get magnifying glass?"

"That morning in the village when the jet flew over."

"Ah, I thought so when we think back after we find magnifying glass and burned ropes. I think it easy to take C-4."

Erik said, "Just lucky, I guess. I'm glad you came out okay. What's going to happen to all of us in Ho Chi Minh City?"

"You will be kept at Bien Hoa airfield. Some will be allowed to leave. My government will get food aid from your country through back channels becaw Americans will feel guilty about lost souls. We will give most to poor people becaw you make so much damage. Everyone will be interrogated by psychology unit. I can't promise anything. Those who stay will work sometime and sit in class lecture sometime." Tran laughed. "Just like university."

"Maybe I can get out of this. Should I say something in the interrogation? How should I handle it?"

"I don't know. It out of my hands."

Erik leaned back and closed his eyes, grateful for the good fortune to ride in comfort. So, Bien Hoa, he remembered, was where he landed so long ago, and then it was on to Long Binh, that cradle of creature comforts, he thought with a wan smile.

Chapter Thirty-seven

The convoy of captives entered Bien Hoa airfield through a gate in a thick eight-foot-high wall of stucco topped with a coil of barbed wire. Erik observed that the wall encircled an area large enough to contain an asterisk of airstrips so that the far side was a barely visible line. He ruled out trying to escape. He was here for the duration, so let's get it over with, he decided.

"*Bonne chance*," Major Tran said.

"*Merci*," Erik said as he joined a line of dazed conscripts ambling toward a large open-air hangar that accommodated a rectangle of cots, with a blanket each, in neat rows. Some were occupied by a doleful-looking lot in various postures—some sitting and others stretched out with a duffle bag for a pillow.

Erik headed for an empty cot and walked by a man whose head was in his hands. He looked familiar. He stopped to make sure. "Marcel?"

Marcel Coronel looked up. He jumped to his feet. "*Mon dieu*! Erik! I am so glad to see you. I wondered if you might have been swept up in zees band of unfortunates."

"I've been drafted before, so it's no big deal," Erik said. "How are you? I tried to reach you but in the hectic last days it was difficult."

"*Oui. Je comprends*. I guess we no longer have jobs. See zat room? Zat is where interrogations take place."

Erik looked at a windowless, single-door redoubt of concrete blocks in the corner. "Not very cheery-looking. What goes on there?"

"In my meeting two majors *et un colonel* sat at a table facing me on a chair in zee middle of zee room. Next to a wall behind me were two soldiers armed wis a pistol in a holstair. Zair were some papers on zee table. To make a long story short, zay told me to go sink about a choice zay were giving me. Sign my company over to *l'état* or stay in camp for one year. Oh, and here is, as you say, zee kickair: zay cannot guarantee I won't have to sign it over in one year anyway. If I choose to sign zee Coronel Coffee Company over to zem, zay have a plane ticket to Paris waiting for me. Not much of a choice, is it, *mon ami?*"

Erik couldn't help laughing. "I guess they're giving you a deal you can't refuse. I'm really sorry, Mr. Cor ..., er, Marcel. I enjoyed working for you. It's unfortunate that you had just put a lot of money into the instant coffee roasters and extractors."

"Ah, it's okay. *C'est la guerre.* My loss is nossing compared to my friend and his son who owned zee Rex Hotel. Zay are gone already. Zay are fellow Frenchmen who were given zee same choice. So, now, zee so-called Democratic Republic of Vietnam is in zee hotel business, one of zee best hotels in Saigon. Many of your newspapermen stay zair during zee war."

"What will you do in France?" Erik said.

"I will start somesing else, I guess. I have put a little money in a Swiss bank account, but not as much as Thieu and his cabal of mountebanks. I will miss zee warm winters here and, *c'est vrai*, a colonial life."

In another corner Erik saw a latrine with no doors. Outside the hangar a company of NVA was setting up a perimeter of security. In the far corner sat a chalkboard in front of about a hundred chairs. Opposite that, by the looks of it, was a field kitchen for dispensing food. "They've got it all figured out," Erik said.

A thin and very tired-looking middle-aged man in jungle fatigues sat on a cot across an aisle. Any rank insignia was torn from his uniform. "The bastards," he said. "I suppose I was reported missing in action in Cambodia in 1972, so I wasn't officially a POW. They will acknowledge me when it suits them. The name's Boyer. I was a helicopter pilot that went down. My co-pilot and I survived, but he died in captivity and they buried him."

A shrill whistle pierced the hum of desultory voices in the sprawling facility that once held jet fighters. "Stand by your cots," an officer shouted. "You will be inspected for contraband."

"Zay are going to take away all writing materials," Marcel said.

"Crap," Erik said. "I was going to try to smuggle a note out or something about what's going on. I have no idea how or to whom." Grabbing one of the ballpoint pens in his duffle bag, he took it apart and stuck the flexible innards with the writing tip in his mouth, bending it around the teeth under his lower lip. He stomped the rest of the pen into little pieces and scattered them around the floor.

Marcel was right. An entourage of cadre systematically walked down the aisles taking passports, notebooks, pens, pencils, magazines, books and billfolds.

When they got to Erik one of the officers said, "Do you have passport?" Erik managed a "Yes, sir" and pulled it out of his pocket.

"Your arms, up." Erik was patted down while another soldier checked his bag, cot, and blanket. They took his billfold. "Personal items will be returned to you at correct time. Do you have any other contraband?" the officer asked while looking into Erik's eyes.

Erik mumbled, "No, sir," hoping the ballpoint wasn't poking into his cheeks. He had a sudden urge to laugh at this absurdity in front of the officer's inquisitive gaze. He bit his tongue to maintain a solemn bearing. The officer peered at him again, shook his head, and moved on. Whew, thought Erik, the guy probably thought this pathetic specimen was uncomfortable in his presence, the conquering soldier.

It took all afternoon to shake down the rest of the rank and file of captives. At least they allowed those who had been inspected to lie on their cots. This is hell, Erik thought as he stared at the roof of some kind of corrugated metal, olive drab in color. Where did the F-105s go? he wondered. They're probably over at Tan Son Nhut, and, no doubt, one or two will end up in a war museum with all the best high-tech military equipment in the world. His stomach growled.

Erik's hope that food was on the agenda was answered with a whistle and unintelligible commands that somebody figured out meant move to the mess corner. While standing in line Erik counted the cots, which came to six rows of twelve. So, he thought, we've got about seventy-two poor bastards here, some of whom will be leaving, like Marcel.

After everybody chowed down on a ball of rice and a cup of water, which they ate in the classroom area, they were herded back to their cots. Erik saw a guard outside the latrine, and, of course a line, which Erik joined to relieve himself. There were three open stalls, three urinals, and the same number of sinks. He went into a stall and was pleased to see that his captors allowed toilet paper. It was, just as he thought, not very soft and could be written on.

Returning to his cot he noticed a senior officer-type moving among the cots and talking to groups. When he got to Marcel, Boyer, and Erik he said, "I'm Lieutenant Colonel Olivetti. I was advising ARVNs around Ban Me Thuot when I was captured in March. I was caught with my pants down—literally. I was using the shitter when the NVA swept through our compound. So I'm one of their recent acquisitions. Anyway, we've got to get organized to make the best of this situation until such time something gets done to get us the hell out of here. So, I've designated numbers for each row. You two guys are in row four." Addressing Boyer, "You're in row five. To alleviate a jam at the latrine before lights out, we'll go one row at a time to piss, shit, brush our teeth, body wash, and the like. Same in the morning for shaving, and so on."

"Lieutenant Colonel Olivetti, I'm Erik Thorvald, civilian. I'm glad you're here. I wanted to talk to somebody about getting the names of you MIAs, like Boyer here, and write them down on a piece of toilet paper. I hid a ballpoint during the shake down."

"Good man." He looked at the floor for a moment. "Here's what I'll do. I'll tell all the MIAs to get over to you sometime and give their info. How are you going to do it?"

"I'll put a square of TP on the floor and lie down. With my right arm over the edge I'll write down names like this." Erik stretched out on the cot and put a flimsy piece of paper on the polished concrete. "What's your name and service number," he said without lifting his head.

As though he were talking to Boyer, he rattled off, "Lieutenant Colonel Anthony Olivetti, 354 45 1622."

Erik wrote it down and the same for Boyer, the first two names of what he guessed were about thirty Americans missing in action.

The screech of a whistle indicated an announcement. One of the officers stood on an empty wooden ammo box. "In honor of Ho Chi Minh birthday, since you are cooperating, we are rifting the ban on books, but no decadent Western magazines. For reasons of happiness in re-education, praying cards and chess game okay. In mess area you get books recovered from retreating imperialist army, but approved by Ministry of Education."

Among the books Erik saw *The Grapes of Wrath*, which he'd read, so he picked *Giap, Young Scholar*. It was either that or *101 Uses for Bamboo*.

Chapter Thirty-eight

The food improved. Apparently the keepers of this little experiment to enlighten the capitalist lackeys wanted to appear magnanimous in their victory. They also probably wanted to avoid emaciated captives if and when the Red Cross should visit with neutral-country officials. Erik was aware that he and the others were but wallflowers at a diplomatic dance. Obviously, the Vietnamese were posturing as self-righteous victims who had suffered the onslaught of American aggression and were doing whatever the hell they wanted.

Everyone got their billfolds back so it was possible to buy cigarettes from guards at exorbitant prices. The hapless internees could smoke if they went outside the hangar at various stations near a bucket of sand. IDs and cards were missing from the returned billfolds, presumably to be used in interrogations.

After breakfast, which was usually *pho*, the national soup of chicken or beef broth with rice noodles, everyone had to police up the area of cigarette butts and wash dishes and pots and pans in the mess area. Lieutenant Colonel Olivetti organized details for those tasks on a rotating basis.

The rest of the mornings were spent on work details. At first they stayed in the airfield pulling weeds, sweeping, and mowing grass with a push mower. After a few days the group was marched to government buildings, such as the post office, in Bien Hoa to do yard maintenance and scrape peeling paint in readiness for painting. All the official buildings were concrete and sometimes stucco painted pale yellow. If the internees felt as Erik did, working outside, despite the intense heat in the sun, was much preferred to enduring the re-education classes in the afternoons.

*   *   *

Erik was struggling to stay awake. The instructor was droning on in broken English about the life of Ho Chi Minh. He was born in rural Vietnam in 1890 during the French colonial period. His father was a Confucian scholar, but Ho had yearnings way beyond his simple rural—*WHAP*—setting. Some poor attendee had nodded off and was smacked somewhere on his head or body with a two-foot length of rubber hose. Ho had traveled the world as a cabin boy, and, while attending a meeting—*WHAP*—of communists in Paris, he immediately adopted their doctrine because one of its canons was the abolition of colonialism.

The lecturer was entertaining only to the extent that every heavily accented sentence was a puzzle that required decoding. Erik just deciphered something about communism being the best form of government because the power is in the people.

Bull! He had to ask a question to fight his sleepiness. He raised his hand. Colonel Pham reluctantly acknowledged him.

"If communism is so great, how do you explain the poor economy of the Soviet Union? Party members at the top have privileges way beyond *the people,* as you say. Basic needs of *the people* are met with long lines every day. Hot water is a rarity in hotels. Waiters at restaurants are rude because they have no incentive to make customers happy. Five-year plans stretch into decades. Famines have—"—*WHAP*. That was the end of questions.

Sonovabitch! Erik vowed to get off square one and obtain a Get Out of Jail Free card. In the last few days he had accumulated twenty-eight names of MIAs and three AWOLs. He pondered what to do with the information. The names were rolled up in several sheets of toilet paper.

The colonel finished his lecture by saying that the assembled guests of his government before him were a form of reparations. Therefore, they owed the Democratic Republic of Vietnam a great deal of labor. Tomorrow, work was to begin on the destruction of the old American Embassy, the symbol of a degenerate, failed system. "You will dismantle everything metal within the building and carry it outside. It will be melted down and forged into statues of heroic fighters and memorials to Ho Chi Minh. When all is empty, the building will be exproded into rubble."

This news, at least, began to plant a seed of an idea as to what Erik might do.

In the evening before lights out, Erik filled out some more sheets of toilet paper.

> PLEASE GO TO
> NORWEGIAN EMBASSY WITH
> ENCLOSED AMERICAN POW/MIAs.

PLEASE FORWARD INFO TO
THE HONORABLE DAVID N. LEVY,
U.S. CONGRESS, WASHINGTON, D.C.
USA.

PLEASE CALL
THUY THORVALD,
FAHASA, QUI NHON,
BINH DINH. ERIK THORVALD
OK IN BIEN HOA.

Damn! Erik thought, he should have given something to Marcel before he left. Oh, well, he didn't have all the names at that time and Marcel would have been thoroughly searched anyway. Whom could he trust? Maybe tomorrow morning at the embassy will provide an opportunity.

After a thirty-minute ride, three deuce-and-a-half trucks pulled up to the compound wall that encircled the abandoned American Embassy. A jeep full of armed NVA led the convoy and similar jeeps followed each truck.

Officers shouted into the green-canopied darkness, "Everyone to get out."

Halfhearted compliance eventually brought the work detail out on the street. A whistle blew and the men fell into a single file with a lot of prodding by AK rifle butts. Onlookers had gathered across the street on the sidewalk and were chattering among themselves at the sight of rag-tag Westerners toeing the line of submission, apparently a "man bites dog" moment. Another whistle and the file began shuffling toward the main gate. That's when Erik thought he heard his name. "Ay-rik." He heard it again. He turned to see a lot of black-haired people across the street. Then his eyes fell on a serene young woman in a pearl-colored *ao dai.*

"Thuy," he said softly. He looked to the front and then smiled back at her. He nodded his head and reached in his pocket and extracted the rolled up paper he had sealed with toothpaste to look like a cigarette. Giving Thuy a glimpse of it, he flung it as hard as he could behind his back. In one last glance he saw it roll into the middle of the street.

Inside the compound the workers were divided by truck into three teams. The first one was told to haul out file cabinets, detach banisters, and grab onto anything metallic and dump it outside. Another team was given a thick 100-foot rope, hacksaws, wrenches, and pliers and directed to the roof. The third team stayed outside to gather the discarded junk and load it on a semi-trailer made in the USA.

When Erik's team reached the roof they were instructed to dismantle the steel stairway and railing which led to the helicopter landing pad atop the elevator-shaft housing. High-ranking Vietnamese and their families had mobbed it to board overworked Huey helicopters during the fall of Saigon. Erik was aware that pictures of this debacle drove certain Americans crazy with humiliation. Erik started unscrewing bolts and supposed those were the people who said we could have won if our hands hadn't been tied by the politicians. Another favored excuse was that if the press hadn't been a bunch of defeatists things would have been different.

What myths they hang on to, Erik lamented, to make themselves feel better about an unfortunate fiasco. His thoughts quickly turned to Thuy. Seeing her was a balm from Gilead. It would keep him going for weeks. He worried that she might not have picked up the messages.

With twenty pairs of hands their task was completed before lunch. When some of his co-workers tied the rope to the unattached staircase, Erik dared to saunter and look down from the twelve-story edifice. He didn't see Thuy. The traffic in the street had returned to normal—a commotion of bicycles and motorbikes.

The officer in charge said, "We keep stairway as souvenir of Reunification. Everyone to pick up and take to edge."

The guards grabbed the rope as their charges hefted the stairs and shuffled toward the edge of the building, and balanced their load on the edge. Erik and the others grabbed the rope and slowly played it out as the symbolic end of an era descended from its majestic heights.

"Now you eat," the officer in charge said.

Munching on a ball of rice in the compound Erik mulled over possibilities. If Thuy picked up the names and got them to an embassy, the wheels of diplomatic maneuverings could be slow to get out of first gear, but he might see some action. He knew there was much gnashing of teeth back in the States about Americans missing in action and prisoners of war. Rightfully so. The Vietnamese weren't living up to the Paris Accord. He guessed they had several other camps out in the wild. He recalled reading in Bernard Fall that many French prisoners were kept for sixteen years after Dien Bien Phu. The group he was in was probably meant to be a showcase for the benefit of citizens in the upstart Saigon. Maybe if something was done about the MIAs, attention would be brought to bear on the rest of the captives.

A jet airliner passed overhead in a slow descent. No doubt landing at Tan Son Nhut, which reminded Erik how some of the internees were allowed to leave, like Marcel, if the Vietnamese got something out of them. What did he have to offer? Not much. The more he thought about it he realized their captors were achieving plenty from this sorry lot. They were benefiting from work, food aid, and self-aggrandizing propaganda. That's why they picked the embassy, for its high visibility.

Boyer said, "I can't take much more of this. I felt like jumping off the roof."

"No!" Erik said urgently. "Don't even think about it. Help is coming."

"What do you know?"

"Just believe me. It might take some time, but your name is on a list and our government is going to know about it." Erik hoped it was working out that way. If he knew Thuy, she would come through.

"I suppose we'll have to endure more of that shit out on the street every time we come here. It's demeaning," Boyer said.

"Yeah, I know. Just pretend you're in a movie. The merciless, inscrutable Asians have the upper hand, but the final reel is yet to come."

Boyer grinned. "Yeah," he said with a wild gleam in his eye.

Erik felt Boyer was close to losing it after three years in captivity. He turned to Andrews, who occupied a nearby cot in the hangar. "So, how did you get captured?"

"In 1971 I was in the 194th MP Company, kind of a misnomer because it was actually an infantry unit," Andrews said. "We were all eleven-B. Our company had platoons protecting remote signal sites, you know, line-of-sight microwave, UHF, and VHF for communication up and down South Vietnam. On a night ambush between Qui Nhon and Anh Khe I got separated from my squad somehow, still don't know how, but I was smoking a lot of dope. I woke up the next morning to five Viet Cong poking me with their AK-47s."

The whistle blew. The three of them groaned. "Back to work, I guess, but at least we don't have to sit in that goddamn class," Erik said.

Chapter Thirty-nine

After evening chow the colonel announced from his ammo box podium that, since the internees finished the first stage of the embassy demolition over the last three weeks, they would receive a Snickers candy bar. And, starting tomorrow, the interviews would continue. The captives would have days off until they were completed.

Make that interrogations, Erik thought. And where's the rest of the food aid? He saw a lot of the soldiers outside the hangar barely able to contain their excitement about something in the boxes they gathered around. Now he knew.

"Thor Vald Ay-Rik." Erik was summoned. He got up from his cot and walked to the corner office. He entered an austere room and stood in front of a table occupied by three NVA officers. A GE air conditioner in the wall made it tolerable. Otherwise it'd be an oven, Erik figured.

The senior officer, Colonel Pham, said, "Sit down."

Erik sat in a single chair in the middle of the room. Marcel was right—two guards stood at the back wall. Be cool, be conversational, not antagonistic, Erik counseled himself.

"Did you ever take arms against the Democratic Republic of Vietnam?" the senior officer asked.

Erik decided to be truthful. They probably had some facts about him in front of them. "Yes, I was a soldier in 1969."

"That is correct. We see that you were in the Twenty-fifth Division."

"Yes, I was. How did you know that?"

"We ask questions, not you," the colonel said. "What you do in the Twenty-fifth Division?"

"I was in a recon platoon. We went on patrols to get information." Erik guessed they had his résumé from the embassy when he first applied for work in Vietnam.

"Why you fight against Vietnam independence?" one of the majors asked.

"I was drafted into the army. There wasn't a lot of choice."

The other major jumped in. "Why you not go to Canada? Why you not refuse to go in army?"

"I didn't have the courage of my convictions. Believe it or not, I was not in favor of going to war in Vietnam. Also, I have to admit that I saw a lot of WWII movies as a kid and fell for the call-to-arms as a rite of passage."

The second major asked, "Why you not leave Vietnam when our glorious freedom-fighters crush traitors to the revolution?"

"For the love of a woman. I married her and she refuses to leave. I like Vietnam. I think it has a lot of potential if you allow development of a commercial class, something the French never did in their exploitation of your country."

"Ho Chi Minh say communism best for people," the first major said.

"Yes, I know you idolize Ho Chi Minh in everything. Just like the Chinese always followed the way of Confucius, but Confucius knew nothing of modern developments and eventually China was a backward country which the world passed by," Erik said.

Colonel Pham said, "We are not your students, and you are not history professor." The two majors laughed. He continued, "We have a message from Hanoi that has all the names of American soldiers in Bien Hoa group. They say Norwegian embassy gave list to Politburo from America. America want release of prisoners of war. We think you do this. You get information out."

"With all due respect, I think maybe you say that to every captive and judge their reactions."

"Did you smuggle out list?" Colonel Pham said, looking steadily into Erik's eyes.

Jeesh, this guy could get more confessions than Perry Mason, Erik thought. "In our country it is written in the Constitution that no one has to testify against himself. It's called the Fifth Amendment."

"In our country that mean guilt," the second major said.

"Why don't you follow the Paris Accord which said to release all prisoners of war?" Erik said.

Colonel Pham smiled. "Your country never declare war on Vietnam, so your friends are not prisoners of war."

Clever answer, Erik allowed, but managed to say, "A rose by any other name is still a rose. Not declaring war shows the character of our Congress. They went along with a resolution instead of voting on a declaration of war, as the U.S. Constitution requires. It may have been voted down, and Johnson knew that. Anyway it's too complex to take up your time. It has to do with precedence by Truman in Korea." That's it, Erik, he said to himself, just bore them to death.

"It seems your great Constitution is followed sometimes, and sometimes not," Colonel Pham said.

Erik decided not to take the bait and argue. Let them feel superior, and don't kid yourself, Colonel Pham is, he admitted to himself. He sat quietly. No one talked as the three Asians steadily observed him. The drone of the air conditioner was more noticeable in the lack of dialogue. Erik recited a mantra to himself that Thuy taught him for meditation and met their gaze.

After what seemed like several minutes, Colonel Pham said calmly, "We know it was you who made list and smuggle out."

"Oh?"

"A congressman from United States sent a letter to First Secretary Le Duan," Colonel Pham said. "He asked for release of listed prisoners of war and missing soldiers. Besides all names of captive soldiers, your name was the only one written who was a civilian. We know it was you."

"Okay, I admit it. Can I ask the name of the congressman?"

"His name David Levy. How did you smuggle out names?"

"Um, I promise I will tell you, but if it pleases you, could I know the contents of the letter?"

The two majors looked at Colonel Pham. Clearing his throat, the colonel said, "Congressman Levy say he would like American soldiers to be released. If not, he will request that Red Cross visit and inspect their welfare. As to you, he asked that you be released and he will urge his Foreign Relations committee not to block Vietnam's entry into the United Nations as a way to begin the long road to restoring relations between our countries. He also say as gesture of good faith, he is sending food aid."

Bless David Levy, Erik thought. He was so smart and always a loyal friend—the deepest kind forged only in the crucible of fighting for each other. "Thank you for that, Colonel. Here's how I did it." Erik proceeded to tell how he got the names and tossed the cigarette-shaped list, but left out the part about Thuy, instead saying he threw it toward what looked like a Western diplomat.

"The Politburo would not like bad photographs of Red Cross visiting prisoners. They will be released. They have served their purpose. As to you, we see you used to work for Coronel Coffee Company, which is now operated by our Ministry of Agriculture. They have trouble understanding directions of new equipment installation for making instant coffee. Since you have indicated a desire to stay in Vietnam, and you have been truthful, and, of course, a United States Congressman has talked about our entry into the United Nations, we are releasing you to the Agriculture Ministry and the Vinacafé Company for any future arrangements. They will send a car over tomorrow."

Thank God, Erik thought. He could hardly contain his elation. "Thank you, Colonel. Thank you very much." He paused. "I was wondering, sir, what will happen to the rest of the internees?"

"It will be decided at appropriate time."

"Do you believe in fate, in chance, the magic of crazy luck?" Erik asked the colonel conversationally, now that he felt a level of mutual respect had been gained.

Pham seemed curious. "It is possible. Why?"

"If I pick a number out of thin air and write it on a slip of paper, fold it up, and set it aside, and you and the majors think of a three-digit number, let's say between 100 and 900, and I will think of a couple of numbers so that we have five 3-digit numbers in a column that we all chose. If the sum of that column equals exactly the number I wrote down on the slip of paper, would you let the other captives go?"

Colonel Pham laughed. "That would be unbelievable luck. Okay, here's a clipboard."

Erik asked a major, "What is your number to see if you got the right idea?"

"Four zero one."

"Good. I'll write my prediction." Erik tore off a piece from the bottom of the paper and wrote 2,399, folded it a couple of times, and tossed it on the table.

"What is your number please, Colonel?"

"Five two eight."

Erik wrote it down and said, "My number is four seven one," and entered it in the column. Turning to the other major, "What's yours?"

"Six three seven," which Erik added to the list.

"For the fifth number I'm picking three six two." He laid the clipboard on the desk.

The column of numbers looked like this:

        401
        528
        471
        637
        <u>362</u>

"Would someone care to add these up?" Eric said.

Colonel Pham said, "Major?" which the junior officer took as a command and added up the numbers.

When finished he stated, "Two thousand three hundred ninety-nine."

His fellow officer reached for the folded piece of paper, looked at it, and broke into a sweat, his eyes wide.

The colonel said, "Well?"

"Two thousand three hundred ninety-nine."

The senior officer grabbed the piece of paper and stared at the number.

Erik said, "With your permission, Colonel, I should go."

Pham waved his hand in dismissal as he looked back and forth at the prediction and the list of addends. He appeared to weigh how it was done because nobody is that lucky.

Erik walked out knowing Colonel Pham was smart and might figure it out. At any rate he hoped the colonel would at least be amused and honor his end of the bargain. By the time he reached his cot he had considered how most Southeast Asians believe in ghosts and some are notorious gamblers who court Lady Luck, so maybe he'll accept it as some kind of wild, howlish coincidence.

Chapter Forty

Erik resumed working in the coffee business with Vinacafé. He told Thuy he hoped he would work there for a long time, unlike the American who got a job with an orange juice company and soon got fired because he couldn't concentrate. She thought that was too bad. Erik explained the pun and she laughed with spontaneous, infectious charm.

Erik opened accounts in the Australian market for instant coffee with bargain prices thanks to low manufacturing and labor costs. Sure, he felt bad for Marcel, but such are the fortunes of war. He reasoned that the French colonials had exploited this part of the world for seventy years. Now it was turn-around time. The Vietnamese benefited by Marcel's investment, and of course, so did Erik, he admitted. His enthusiasm and straightforward approach earned accounts in major hotels as he convinced management that instant coffee packets in every room is an amenity that customers would enjoy and remember.

Each decade had brought more hotels on the most beautiful beaches in the world. Soon, Australian tourists flocked to enjoy package deals on charter busses from Ho Chi Minh City to Hanoi, stopping along the way for surf and sun and a little history at Nha Trang, Qui Nhon, Hoi An, Da Nang, Hue, the old DMZ, and into the former North Vietnam. How those places tripped memories of intense fighting, Erik thought, but now, according to the few Americans who came back to travel, the Vietnamese have put the war behind them and hold no animosity against them. As the manager of one of the hotels, whose name was Huong and with whom Erik became friends, told him, "Let bygones be bygones."

Some of the hotels were government owned. Several high-rise luxury hotels in the cities were built by Japanese or Chinese investments, and some were privately owned by Vietnamese businessmen. Private enterprise made inroads into the economy, especially for those in power, who made huge profits. Huong told how his hotel was the result of under-the-table wheeling and dealing by a top government official in the Communist Party.

"How did he do it?" Erik asked.

"When my boss was in the Politburo he knew Vietnam was going to place an embargo on Japanese electronics, so he bought millions of dollars' worth of televisions, VCRs, and you name it, on credit from Japan. When the embargo went into effect, he had warehouses full of this stuff which he sold all over Vietnam and made profits beyond the wildest dreams of most Vietnamese." Huong's salary now, thirty years after the war, was the equivalent of $400 per month, but way above the average worker's income of about $100 per month, or two million VND (Vietnam dong).

Erik laughed. "Once upon a time, conservative Americans trembled at the thought of a Communist Vietnam. They pressured Johnson and the military into a war, and the public bought into it."

"Yes, we never understood why you come so far to fight us. We were always one Vietnam, not South Vietnam and North Vietnam," Huong said. His English was excellent from his student days in Australia.

"Power corrupts, absolute power corrupts absolutely," Erik recited the well-known quote by Lord Acton.

"Oh, yes. It is widespread. When officials know where a new road will be built, they buy up land at cheap prices from simple, poor people who aren't in the know and make a killing," Huong said.

Erik was reminded of *1984*. The Party seeks power entirely for its own sake. "So much for caring about the people," Erik said. "At least the Central Committee recognized the failure of collectivizing all the farms."

"That's right. Le Duan lost all credibility when rice production was very bad in several five-year plans of pure communism," Huong said. "There has to be some reward for working harder than the next guy and benefiting from it. Otherwise the peasants will do the bare minimum. Now the government allows some land ownership and small private businesses."

Since he was in Da Nang, Erik decided to play golf at the course south of the city, one of the few in the whole country. He drove through miles and miles of urban blight and abject poverty the farther he got from modern downtown Da Nang. Marble Mountain loomed on the right with numerous shops in its shadow displaying objects sculpted from the mountain's pure white marble into statues of Buddha and other Eastern themes. The mountain itself was honeycombed with caves that once hid Viet Cong and North Vietnamese regulars and even a hospital that was a par-five away from a marine base camp during the American War.

Turning into the Da Nang Golf Club, designed by Greg Norman, was as if a light of affluence had been switched on. The manicured fairways were lined with expensive homes of Korean businessmen and their families. They made up half the club membership to escape the brutal winters at home. The rest were wealthy Japanese and Chinese with a sprinkling of Vietnamese party officials and high-ranking army officers.

The only other Vietnamese were waitresses, bartenders, groundskeepers, female caddies, and desk clerks, one of whom was very forthcoming with information. Erik played the front nine, sometimes overlooking the South China Sea. On Vietnamese maps it's labeled the East Vietnam Sea. The dislike, nay, hatred for China by the Vietnamese was evident in conversations and newspaper articles about trade disputes of one kind or another, which led Erik to wonder, what was that war about again? The cost for nine holes was one million VND, the equivalent of fifty American dollars. He tipped the caddie, who really knew her distances, one hundred thousand VND, or five USD. Tips were the caddies' only compensation.

Driving back to Qui Nhon Erik couldn't get over the sacrifices made by the Vietnamese people in their struggle for independence, only to be owned by foreigners. If it lifted all boats, fine, but Erik hadn't seen it yet. The gap appeared to be widening. He wanted to pay the coffee pickers more, but the CEO couldn't see it. Erik's income, based on commissions and a small profit-sharing arrangement, was comfortable at fifty million VND per month, or twenty-five hundred USD. Most of the native population couldn't dream of playing golf or traveling abroad. First of all they couldn't afford it, and secondly, the government did not grant visas in their tight control of the populace.

The funny thing is, everybody is happy. The university graduates who live in cities work in offices, hotels, banks, retail stores, schools, and hospitals for about four million VND per month, or two hundred USD. The less educated are fishermen, cleaners, cooks, odd-jobbers, motorbike repairers, drivers, farmers, and construction workers for about half the income. In the small villages they own their homes of simple concrete structures along rudimentary streets. Those who work in the cities pay anywhere from twenty-five to one hundred USD to rent an apartment. Erik had paid one hundred USD for a fairly spacious apartment when he and Thuy raised their two children until he saved enough to build a home along the coast of Qui Nhon.

One term in the communist dogma that Erik thought was spot-on was "proletariat," meaning the mass of people whose only wealth was their children. That was the case in Vietnam where the value of material possessions was secondary to the primary importance of family. In the humblest of surroundings and little accumulated wealth, the Vietnamese loved their children and spent a great deal of time with them, a practice not lost on Erik, who felt he and Helen were raised in emotional austerity when they moved from Gainesboro. Maybe that was a Scandinavian thing, but certainly not a Vietnamese habit.

Every day when Erik was home, he and Thuy played with Kai and Natalie. They accompanied them on walks on the beach or watched them play in the sand. They went on bike rides and hiked to interesting places, such as Vung Chua Mountain which overlooked Qui Nhon when it wasn't shrouded in clouds. It was once a U.S. Army communications base. They walked on abandoned concrete slabs that once held barracks or signal equipment. The wind moaned through some trees that had reclaimed the mountain as though ghosts were searching for peace from a violent death in a monsoon fog. The older generation in Qui Nhon talked of a time when Viet Cong overran the site and both sides suffered casualties and KIAs. Erik felt the fear. He wondered if he wasn't going native by believing in wandering spirits.

It was a long drive from Da Nang to Qui Nhon. Erik was covering a lot of miles, and time, too. He chuckled at the memory of finally getting through to David in Washington after he was released from the re-education camp.

"David, this is Erik."

"Erik! So, the student has graduated or are you on spring break?" David said.

"Ha, ha. Pardon me if I laugh," Erik said. "I can't thank you enough. Now we're even."

"Even?"

"Yeah, you know, I got you through Vietnam, and all."

"My turn to laugh, you reprobate. How is Thuy?"

"Fine. And your family?"

"The boys love Washington and Aviva is working in the Department of the Interior on a Jewish memorial of the Holocaust, so we have had some interesting discussions. If we come to Vietnam can you show us around?"

"Absolutely. I hope you will come. Again, I don't know how you did it, but I've been sprung and now work for my old company, under new management, of course."

"It was nothing. Just don't tell anybody *everything* we did during that fucked-up war."

"So, you're running for senator or something?"

"Ha, ha. You never know."

"David, it is great talking to you. I know you're busy. I'll say goodbye until we meet sometime. Again, thank you. You are tops!"

"Don't mean nothin'," David laughed. "See you, Shrap."

*   *   *

Erik wondered how much David had to do with Vietnam's acceptance into the U.N. It was just a couple of years later that they were admitted, in 1977. Full diplomatic relations were established in 1995. The old high-rise American Embassy fortress in Saigon was replaced on the same spot by a friendly single-story consulate of forest green and beige in a very inviting compound. Funny, he thought, how that stairway we tore down ended up in the Gerald Ford Presidential Library in Michigan.

He read in the newspaper that the former Colonel Pham retired from the Central Committee but remained in the General Assembly as a senior member with venerated status as a fighter in the Reunification. Erik figured he was destined for higher office. He was surprised when Pham released the other internees a week after him. It was probably because they had provided enough propaganda pictures, but he wondered if it was because of the deal he made with the colonel. He wanted to think so, but he never did learn if he figured out the trick.

One of these days, if he ever expanded into the Hanoi market, he planned to look up Doc, probably a general by now, and get his billfold back. He wondered how many children he and Lolla, that is, Mai, had.

A few years before he died Harold bought plane tickets to Vietnam for everybody in his stateside family. Erik took them on a tour, including part of the Ho Chi Minh Trail where he once trekked with a cast of characters he would never forget. Bernie was ecstatic to be on the hallowed ground that allowed Marxist insurgents to stick it to the capitalist man.

They visited the popular tunnels of Cu Chi. Even the octogenarian Harold and Doris were game enough to crawl through a small section made available for tourists. Thuy was the right size and made it easily. An afternoon at the War Remnants Museum in Ho Chi Minh City left them all a little depressed at the portrayal of needless American involvement in Vietnam's history. The weapons on display throughout the grounds, from F-105 jets to helicopters, were grim reminders of the high-tech war unleashed on a tenacious foe.

In sidewalk cafés, Helen was funny with erudite witticisms and obviously delighted with her two children. She loved Bernie even if he was an eccentric philosopher who never quite left the '60s. What struck Erik the most was how his father was so animated and engaging with his four grandchildren. It warmed his heart. Doris and Thuy really hit it off and became pen pals.

When Harold died at age 90, Erik took his family back to America for the funeral. On a side trip to Gainesboro, he was surprised that no kids were playing outside, and it was a beautiful summer day. That was unheard of, Erik explained, when he lived there. All the stores downtown were empty save for a bank, a post office, and a convenience store where

Freddie's Standard used to be. He drove out of town a few miles and showed his family some connected ponds in a secluded valley. "What's this?" they asked. Erik said he would tell them about it sometime.

When Doris wrote in a letter to Thuy that she was dying, Erik said he didn't think they could go to her funeral. Thuy told him that he must go. Doris, having no children, named him executor of her estate. They arrived in time to tie up loose ends and be with her when she passed. Naturally, Thuy was correct. Erik was glad he went to do right by his late father's wife, although longing for his real mother. Life is interesting, he decided, and full of surprises without a master plan that he could figure out, except maybe: Don't count the years, make the years count.

Erik pulled into the carport. He got out and stretched. A glow on the eastern horizon reminded him of last night. He and Thuy had sat transfixed for about fifteen minutes while an orange corona set the stage over the South China Sea for the sudden appearance of a rising full moon. It was a breathtaking demonstration of the Earth spinning on its axis. He stood for a moment and listened to gentle waves that had probably lulled Thuy to sleep on the veranda. Yes, that's it, he thought, make the years count.

Chapter Forty-one

Thuy arrived from market. Natalie's thumbs were doing a tap dance on her mobile phone. "Did you practice?" Thuy asked.

"Mmmm," Natalie said without looking up.

"Natalie, I said did you practice your violin?"

"Hmm? Oh, yes, I just did it." She looked at her phone and Erik could see her blush from across the room.

Erik sighed. She's obviously texting that boy who's a desk clerk at the Sea Gull Hotel. He has potential, allowed Erik, as a graduate of Saigon University in business. He shook his head, thinking about those smartphones that everybody had, well, the young ones anyway. Kai often called him on his as though he sought his advice. "He's a better kid than I was at that age," Erik said softly.

Thuy walked out onto the veranda. "Hello, dear. Did you say something?" she said.

Her sweet voice still tripped affectionate responses in Erik's feelings for her. "Hi, honey," he said. "Come sit," he patted the space on the settee next to him. She wore her *ao dai*, as usual, since she was the manager. "How was work?"

"Fine except when I went to the library, since they were buying books, it was hinted by the purchaser that you don't need to donate books to them anymore," Thuy said.

"Really, why not?"

"He said somebody at the library did not like a map which showed the Paracel Islands as belonging to China and not Vietnam."

"My, they're touchy, aren't they?" Erik said.

"When it comes to China, yes," Thuy said.

"Okay, I won't anymore. Anyway, I've been doing a lot of thinking as I drive along and was filling in all the spaces about how lucky we are. Remember when I saw you at the embassy when I was in that work detail?"

"Yes."

"How did you know we were going to be at the embassy at that particular time?"

"Are you kidding, Ay-rik? Information alway pass through Vietnam people faster than typhoon, like waves of wind in a field of rice. Everyone know what would happen before the Americans did during the war. When I hear that trucks taking you to Bien Hoa I wait one week and ride bus to Saigon. When I get there I wait and listen. You know I stay with sister in Saigon, but I not tell you every day I ride her motorbike to Bien Hoa. One day I hear that tomorrow they start to tear down American Embassy. So I go there the next day. That when I see you."

"You are amazing," Erik said.

Thuy smiled such a knowing smile that Erik, for a brief moment, felt he was communing with Da Vinci.

Out in the bay, lanterns on the blue fishing boats grew brighter as the day was ending. Erik thought they looked like reflections of stars. He smiled.

"What you smile abow?" Thuy said.

"I found my perfect ice."

Thuy looked at him quizzically, and then at the water as though that would explain it.

"Never mind, my darling. It's a long story."